NOWHERE TO HIDE

Chris Billett

For Dad

It wouldn't be fun if it wasn't a challenge.

Chapter 1

The afternoon sunlight glinted on chrome letters as tarnished as the dreams of the company's founder. Beneath the once proud sign, the double doors leading to the foyer were chained and padlocked shut. Painted plywood squares blanked the windows of the low, stucco office building. Near the sidewalk, Orange Commercial Realty had planted their sign, staking claim to the foreclosed property.

Seated in his parked car, less than fifty feet from those doors, Charles Maitland remembered when the lawn had been a lush, verdant green, not this unkempt tinder, baked brown by the relentless California summer. He let his gaze linger on the tainted words, "Maitland Construction".

Surfacing from his reverie, he checked the time. Damnit! He'd sat here far longer than he'd intended, and he could not be late for his appointment at the bank.

As he pulled out the parking lot, Maitland couldn't help staring at the rearview mirror, one last farewell. His business, his dreams left behind in that silent building where once he'd employed a dozen people. It had been a good company, the employees his friends. Maitland wondered briefly what they were doing today, three months since the layoffs. He hoped they were doing better than himself. Not that he had much doubt on that score. He couldn't imagine anything worse than his own fate.

Maybe he could have done something before it was too late. Now he was simply out of options, for which he cursed himself. Though he saved most of his bitterness for the man who had destroyed everything Maitland had worked so hard to build. That son of a bitch.

Soon everything would be gone. First it had been the boat, then his Mercedes, and in their wake, his wife of thirty years. He should have told her everything, but again, it was too late to change things now. His business folded a few weeks after their divorce. Jennifer had kept the house on Balboa Island, and he'd taken the condo they owned, their income property, in Huntington Beach. He kept it for about a month, before the bank foreclosed on his life.

A wave of hatred as foul as bile rose within him. Today, he would exact a token of revenge against the stranger who had come into his life and ruined it all. He felt inside his jacket pocket, touching the cool metal barrel of the small caliber Smith & Wesson. His hands had trembled in the pawnshop when he'd picked up the handgun the previous week. Loading the weapon, his hands had shaken even more violently. But he was determined to hold the weapon steady when the time came to pull the trigger. Two bullets.

The second bullet would write the final page in his life. But before he fired that fatal shot, the first bullet would exact his revenge. At least it would if there was any justice left in the world.

He turned off Alton Parkway and into the strip mall, finding a space near the mirrored glass entrance to Pacific Security Bank. Feeling almost lightheaded, he walked across the lot, the automatic doors sliding open before him.

Leaving the oppressive heat, he entered the glacial chill of the bank.

*

The manager, a youthful forty-something MBA, stood as Charles Maitland crossed the polished marble floor, and shook hands with the businessman.

"Please." Tom Stinson beckoned his customer to a seat. He was shocked and disturbed by the fatigue and defeat in the older man's eyes. What the hell had happened to the guy? Up until six months ago, Maitland had been a success, and one of PSB's best customers.

"Coffee?" Tom asked.

Maitland didn't bother to look up, merely shrugged, and continued to stare at the cluttered desk.

Tom felt a pang of guilt. Christ, I hope we didn't do this to him. But the bank had to foreclose. No choice. Maitland had understood. Hadn't he?

Tom excused himself and strolled over to the coffee percolator. He returned with one cup, black and strong. As he placed the cup down on his coaster, Maitland put a hand inside his pocket and the color seemed to drain from his face.

"Everything all right, Mr. Maitland?"

A moment, then Maitland pulled out a Kleenex and patted his feverish brow. "Hot," he explained with the faintest smile.

Tom sat down. "Sure is out there. Heard on the radio it might hit a hundred this week with the Santa Ana winds." He forced a smile, but Maitland didn't respond in kind. Fair enough.

"Well, we've been through everything. You know you're going to walk away from all this with over fifty thousand. I know that doesn't seem like much." Tom faltered when his gaze met Maitland's empty, lifeless eyes. "Maybe it'll help you start over."

Tom keyed the computer. His typing wasn't even up to his one-fingered best. Instead he kept glancing at the man seated a few feet away. Finally, he pulled Maitland's account details up on the screen.

"I've authorized a cashier's check -"

"I need cash," Maitland interrupted.

"I didn't think you'd... Of course. I'll just need a few minutes."

Flustered, Tom Stinson hustled off and disappeared from view.

It took ten minutes before he returned and laid the money and a small canvas bag on the table.

He started counting hundred-dollar bills.

"Doesn't matter," Maitland said, reaching for the money and stuffing it into the bag.

"It's policy," Tom began, but one look at Maitland was enough to deter the manager from pressing the point. Besides, he'd double-checked the amount. Counting it now was merely a formality for the customer's benefit.

"I'll need your signature to close the account."

Maitland picked up one of the bank's black and gold pens and signed.

"Mr. Maitland, thank you. And good luck," Tom reached across to shake the man's hand. No hard feelings. Just business.

But Maitland simply stood, ignoring the outstretched hand, and walked away.

Poor guy, Tom thought as he watched Maitland shuffle out the glass doors and across the parking lot.

*

Once in his car, Maitland dipped his hand in his pocket. He was still in shock. What a fool he'd been. He couldn't believe he'd walked into the bank with a loaded gun. His heart had raced the moment he'd touched the small caliber weapon. God, what if they'd had metal detectors at the door? He took a few breaths to steady his nerves. Though what he wanted, needed, was something far stronger. Still shaken, he placed the gun under his seat and started the engine. He had a long drive ahead before his final appointment with the man who'd torn apart Charles Maitland's life.

He roared out the parking lot, and moments later took the ramp onto the 55 Freeway, headed inland.

In an aimless twilight zone, freeways merged and blurred as he passed by planned communities of Spanish tile and stucco which were slathered over the arid hills. Eventually, the suburbs relented and gave way to the desert. In his rearview mirror the dying embers of sunset faded, and Maitland felt a momentary regret for not having taken the time to watch the setting sun. Most people didn't know when they were watching their last day end. Most people were lucky.

He stopped once, to buy a small bottle of bourbon from a store situated less than fifty yards from a gas station. Taking a long pull, he rejoined the highway as it rose, threading its way through the mountain range that separated the coastal weather from the inland desert communities, Palm Springs, Rancho Mirage and the other towns that had blossomed around numerous golf courses.

He pushed the gas pedal deeper and accelerated past the slower traffic.

Ahead lay the night.

*

In the dark the killer waited for Maitland to arrive.

The night was the time for hunters.

Its darkness made him feel invisible, a figment in the pale light of a waxing moon.

Ever since the night long ago, when he had slipped away from home, avoiding the watchful eyes of the local cops, he had lived in the hours between twilight and dawn. Hiding from the day. Hiding from his memories.

But tonight, while he waited for Maitland to arrive, his memories surfaced and swirled around him. Ghosts of another time and place, another life. As if some other child had pulled the shotgun trigger and blown away half his father's skull.

The killer shook away the distracting memories, cramp gnawing at his legs and forcing him to shift position. He'd left that cabin so many miles, so many years behind. Time to move.

A furtive shadow, he crept across the moonlit desert. The sand like silver snow.

He felt a surge of excitement, his chest tightening. But he knew how to keep his emotions under control. He relaxed, focusing on his breath, and contemplating the events about to unfold.

The game always played out differently. That was one of the things that made it so rewarding. The unexpected danger. Once, in the beginning, he had made a mistake. But he was far more careful now when he selected his target.

He followed one guiding rule above all else. Only the guilty man would pay his price.

A steady susurrus beat whispered above the breeze blowing through the desert pass. An eerie mechanical breath which throbbed in the distance as regular as a heartbeat.

As he drew closer to the familiar sound, a feral smile touched his thin lips. He would arrive on foot long before his prey appeared.

*

The bottle of bourbon lay empty, a few drops spilled across the Cadillac's faded upholstery.

Maitland snored, then twisted in his seat. A troubled slumber brought on by too much alcohol. He moaned softly, and turned again, this time banging his head against the door pillar. His phone's alarm bleeped.

Startled, his eyes blinked open, unfocused for a moment.

He wasn't at home, he realized, because home no longer existed. He was sitting in the middle of nowhere awaiting his fate. He glanced at the digital clock, the numbers glowing 11:50. Just over an hour before he was due to meet the son of a bitch who'd ruined his life.

Maitland reached down, feeling under the seat, his fingers brushing against steel. He picked up the gun. Moonlight glinted on the slender barrel, making it appear fragile. Maybe he should have brought something bigger. But it was too late now. The .22 would have to do the job.

Or was it too late? Why not start the engine and drive away. Take the bank manager's advice and start over. Easy to say, Maitland thought, and perhaps some people could do it. But not him. He'd gone through too much to build his company, only to see it crumble away. The sooner this was all over the better. But first he would make sure the bastard who'd caused him such anguish paid the ultimate price.

He clicked off the safety and placed the gun inside the bag of cash.

"Last payment you'll ever see," he swore.

*

Silhouetted against the night sky, the man stood at the crest of a hill and looked down. Below, a hundred windmill generators scythed the night air, their giant propellers revolving with mesmerizing monotony. He started down the incline, toward the valley floor.

Long ago he had learnt the fastest ways through the maze of windmills. He crept by one generator, its thirty-foot blade cutting a graceful arc, catching the quicksilver light at its zenith, then falling.

Suddenly the man crouched low.

Headlights lanced the ground below as a car crossed the rutted track used by maintenance vehicles. It traveled slowly along the winding track.

Maitland had appeared before his appointed time, no doubt hoping to gain the element of surprise. The man smiled. He could imagine Maitland swearing he had no more money. Begging, pleading. It didn't matter. The money, this time, was irrelevant.

The time had come for Maitland to die.

Tomorrow, a passing police patrol would discover a car abandoned on the shoulder of a seemingly random freeway. The driver missing. Later they would learn of Maitland's divorce and bankruptcy, and they'd assume he was another statistic. Perhaps dead, perhaps one of the faceless, nameless thousands living on the streets. Either way, there was no one who cared.

Keeping low to the ground he neared the prearranged meeting point and watched the Cadillac cruise to a halt.

His night vision ruined by the passing headlights, the man unfastened a pouch strapped to his belt. The belt held a hunting knife, plastic sheeting, and a compact night-vision scope, one he'd purchased using a bogus identity on the Internet. He held the single lens scope to his eye and focused on the car.

*

Maitland had deliberately driven this far with his headlights on full, watchful in case the man was waiting to ambush him. But Maitland had seen nothing untoward along the rutted track.

His palsied hand betrayed his fear as he grabbed the bag from the passenger seat. He killed the headlights, unlatched the car door, and stepped outside. His shoes crunched on gravel. His breath came in ragged gasps.

He half expected his nemesis to leap from the night-shrouded shadows. But after standing motionless for a few minutes, he concluded he'd arrived first. He cast about for a place to hide and wait.

He had parked close to a sprawling Agave plant, but as he hurried toward it, he realized how insubstantial the thing was. Hardly the cover he wanted. Perhaps he could hide behind one of the windmills.

He slipped into the support's shadow. A kiss of air touched his face as the steel blade swept by overhead.

His mouth still burned from the bourbon he'd drunk. A little Dutch courage, he'd told himself. He squeezed the bag, feeling the money, then the reassuring solidity of his gun.

He never heard the figure that loomed behind him.

"Good evening, Charles."

Maitland spun around, almost dropping the bag in surprise.

"A little jumpy tonight, aren't we?"

The man was dressed in black, always in black. Maitland stared at the stranger who'd ruined his life.

"I br-brought it all, like you said," Maitland stammered. His chest was pounding, adrenaline pumping his heart faster and faster.

The man in black nodded, as if he had expected nothing less.

"Here," Maitland added, opening the bag and starting to reach inside.

The man smiled. An evil distortion of his face. Pale, scarred muscles across the man's left cheek turned the flesh to white clay.

"Take it. You can count it if you want." His fingers touched the money.

"Is there a need?" the man said.

Hardly daring to breathe, Maitland pulled out the thick stack of bills and handed them over.

"There's more." He reached inside the bag again. This time he felt for the pistol intending to shoot the man who had destroyed his life.

Perhaps something in Maitland's eyes gave him away. Whatever the reason, Maitland would never know.

The man moved fast and silent as a wraith. Closing the gap between them in a heartbeat. The killer's knife slashed the air.

Charles Maitland heard a single gunshot from his weapon in the instant he felt the blade pierce his chest, angled up between his ribs, spearing his lung. Maitland's mouth gagged like a fish drowning in air. The gun and the bag slipped from his grasp. In disbelief, he clutched the knife protruding from his chest, his strength ebbing as warm blood trickled down the haft and over his hand. He willed his cold fingers to pull the knife free.

Maitland's legs buckled, and he staggered backward as the endless night embraced him.

Chapter 2

Sam Grady glanced around at the enigmatic faces staring back across the elliptical conference table, and sat down. Surely they had all heard his nervous stutters during his presentation. He only prayed it wouldn't affect their decision. He needed this account. Desperately needed, would be more accurate, he thought. As always, Sam had dreaded making his pitch. He had to persuade the half dozen network executives that they should use a small upstart company rather than going with one of the established digital special-effects houses. It had taken months to get this far, ending up as one of three companies the station had short-listed.

At the head of the conference table Marcel LaCrosse, network manager, scribbled a note inside the cover of Sam's proposal. LaCrosse stroked his stubbled chin and offered up a vague smile.

"Sam, thanks for coming all this way."

"It's no problem. It's not so far when you time the traffic," Sam tried to sound casual. The traffic was the least of his concerns. The graphic intensive demo had taken two valuable and arduous weeks to prepare. He hoped it hadn't been time wasted.

The lines around LaCrosse's eyes pinched tighter.

Sam looked at the other executives, hoping to see some spark of approval, or at the least some sign that they were individuals with ideas of their own. He should have known better. The silence lengthened.

Sam reached for the water jug and refilled his glass. He was about to take a sip when LaCrosse spoke.

"This is good work."

The glass poised at his lips, Sam awkwardly returned it to the table without tasting the cool Evian.

"Thank you," his voice sounded hoarse, his throat dry and tight.

"We'll be in contact," the manager said, standing and offering a perfunctory hand.

Sam scrambled to his feet, lunging across the table to shake hands. As he did, the bottom of his jacket sleeve caught his glass, spilling water across the pristine table. Shit. Sam winced, feeling everyone staring at him, admiring his incompetence.

"Sorry." He fumbled in his pocket for a clean handkerchief and ineffectually mopped the pool of water. He lifted up LaCrosse's copy of the proposal, peeling the limp, waterlogged pages from the desk. He glanced at LaCrosse. "I've got a spare copy in my case."

"Don't worry. These things happen."

"Yeah, they seem to happen to me all the time."

"Leave it, really. You can email a copy over."

"I'm sorry." Sam held up his soggy handkerchief. Searching around, he spotted a trashcan and dropped the dripping cloth into the bin. "It's no trouble."

Reaching down to the floor, Sam retrieved his attaché case. Click, the left catch flipped open. Sam pressed the other without effect, then realized it was locked. With an apologetic smile, Sam thumbed the revolving lock open. Damn it, he was looking like a complete moron. "But I can do that, I'll email a PDF. And I really appreciate your, well, everyone's time."

Sam shook LaCrosse's hand and nodding his thanks to the others around the table, he backed out the room.

Closing the conference room door, Sam let his shoulders sag.

"Idiot," he whispered to himself.

"Sorry?"

Startled, Sam spun around. The young receptionist was watching him with concern.

"Are you feeling okay?"

Sam nodded as he strode past her desk.

Christ, thought Sam, the whole day had been a disaster. He'd ruined his chance. And his reward, his consolation prize, the horrendous 405 freeway traffic, and the interminable crawl south.

He glanced around, looking for the stairway he'd used on his way in, and spotted the door to the left of the bank of bronze elevators. A chirpy ping announced the elevator's arrival just as Sam strolled past.

He hated elevators. The confined space, no windows, no escape. He shook away a dark, distant childhood memory.

Sam stood, staring into a sea of faces. A woman reached to hold the door open for him.

Sam gestured not to bother, and watched the polished doors slide shut.

A moment later, he opened the stairway door and hurried down the long flights of concrete steps.

Leaving the glass tower, Sam was rocked by the oppressive heat that stifled Burbank. From the ground, the sky looked surprisingly clear, a cloudless azure. But Sam knew, if he glanced back on his way south he'd see a pall of brown smog hanging over The Valley, trapping the ninety-degree heat and the day's uncommon humidity.

"Let's move, guys," he cursed the stifling traffic, feeling impotent.

He had planned to arrive back at his office by lunch. But the meeting had started late and taken longer than he'd expected. Now, if he made it back much before four he'd be lucky. On top of everything, he knew, Ellen was going to be more than upset, especially after their argument earlier that morning.

A queasy guilt settled in his stomach as he remembered charging down the stairs two at a time and breezing through the kitchen with a brusque, "No time for breakfast, hon. Sorry."

Then he'd noticed two glasses of fresh orange juice on the small pine table.

Ellen, dressed in her robe, was watching him.

"What?" he wondered.

"Nothing."

Sam sighed inwardly. He had detected more than a hint of annoyance in her voice.

"I've got to get to Burbank. Traffic's going to be killer." His voice sounded pitiful as he tried to explain his hurry. "You said, you wanted to get away by early this afternoon."

Ellen didn't reply.

Christ, he hated it when Ellen went silent like this. That meant things were serious.

A horn blared, jolting him back to the present. Sam's eyes shot to the mirror, then to the gap which had opened ahead. As he rolled forward another car cut in front, filling the space.

The driver behind hooted again.

"Yeah, yeah," Sam muttered under his breath.

Steeling himself, he accessed his Bluetooth on the steering wheel. He couldn't put off calling Ellen any longer.

*

Ellen Grady had driven her forest green Explorer from their Tustin town house to the Laguna Beach restaurant overlooking the ocean where she'd arranged to meet her mother for lunch. Her mother had spent the last two days attending a watercolor class in Laguna, the arts capital of Southern California. Once they'd eaten, they planned to return home and collect Jason's things, ready for his weekend 'camp' at his grandmother's home. Their young son had been eagerly anticipating the event ever since he'd found out about it, asking Ellen every few minutes how many more days until the weekend.

Her own excitement about the upcoming trip had been dulled by Sam's attitude, especially when he'd left the house that morning.

As she entered the restaurant, her cell phone rang, and she let go of Jason's hand to search inside her handbag. From the ringtone she already knew it was Sam, and was equally sure she knew the reason for his call.

"You're running late?"

"I'm sorry, honey. Traffic's a nightmare," he began. "Might be a couple of hours before I get back, and—"

"Sam, I don't want to hear it."

"Look, I'll be like two minutes in the office. In and out. I promise."

"Okay. I'll see you whenever you get home." A moment, then she added, "Drive safe," before hanging up.

Ellen looked beyond the bar, searching for a waiter. A casually dressed guy in his early twenties strolled over. She decided he was most likely a college student working the busy summer season. "Table?"

"Actually, I'm meeting my mother. She's probably out on the patio."

"Of course." His eyes flitted to Ellen's tanned legs and he smiled with unabashed guilt when he realized she'd caught his glance.

She smiled back out of politeness rather than any sort of come on.

"This way, please."

Ellen spotted her mother sitting in the shade, checking her watch.

"Hi, Mom," she pecked her mother's cheek.

"Ellen," Lucy Hamilton reached across the table and patted her daughter's hand as Ellen sat down. "You look," she paused, her gaze fixed pointedly on Ellen's dress.

"I look, what?"

"Isn't that a little on the skimpy side, don't you think? For a mother?"

"I bought it for Palm Springs, it's going to be hot out there. And I thought Sam would like it."

"I'm sure it'll attract attention."

Ellen turned to Jason. "Would you like a toasted cheese?"

"And fries?" he asked eagerly, bouncing around in his chair.

"Absolutely. But I think we should sit still don't you?"

Jason pulled a cheeky face, and settled down thanks to the promise of his favorite food.

Ellen watched the surf beyond the glass wall, but her appreciation of the timeless view was interrupted by the waiter's arrival.

They ordered, Ellen earning a frown from Lucy when she asked for a glass of Chablis.

The two women lapsed into silence interspersed with small talk which continued once the waiter returned with their meals.

As the sun crept across the sky, Ellen shifted in her chair, maneuvering so she was in the shade once more, having forgotten her sunglasses. The flimsy cotton fabric floated up her thigh, and she felt the attention of a man in a sharp business suit. Maybe, she admitted, her mother's disdain hadn't been totally misplaced.

"You know, I often wonder what it would have been like if you'd had a brother or sister."

The remark came out of left field, and Ellen wasn't sure what to make of it. "I don't know, Mom. Being an only child had its advantages."

"Well, it's good Sam's finally taking a break," Lucy said.

Ellen nodded, slightly concerned that her mother seemed to jump from topic to topic ever more readily these days. "That's what he said."

The atmosphere surrounding them chilled.

"You two are getting along, aren't you?"

"We're fine, Mom. Except, I hardly get to see him. Sam's great at making promises. He'll be home by six, then it's eight, nine o'clock by the time he walks through the door, and Jason's in bed, so he doesn't get to see his dad. It seems so unfair."

"Unfair on Jason, or you?"

"Both," Ellen nibbled her chicken salad. "Is there something wrong or horribly old-fashioned about wanting to see your husband, to eat dinner together in the evening?"

"Now you're being silly, Ellie. I'm sure he's doing what he thinks is right."

"That's what makes it so hard. I know the company's important. And I promised we'd give it time. But he doesn't have to spend every hour there, does he?"

Her mother turned away. "I'm hardly the one to ask for advice."

Their conversation trailed off as the waiter returned with the check, which Ellen picked up.

*

Forty miles away, California Highway Patrol Officer Claire Sawyer took the 91 freeway on ramp, momentarily forced to a crawl by the stationary line of vehicles that had been about join the Eastbound traffic when the incident had occurred. She squeezed her patrol car past a wide, double-decked car transporter, as she traveled down the shoulder. Ahead a line of flares cut a swathe across the right lanes, creating a substantial bottleneck for everyone trapped behind the accident scene. A local radio station chopper flew overhead, the deep bass thrum of the helicopter's blades reverberating through the car. She didn't need a news flash, or a CHP report, to know the afternoon commute was probably backed over a mile already. But all those people whose journey had been interrupted were not her concern. Claire and the accident investigators she worked with had been called in to figure out what had happened and why. From the preliminary information it sounded straight forward, and not necessarily the sort of thing CHP's Multidisciplinary Accident Investigation Team would typically look into, of course everything changed if there was a fatality involved. And a comment from dispatch made it clear that one of the driver's involved had been well connected in the Riverside community. Her death would be fully investigated.

Claire pulled around a tow truck and stopped near the crash. She climbed out, gathering her equipment case, and formed her initial impression of the accident. Three cars involved. She walked past a delivery van; the front driver's side had taken the brunt of the impact, but the damage, Claire decided, was superficial. Minutes earlier the driver had been taken by paramedics to the nearest hospital complaining of neck spasms. The injury report had sounded minor, and Claire was pretty certain it would be nothing compared to the pain he'd feel when he realized how much shit he might be in.

Don't judge the book, Claire chastised herself, recalling the clichéd words of her college professor when she'd studied accident investigation. Striding around the van, Claire got her first proper look at what remained of the Acura sandwiched between the van and a pickup truck. Despite the car's rigid construction and its driver safety cell, the vehicle looked as if it had been pummeled by a giant fist.

Claire grabbed her DSLR camera out of her case, and started shooting. She circled the vehicles taking a series of general photographs to document the scene, then the details. A shot of the bumper impact on the Acura's passenger door, another of the broken right front wheel, shots all around the van. Moving back up the freeway, she studied the intricate skid and scuff marks on the pavement. As she removed a heavy cardboard square from her bag, Officer Carlos Sroka, the team's Motor Carrier Specialist, waved to her and strolled in her direction.

Claire unfolded the white portable grid and placed it on the ground before stepping back. The two foot square was divided by a series of black horizontal, vertical and forty-five degree lines, which would appear in the foreground of her photograph. These would enable her to overlay a perspective grid on the computer for later analysis and saved considerable time attempting to measure the road marks while tying up freeway traffic.

"What are you thinking?" Carlos asked, flipping through a sheaf of papers. Despite his youthful looks, he was definitely old-school. "I got a statement from the guy in the F150."

Claire snapped another picture, and picked up the cardboard square, shifting it to another location. "And?"

"And, he said the Acura shot out of its lane—"

"After the van shunted it."

Claire kneeled down to take a close-up of scuff mark left in the Acura's wake. The mark indicated the car had yawed to the right prior to impact.

Carlos continued. "Nothing the pickup could do to avoid the collision."

Claire mumbled noncommittally and shot another close-up. The camera's memory card beeped and flashed 'FULL' on the screen, interrupting her flow and forcing her to fish around for a spare.

Standing, she strode toward the front wheel drive Acura. She noted the heavy, intrusive damage inflicted when the pickup had impacted the driver's door. She steered clear of the Firefighters who were busy extracting the deceased victim. Moving around the car she peered in through the shattered passenger window at the driver's body. From this angle, the cause of death was readily apparent, a piece of metal had sheared and been driven through the driver's sternum, piercing her heart. Death had been instantaneous, Claire suspected, and so the driver had been spared the agonizing demise Claire had witnessed so many times before. She recalled comparing notes with a homicide detective a year ago, and he'd agreed his cases were typically far less gruesome than the average car fatality. At least this time, Claire thought gratefully, there weren't dismembered body parts to be retrieved, or worse still, the horror of a dead child or infant. Those were the scenes which haunted her.

"Officer," one of the Firefighters indicated to her that they were about to resume cutting, and Claire stepped away as sparks fireworked from the tortured steel skeleton.

"Gloria Weston," a familiar male voice spoke behind her.

Claire turned to see Sergeant Mike Stadler, the team's leader, standing beside Carlos. He rubbed his stubbled chin, and continued.

"Fifty three. Married to Malcom Weston."

Claire nodded, she had heard of Weston, a local real estate developer who had run unsuccessfully in the last city election.

"We got anything suspicious here? Any HBD's?" Mike asked.

"Nothing apparent. We'll get her blood work. Right now, she looks like another statistic. Only, maybe this one'll make the news," said Claire.

"But it won't make any difference," Mike echoed what Claire was thinking.

"Do they ever?"

They'd both been at this long enough to know the answer to that. Claire stared through the broken glass at the woman's body. She would have been on her way home, or maybe a fundraiser. Whatever her destination had been, one thing was certain — she hadn't been planning a trip to the morgue.

Mike tapped her elbow. "Let's get this wrapped," he glanced meaningfully at the long line of traffic.

"They didn't need us for this one," Claire commented as they moved aside, allowing the tow truck to maneuver ahead of the pickup.

"Politics, Claire, you know that." Mike shrugged. "You want to talk to the van driver or the wits?" he pointed to a couple of bemused witnesses who were standing near their parked cars.

"I'll take the van."

Stadler glanced at Carlos. "They're all yours."

With a last look at the wreckage, Claire headed back to her car. With any luck she'd get to talk with the van driver soon, before he realized how badly he needed a good lawyer.

Chapter 3

Wavering shadows shifted across saffron walls of the master bedroom. Outside the balconied window, palm fronds rustled in the sea breeze. The multimillion-dollar house was situated in a private cul-de-sac not far from the water, overlooking Newport Beach harbor. Hundreds of sailboats and motor yachts, floating gin-palaces, could be glimpsed bobbing at their moorings. The boats waited for the weekend, when the titans of industry would crowd the harbor, circling the man-made islands and the prestigious waterfront homes. Although surprisingly few captains seemed confident enough to venture out to sea or across the water to Catalina.

The sleeping figure hidden beneath a silk sheet stirred. The man's scarred face emerged, blinking against the harsh daylight. The face was gaunt, hard-edged, and his nose had once been broken. A twinge of pain in his shoulder reminded him how close he'd come to a fatal error. Something that would not happen again.

He remembered two nights ago when a flash of searing heat had kissed his shoulder.

His eyes had narrowed as he'd watched Maitland's body fold to the ground.

Satisfied his work was done, the man had peeled his black leather jacket away from his injured shoulder and examined the wound. It didn't look bad. The wild shot had literally grazed his flesh, the heavy leather coat saving him from a more severe injury.

He'd suffered worse.

But Maitland's execution had been messy. Too damn messy, the man reprimanded himself. He'd wasted precious time scuffing the blood-soaked sand where the body fell, with only partial success. He laid Maitland's bloody corpse in the trunk of the man's rented Cadillac, wrapped in the polythene sheet the killer had carried with him. The plastic would keep the trunk clean, leaving no evidence for the police when they later discovered the abandoned vehicle.

He'd slammed the trunk shut and climbed behind the wheel…

The car sped across the desert plateau, a favorite ground for off-road vehicles during weekends and vacations. No one would ever notice another set of windswept tire tracks, even if they had reason to look.

Twice the Cadillac hit soft spots, tires sinking deep into the sand. Both times he fought to keep the vehicle moving. To get stuck would mean disaster.

After fifteen minutes, he reached his destination. He drove along what had once been a riverbed, now a gully of sand with low, ragged cliffs rising like worn teeth along the banks. He kept close to the base of the cliff for perhaps a mile, then stopped.

Going around to open the trunk, he grunted as he hoisted the plastic-clad corpse over his shoulder. He staggered under the lifeless bulk, trudging toward a splintered opening in the cliff face.

Entering the cave, he dumped the body. He proceeded to scan the darkness using the image intensifier. Details of the rocky walls swam before him, a dim green-gray haze. Certain no animals or snakes were lurking in the gloom, he lifted Maitland's shoulders off the ground and dragged the body across the dusty floor.

The craggy roof dipped lower as he moved deeper inside the cave, until he was bent double, with scarcely four feet between floor and ceiling. Straining as he pulled the corpse, he heard the steady, monotonous drip of water that marked his destination.

Vestigial traces of moonlight beyond the entrance faded, and Stygian darkness closed around him. He entered a narrow passageway hidden at the rear of the cave. Leaving the body for a moment, he felt along a gritty ledge near the low ceiling. His fingers curled around a familiar metal cylinder - his sturdy flashlight. He switched on the powerful Maglite, the beam bouncing off the ceiling, illuminating the passage. He was far enough inside the cave to ensure no light strayed outside.

He resumed his struggle, inching through the secret passage, hauling the body.

Abruptly the shaft opened into another cave. A domed cavern fifty feet across and a dozen feet high.

A cathedral for the souls of the damned, he thought.

Water dripping into an unseen pool broke the silence.

The flashlight played over the rocky floor, then stopped. The beam touched the lip of a crevasse splitting the cavern in two. Far below echoed the steady drip. Water seeping through the domed ceiling fell into the fissure and disappeared into an underground lagoon.

He dragged Maitland's body to the edge of the abyss and gave the corpse a final push.

Moments later a splash erupted from below. The underground lake had claimed another victim.

Moving quickly now, he returned the flashlight to its hiding place, then made his way outside and back to the Cadillac.

There was still much work to be done, he told himself.

He glanced at the time, surprised to see it was past two. In a few hours the russet dawn light would rim the horizon. But by that time he planned to have left the desert behind and returned to his luxurious home on the Pacific coast.

Dumping the car in one of his chosen locations had become as routine as disposing of the body. Over the years he had perfected his methods, although there remained an element of risk.

Once he'd been spotted as he abandoned a vehicle, when a foolish good-Samaritan had pulled over to help, even offering him a ride. He'd accepted, and let the student drive him to a gas station. Later that day on the TV he heard the police ask for witnesses who might have seen a man abandoning his car around midnight on the 91 freeway. The following day, a report mentioned the student who gave the missing driver a ride. A man he described as average build, dressed in dark clothing, a scar on the man's cheek being the only distinguishing feature.

The man knew he'd been lucky that time. And it didn't pay to trust your luck. You only had so much.

The killer swung the Cadillac into a gas station that offered twenty four hour service. He pumped a couple of bucks of gas at the self-service and paid cash.

"Wash working?" he asked the cashier.

The girl nodded. "Three bucks," she mumbled, barely noticing the man dressed in black as she turned the page of a romance novel.

The Cadillac emerged a few minutes later, the sand washed away, water dripping from its spotless coachwork. The man drove out the gas station and back to the freeway.

There was little traffic so early on Friday morning, but he still had a long journey before he abandoned Maitland's vehicle. He kept to the speed limit, needle fixed on sixty-five. This was no time for a stupid mistake.

Joining the San Diego freeway he headed north. He stayed in the right hand lane, as the first of the morning commuters headed to work, or to catch a dawn flight out of LAX, overtaking him in their rush to beat the buildup that would soon begin.

Eventually, the Cadillac pulled onto the freeway shoulder, its headlights dying.

The man waited until a gap in the traffic and climbed out, marching away from the car before venturing into the thorny brush at the roadside. Beyond the brush a bank dropped sharply away. He bounded down the slope, leaping high onto a wire fence. Swinging himself over, the killer winced as he strained his injured shoulder. He dropped to the far side, crouching. The flesh wound was not severe, but he needed to sterilize the cut to prevent infection. Once he arrived home, he would contact his doctor. His physician had a legitimate practice, but enjoyed a substantial tax-free income from an occasional house call to his wealthy, secretive client.

The killer was about to head off when strobing lights pierced the darkness.

Blue and red pulses flashed through the branches above him. Gravel crunched under tires as a police cruiser pulled off the freeway.

Glancing over his shoulder, the man glimpsed the patrol car as it came to a halt behind the abandoned car. Inwardly, he cursed the cops' timing.

The car door opened. A pair of spit-polished boots walked along the road, approaching the Cadillac.

He saw a flashlight, reflected in the chrome wheels.

"Don't see no one," the officer's bass voice called out.

"I'm running it," replied his partner.

The killer edged down the slope, careful to avoid any twigs or dry leaves, heading away from the abandoned vehicle.

The man reached the bottom of the slope. The freeway was some thirty yards behind him now, and he was no longer able to hear the officers' conversation.

He stood at the dead end of a no-through road. Decrepit tract houses on either side were boarded up, sprayed with graffiti. He didn't know if anyone lived in them, not that he cared one way or the other. His only concern was the car parked less than a dozen paces away. It was not the car he usually drove, it was a rusted Volkswagen Rabbit, equipped with threadbare tires, no radio, slashed cloth seats and a stone-chipped windshield. If he'd been lucky, maybe someone would have offered to scrap it for twenty bucks. But the little car's value was far higher to him. Even abandoned on the border of L.A.'s gangland streets, the car had never been touched by thieves.

He hurried across the street to duck behind the VW.

Behind him, he heard the fence rattle. He risked a glimpse and saw the swaying beams of their flashlights probing the trees. He caught a few muffled words.

"… get it towed." Then, "Need to roll…"

Then silence.

The beams of light vanished.

Only when he heard their doors slam and the patrol car pull away did the man emerge from behind the VW. Climbing in, he too started his engine and drove along the desolate street, turning right at an intersection. A minute later he passed a Greyhound bus station, an oasis of lights ablaze. The previous morning, after parking his VW, he'd strolled to the depot and caught a ride to Palm Springs.

The final danger came when he neared Newport Beach in the early hours. Driving such a dilapidated car in such upscale neighborhoods risked drawing the attention of the police, or a private security patrol. So he kept judiciously to the speed limits, making sure he signaled at every turn. He drove to a condo, which he'd purchased for cash four years ago, and unlocked the double garage. Inside, he parked the VW and climbed into his five-liter Mercedes coupe. And resumed the final leg of his journey home.

At the gated entrance to the exclusive cul-de-sac community, he nodded a curt hello to the security man, who was outside his booth stealing a smoke.

"Long night, sir?" the man said, as the wrought iron gates opened automatically after scanning the Merc's license plate.

"Felt like a lifetime. You take care, George."

*

Dr. Andrew Bernard paused to listen for a moment. He heard his wife, Stephanie, downstairs chatting on the phone, then he stepped into the walk-in closet, and opened a drawer. Nestled among the neatly regimented stacks of socks was a box of Trojan condoms. Shoving four of them into his pocket he flicked off the light and hurried downstairs.

"I really need to check our calendar, it sounds like a wonderful idea, but you know how busy the boys are," she smiled as Bernard entered the room.

He strolled over to kiss his wife goodbye.

"Yes, hold on one minute," lowering the phone she permitted him to kiss her cheek. "Mary Beth wondered if we want to take the boats over to the island anytime soon?"

Bernard shrugged. "Sure. I'll give Rob a call and fix a date, maybe next weekend. I've got to skedaddle, Mrs. Connelly insisted on another consultation before we go any further."

"Now? Andy," an edge of exasperation crept into his wife's voice.

"What?"

"We've got tickets, for the theater. This evening, remember? God, I reminded you on Monday, you said you were clear."

"I'm sorry," he sighed, as if he shared her exasperation. "Maybe I could reschedule, or something. Let me try and get her on the phone."

Mentioning the phone had the desired effect, and Stephanie hurriedly spoke into the receiver. "Mary Beth? Yes, I'm sorry. Look, can you hold on just one more minute?"

Her eyes narrowed as she stared at Bernard.

"No," she said finally, "you better go. Please, just see if you can get back in time. If we leave by seven we should make it."

Bernard gnawed his lip. "Darling, you know I'd love to, but I don't think that's going to work. Wait, does Mary Beth want to go? You two go, make an evening of it?"

But Stephanie shook her head. "No, that's okay, it doesn't matter."

You're such a martyr, thought Bernard while nodding his head as if he sympathized with her disappointment.

"Bye, darling. You're a trooper, you know?" he kissed her once more then added, "If you need me call the cell, the service'll be picking up the regular line."

With that he ambled out to their four-car garage. His immaculate Lexus sedan was parked beside her polished Jaguar F-type R — a machine, she delighted in telling him, that would burn his car off the road any day. Anyone looking at his once glamorous wife, thought Bernard, might have taken her for a grandmother, a kindergarten teacher or perhaps a fading movie star, but he doubted anybody would have guessed her passion; cars and speed. She had more tickets than anyone he knew, yet somehow she still retained her license.

The garage door rumbled open, and he tossed his case into the passenger seat.

Passing the cliquey community's gatehouse he turned onto the street and inched up the music, basking in the afternoon sun accompanied by Vivaldi's *Four Seasons*.

He took the 261 Toll Road, at first heading in the direction of his practice, but after only a few miles he took an off ramp, and drove the wide, winding avenue through Tustin.

A thrill of anticipation tingled his flesh and his foot pressed down on the gas pedal.

Ten minutes later, Bernard was jogging up the steps outside a refurbished condo. Reaching the second floor he pressed the buzzer. The front door swung open, and a delightfully cherubic face beamed at him.

Celia Provenzano had been his nurse and assistant for two years. When she'd landed the job their relationship had been suitably platonic, but it had only taken a few weeks for them to discover they shared certain peccadilloes. A discovery Celia had made when she walked in on Dr. Bernard as he surfed the web one evening after his last patient had left. At first a nauseated panic had flooded Bernard's body as he tried to hide the pictures on the screen. But far from being shocked, Celia had gazed at the explicit images and smiled, then she had marched toward him. The prospect of lawsuits and sexual harassment charges and MeToo crucifixion had raced through his mind, until she spoke and asked him if he'd like to perform one of the acts so vividly displayed on the computer screen. Startled and delighted, he'd eagerly undertaken the task, and had subsequently spent many late evenings serving Celia in whatever manner she saw fit.

A whimper escaped his dry lips as he admired the woman standing before him.

Celia stood in the doorway dressed in her nurse's blouse, suspenders, stockings and five-inch stilettos.

"Good afternoon, Doctor," she said with a saucy wink.

"Nurse. I hope I'm not late for my appointment?"

He removed his shoes and stepped across the threshold.

"And I hope you haven't been a naughty boy," she spanked him lightly as he walked past her. "You better run along, your clothes are in the bedroom. This is going to be such a long, but very rewarding evening."

"Mmm, sounds wonderful."

She nudged the front door shut. "Get changed — now!"

The bedroom walls had been painted black and the shades partly lowered. Bernard's hands trembled with a thrill when he saw the 'clothes' she had selected for him and left on the satin sheets. He picked up a studded leather thong and caressed it. So soft, so good.

"Hurry up," she barked from the bedroom door. "It's time for your examination."

Bernard felt a powerful surge course his body as he stripped before her. His heart pounded as Celia's eyes swept dismissively over his naked body. He stood before her, vulnerable, aware of nothing beyond the rapid beating of his heart. He followed her as she circled around him, forced to squint as she passed before the window when the low sun's piercing glare reflected from a parked car's windshield. He took a step toward the shade, intending to lower it the rest of the way.

"Where do you think you're going?" Celia demanded. "You ask permission before you move. Do you understand?"

"Yes, mistress."

"On your hands and knees."

Bernard sank gratefully to the ground, ready to accept his punishment.

Chapter 4

He had closed the books on Charles Maitland, and in the course of a few months had netted over four hundred thousand tax-free dollars. Not bad.

Only in their final meeting had Maitland ever surprised him, carrying a gun, intent on revenge. His error in judgment concerned him more than the injury he'd suffered. It raised an unpleasant question in his mind. He had to pay more attention to the warning signs. Maitland had seemed on edge the last few meetings. The trickle of blackmail money he'd paid at the end had not been worth the added risk.

He would take more care with Dr. Andrew Bernard, he promised, reflecting on his previous afternoon's work as he glanced at the Nikon digital sitting atop an antique chest-of-drawers.

Slowly he rose from the bed and crossed the huge master suite.

Before entering the bathroom he turned and looked back, at the huge painting hung above his bed. He'd commissioned the expensive artwork based on a photograph, the only picture of his mother he possessed. She was, if anything, more beautiful in the painting than in his memories. The artist had interpreted her image wonderfully, casting aside the background, so his mother stood waif-like, a timeless beauty bathed in a golden, heavenly aura beyond which was only the darkness of eternal night.

"Good morning, Mother," he said.

As he strolled into the bathroom he smiled and contemplated how much Dr. Bernard might be worth. Having only met the man twice in the past, it was difficult to judge. But his research revealed assets close to five million dollars. To get anything like that amount would take some time. Wear the doctor down, force him eventually to sell his house, and his rare coin collection. The latter fact was something he'd overheard quite by accident at a recent gathering of Newport socialites. The doctor had not attended, but a couple of his female patients had, and they'd eagerly discussed everything they knew about the man, speculating if a divorce was in the air, until finally concluding it wasn't and moving on to another target. Two young and vapid women, was the opinion he had formed, eavesdropping on their inane chatter. Their silly plots to snare a wealthy husband. As if mommy and daddy weren't worth millions, and wouldn't give them whatever they wanted for the rest of their lives, just for the asking.

He despised attending such functions, yet it was a necessary part of his work. For once there, mingling with the high-class elite, he would find his prey.

Gilded invitations to parties held at exclusive residences, or on million-dollar yachts, dropped through his mailbox every week. He was well known in the area for his philanthropy, giving to a variety of charities, knowing his generous donations would spawn future invitations.

Arriving once the party was well under way, he would slip into a quiet corner and observe the rich and powerful men with their sculpted and scalpeled wives, women who clung desperately to a vanished youth. His concentration focused on the husbands. On those handful of men who made frequent journeys to the bar. Their conversation grew louder and more boorish as the night grew old. He watched and waited. And as the guests trickled away in the early morning hours, he would follow his prey. He remembered following Maitland and his statuesque wife outside, leaving the sprawling Pelican Point villa where a Friday night party had been held. He followed them down an avenue of Cyprus trees to the valet, watching as Charles Maitland proclaimed himself fit to drive, and stumbled around the car to climb behind the wheel.

Discarding the memory, the man twisted the gold-plate faucet and splashed his face. He decided to pay Dr. Bernard a call later that day.

It really was a wonderful thing, watching such powerful, self-assured men like Maitland and Bernard crumble under a little pressure. Watching their lives disintegrate. Of course, he was careful only to select those who deserved to be punished –

Abruptly a needle of light stabbed his eye. Pain lanced through his head, causing him to stagger. He gripped the sink as he tried to maintain his balance. The migraine intensified, as if a finely honed drill had pierced his right eye, scoring deep through the socket. His knees buckled and he collapsed, clutching his head in his hands, trying to squeeze the agony from his mind. Closing his eyes didn't help. Hundreds of bright pinpoints of light flickered and died, each one a burning red pain searing through him. Doubled over, he rolled onto the floor, his body in a fetal curl.

A low moan escaped his lips. The unholy sound bearing witness to the agony that engulfed him.

Then he saw her.

The woman's face swam before him. She smiled gently, a warm smile that filled him with happiness. She looked old, crow's feet stretching her kind eyes. Yet she was beautiful.

His mother reached out to him. Her smile vanished. Her eyes suddenly revealing her own suffering.

The man's pulse quickened.

"No," he breathed.

He didn't want to see.

Not again.

The man didn't know how long the attack lasted. His muscles ached, his head throbbed. Both his body and mind felt weak with exhaustion. It took all his effort to grasp the edge of the bathtub and lift himself off the cold tile floor. He swayed, his legs trembling.

He hated himself, hated his body, for its weakness, its lack of control. The self-discipline he had learnt throughout his life failed him utterly at such times. It was a weakness he could not tolerate. Yet he had no choice.

He glanced at his watch, shocked to find only twenty minutes had passed.

His legs unwilling to support him, he dragged himself back to the bedroom where he collapsed on the bed. He lay, listening to the rhythm of his pulse and stared up at the painting.

I'm sorry, he told her for the thousandth time. I should have been there. If I'd been home I could have stopped him. His breath quickened as he fought against the memory.

All my fault, my fault, his mind insisted.

Cautiously he sat as the incessant inner voice gradually faded, returning to wherever it dwelt, then he swung his legs off the bed.

After pulling on a cotton shirt and pair of slacks, the man picked up the Nikon camera and marched downstairs.

In the sleek, stainless steel kitchen, the man sat at the breakfast bar, and plugged the Nikon into a laptop computer, ready to review the photographs he had taken the previous evening. Before settling down to select those glossy images he would print, the man helped himself to a freshly brewed Crema Coffee from the automated maker. The impressively efficient machine was one of the luxuries he afforded himself. Caffeine, the doctor had warned him would most likely contribute to his migraine attacks, but then such was the flux of medical opinion, he'd read the opposite findings on the internet, and drawn his own conclusion.

He scrolled through the thumbnail images on the laptop. What they might have lacked in composition, they more than made up for in their explicitness.

Sipping the steaming drink, he recalled the previous day. After disposing of Maitland and returning home, the man had endured a brief, restless sleep before awaking mid-morning. He'd felt the familiar surge of renewed determination fueled by anger. Determination to pursue those who thought themselves above laws or morality. In his study, he'd reviewed his elaborately detailed files of the men he had decided would one day pay for their sins. Men like Dr. Andrew Bernard. Yes, doctor, he thought, your time is now.

He had called Bernard's practice, and learnt that the doctor was at home and would not return until Monday. It didn't take a genius to guess what the doctor was up to. So the man had parked his car and staked out the Provenzano woman's townhome from the quiet, tree-lined park across the street. He armed his camera with a 500mm lens, and waited. Less than two hours later, the doctor made his house-call and the illicit lovers disappeared inside for a grueling evening's entertainment. During their adventures the man had taken dozens of digital photographs as the physician and his dominatrix let their insatiable passion override their desire for privacy, neglecting to fully close the shades. Or perhaps, thought the man, that was also part of the thrill, there was no way to know how such depraved minds worked.

The man clicked the print icon and the laptop relayed the command across his WiFi network. Moments later he could hear the color laser printer in his office as it churned out a few glossy high-resolution pictures.

*

Officer Claire Sawyer continued to stare at the Computer Aided Design monitor. On the display was a high-contrast image of the tire marks left on the freeway by Gloria Weston's car. After leaving the scene, Claire had driven to the Inland Medical Center and waited until she could interview the driver of the van, the man believed to be responsible for the crash that had killed Mrs. Weston.

As Claire and Mike had predicted, the press had jumped all over the case. Though, headline news one day, it seemed it was barely worth a thought the next. Except for the family and friends of the deceased, the only other people who still appeared interested were the other drivers who'd been involved, and the M.A.I.T team.

Earlier, while eating a stale brownie and a downing an espresso triple shot, Claire had reviewed the eyewitness statements. Such statements were useful, but most of the time people saw the same accident in surprisingly diverse ways. In fact, most of the time they never actually saw the accident. She remembered her first case all too well. A head on collision, a speeding car straddling the median, the driver DUI. There had been plenty of witnesses, or so it seemed at first. They'd given their statements, some at the scene, others within twenty-four hours. The problem was, none had actually seen the collision occur. Only after hearing the crash had their attention focused on the street. What they saw was a red Mustang facing the wrong way, having piled into an old Volvo wagon. Obviously the Mustang had been driving recklessly, they surmised. Claire's investigation discovered it was the Volvo, not the Mustang that cut into the oncoming traffic, overtaking a taxi, racing somewhere, who knew where. Claire doubted if the driver of the Mustang ever saw it coming. The Volvo had been traveling at over seventy miles an hour she estimated from the distance the cars finished apart. The off-center impact had spun both cars around, facing the opposite direction, as often happened.

The driver of the Mustang was a young nurse on her way home after a twelve-hour shift. Pronounced DOA at the hospital. The Volvo driver was a forty-year-old businessman who, after recovering from minor injuries, was able to afford a semi-competent lawyer. Claire had pushed for vehicular manslaughter. But the case had gone before a jury. Twelve good people, no doubt, but some of them could empathize with the executive. After all, who'd never driven after one or two drinks? And that was all it took.

A thousand dollars, she recalled. Not exactly a heavy fine to pay for murder.

"Can I sign this off?" Mike Stadler's question brought her back to the present case.

"I still don't like her phone record," Claire said, referring to the report that showed Mrs. Weston had been on her cell for twenty minutes prior to the collision.

"Come on, seriously?" he prompted. "What else is nagging at you?"

She pointed to the photograph on the monitor. "You see the yaw mark here, we've got stuttering a long way back, crossing the lane-stripe, along with minor glass debris. The van driver told me he felt a vibration from the back of the vehicle, which caused him to over-correct and enter her lane."

"Got a witness who says otherwise. Stated the van blew down the on-ramp like some Nascar Challenge and cut straight across two lanes and into Weston," Mike pointed out.

Claire looked at him. "Devil's advocate?"

"That's my job. Yours is figuring this out. But if you conclude Gloria Weston was at fault, you better be damn sure 'cause the lawsuits are going to be flying thick and fast. The department can't afford to have its blood in the water along with Malcom Weston's." He paused, staring at the image, the faint scuff markings on the pavement. "I tell you, this sure must've been easier before ABS."

"True, but that's why we get the big bucks," she smiled.

"Yeah, I wondered why that was," the levity left his voice. "I need this wrapped, Claire; whichever way it goes."

Claire nodded her understanding as Stadler strode back to his desk. Subtle, outside pressure was no doubt being applied, she knew, recalling Mike's warning at the start, that this one was political.

She continued to work through the entire series of photographs, using the software to enhance and zoom in on portions of the image. Once again her attention focused on the staccato skid marks. Weston's car was yawing, but why? Unless I'm reading this the wrong way, she thought.

She trekked back through the Department's database, searching the files from the evidence lab, and pulled one particular photo onto her screen.

Thirty minutes later, Claire laid her summary report on Stadler's desk next to a framed photo of his teenage daughter.

"What we got?"

She flipped the pages to the evidence photograph of Mrs. Weston's right shoe, an impression on its Italian leather sole.

"We've got a heavy imprint of the gas pedal and," she turned the page to reveal a zoomed image of the tire scuff marks.

"We've got Mrs. Weston, chatting on her phone, cruise control on. Suddenly, she sees a van racing down the ramp. She stands on the brakes, only she hits the gas pedal by mistake. There'd likely be some torque steer, but either way she's startled and she crosses the lane divide and bumps the rear side of the van. After that, she's ricocheted between the van and the F150."

As she'd outlined her conclusion she'd watched for Mike's reaction. As always, he remained enigmatic.

"Any doubt in your mind?" he asked.

"No reasonable doubt."

"Okay," he mused and she started to walk away. "Claire, good work here."

Claire smiled, the M.A.I.T team's record solving such puzzles might not be one hundred percent, but it was damn close, and everyone worked hard to keep it that way.

Chapter 5

Sam Grady awoke uncharacteristically late, his back aching, stiff from a night spent on the soft, unfamiliar mattress. He rolled on to his side, surprised to see Ellen had already risen. Stretching languorously across his wife's half of the bed, he found the sheets still comfortingly warm.

He glanced out the French door at the clear blue sky over the apartments and glimpsed a trio of palm trees, fronds waving in a light breeze.

"Hey, sleepy head," Ellen said, entering the room, carrying a glass of orange juice, which she handed to him.

Propping himself on one arm, Sam sipped the chilled juice. His eyes wandered over Ellen's body, her silken wrap clinging to her curves rejuvenated by frequent visits to her fitness club ever since Jason's birth.

"God, I must have been tired," he said, vaguely remembering collapsing into bed the previous evening, around nine-thirty after the interminable drive. Although the distance wasn't so bad, the traffic had been awful. He hoped his hosts hadn't thought him rude, disappearing so soon after dinner.

"You looked exhausted," Ellen said. "You work too hard, Sam."

Sam didn't detect any implied criticism, although it might have been in her voice. Either way, he didn't want to start an argument.

Placing the empty glass on the bedside table, he lay back down, head sinking into the pillow. His hand beckoned Ellen closer, and she sat on the edge of the bed as Sam's fingers combed through her hair. Sunlight limned the blond strands, flaring them with brilliance all their own. When he touched her waist, trying to pull her to him, she half-heartedly attempted to ease his hand away.

"Sam," she hissed. "Pete and Anne are up already."

"So am I," Sam said, and grinned.

"Really?" She peeked under the sheets.

"Well, almost."

Ellen looked at him, a playful, girlish glint in her smoky eyes. "I think you can do better than that."

"Yo, folks?" Pete Shelby's voice called through the door, startling them both. "You decent?"

Ellen hurriedly stood up as if caught with her hand in the cookie jar, and the next moment, Pete strode in, swinging a tennis racket, dressed for the court. Lean and lanky, Pete had excelled at a variety sports, Sam knew, before settling on tennis. He'd been close, or so Pete liked to often brag, to turning pro.

"Come in," said Sam belatedly.

"Thought you wanted to play early, Sam. You know, by the time it reaches eleven it's gonna be kinda hot here. Not like your neck of the woods."

Ellen remained perched on the edge of the bed, a picture of innocence. But when neither she nor Sam spoke, Pete's edgy gaze flitted suspiciously between the couple.

"Ah, 'scuse me." He edged backward, bumping into the doorframe and then stepping into Anne, who appeared behind him.

"Watch out, Pete. Sheesh. So what's happening? Where are they?" she asked, nudging Pete aside. "Let's go, guys." Despite encroaching on forty, Anne seemed to possess boundless energy, and insisted on dressing like a woman half her age. Fortunately she had the lithe physique that meant such outfits usually looked great on her. Today she was ready for game, set and match Palm Springs style, dressed in her designer skirt, shirt and pale pink tennis shoes.

"I think Sam's looking a bit peaked," Pete suggested, trying to usher his wife out of the room.

"Nonsense." Anne shrugged him off and stepped into the bedroom.

"I'm fine. Give us five minutes," Sam said.

Pete tugged at Anne's sleeve. "Let's go warm up, honey."

"We'll see you both out there."

As they left the room, closing the door behind them, Sam could hear their low voices. Then, "Oh!" exclaimed Anne, and a moment later the front door closed.

"Alone at last," Sam said.

"Five minutes, Sam. And that includes getting washed and dressed. Next time, stud."

Ellen stood, gathering her clothes. Then she let her robe slip tantalizingly to the floor as she disappeared into the en-suite bathroom.

"Tease," he called after her.

Sitting up, Sam stretched, rolled his shoulders and arched his aching spine again. He stood, feeling ancient, his knees creaking as they sometimes did early in the day. He wasn't sure what he wanted to do, though he was pretty sure he didn't particularly want to play tennis. But, he thought, it was kind of Pete and Anne to let them stay the weekend, and they were good friends, so, to keep the peace, he'd go along. Even if his body protested.

He and Ellen lost the first set without winning a game. And what marginal enthusiasm he'd mustered at the outset soon faded.

His desperate lunges to return Pete's ballistic forehand only earned him a frustrated glare from Ellen.

"It's only for fun," he said, trying a smile.

"Sure, but can we try and win one game?" Ellen said beneath her breath as the two couples swapped ends.

"Can I help it if I'm a grass player?" Sam said jovially, scuffing the concrete surface. He wiped the sweat from his forehead and face, using the front of his shirt.

"Très amusant," Ellen said.

Sam sighed, and helped himself to the bottle of spring water sitting in a small ice chest beside the net. He swallowed a great gulp of the deliciously cool water, and wiped his mouth with the back of his hand. He offered the bottle to Ellen and, after a pause, she accepted.

Finally Sam and Ellen found a groove and managed a minor counter-attack, fighting back to take a couple of games in the final set. All four players were flagging under the dazzling sun when Pete dropped a clever volley over the net for victory.

"How about a swim?" Pete suggested as they gathered their gear and abandoned the baking court.

Sam didn't know if Pete was kidding or not, but he didn't want to take the chance. "How about brunch?" he said, his stomach protesting loudly.

Pete laughed. "Sure. Feeling your age, eh?"

"And the rest."

"I'll catch up in a minute, after a quick coupl'a laps."

With that he trotted off to the pool. The others headed along a shady path lined with citrus trees, and back to the Shelbys' second-floor apartment.

"I'm going to hit the shower," said Sam as he disappeared through the kitchen, leaving Anne and Ellen to prepare the meal.

"Things seem to be working out for you guys," Anne commented, slicing a cantaloupe in half.

"I don't know. Even when he's home, I can tell he's thinking about work. Half the time, if I ask him something I need to say it two or three times before I get an answer."

"I know, I mean Pete's the same way. Maybe it's a man thing."

"It's a damn annoying thing," Ellen said. "Where do you keep the plates?"

Anne pointed to a cupboard.

"And," Ellen continued, "heaven forbid if you don't hear one of their questions, and don't answer within a fraction of second."

"Answer what?" Pete asked as he returned from his swim.

"Was I talking to you?" asked Anne, playfully wielding the knife.

*

Behind the wheel of his Mercedes S500, the man thumbed through the selection of photographs. The plastic surgeon's penchant for S&M games was vividly revealed in the set of color glossies.

Slipping them back inside an envelope, the man gazed out at the harbor, at the row upon row of motor yachts and sailboats moored at their berths.

The doctor often spent his Saturdays down at the marina, cleaning and tidying his forty foot Bayliner, *Skin Deep*, one boat among the thousands that ensnared the waterfront homes of what had once been a quiet vacation city. Sometimes the doctor's wife would accompany him, but usually he came alone and stayed for a few hours. Rarely, it seemed, did the boat actually leave its mooring. But it made a fine place to sit back and watch those daring souls who took to the calm waters and sailed the bay.

Leaving his car, the man strolled along the dockside. A breeze swept off the water and rustled his blue and white Nautica clothing. While he would have preferred his accustomed black attire it was more important to blend in, especially here where appearance was everything.

"Ahoy, there," he called stepping onto the floating jetty, acting the cheerful ocean-loving neighbor.

Dr. Andrew Bernard glanced around, arms lathered with soapy water as he washed down the transom.

The man approached, feeling the wood planking sway lackadaisically as he walked.

"Hello?"

"Mind if I come aboard?"

The doctor returned the stranger's smile but couldn't hide his puzzlement. "Well, I... suppose," he said, wringing out the chamois leather he'd used to wipe down his boat.

"Name's Nick," the man said.

The doctor frowned, then shook the man's outstretched hand. "Dr. Bernard. Er, may I help you with something?"

"Nice vessel," he commented as he stepped aboard. "Wondered if I might have a moment of your time?"

"Oh." A realization seemed to dawn on the doctor's face. "I don't think I want to buy anything today, thank you. You know, these are private docks."

The man who, for now, called himself Nick nodded, and handed over the manila envelope he was holding.

"What's this?" Bernard frowned.

"Why not open it, Doctor?" the man was amazed at how obtuse supposedly intelligent men could be at times.

"Do I know you?" Bernard fingered the package. "Is your wife a patient?"

The man did not reply.

"Listen," Bernard continued. "If this is some legal matter then you should contact my attorney."

Slightly unnerved, he slid his finger under the flap and tore open the envelope.

One of the glossy enlargements slipped from his limp fingers and floated onto the deck. The doctor staggered as if kicked in the groin, his eyes bulging, face ashen.

"Hey," the man spoke, feigning sympathy. "Don't have a heart attack yet, Doctor."

He smiled broadly as Bernard slumped down on the captain's chair.

"That's it, you take it easy there. I know this must be a shock for you." He paused. "Of course, it would be more of a shock for Stephanie. I take it she doesn't enjoy these particular activities?"

Drawing a deep breath, Bernard looked up. "What do you want? How much?"

The man nodded. Perhaps the good doctor wasn't so dull witted after all.

*

Mercifully for Sam, there was no more talk of exercise during the rest of the day. Their sole activity was a gentle stroll along The Strip running through Palm Springs. Here, tourist shops and restaurants vied for passing trade with such notable stores as Chanel and Versace.

Money, it quickly appeared, was not tight in the Shelby household, and Sam and Ellen watched as Anne amassed several hundred dollars' worth of clothes in an upscale boutique.

"Don't you just love silk?" Anne asked Ellen as she handed her purchases to Pete.

"Lovely," Pete interrupted.

"I was talking to Ellen."

Pete snorted.

"Are you positive you don't want to try on that jacket? I'm sure it'd look wonderful on you, especially with your figure," Anne prompted Ellen.

"Absolutely," Pete agreed.

"Will you shut up, darling?"

"I don't think I really need anything right now." Ellen glanced at Sam long enough to catch his eye. "I bought an entire wardrobe once I got out of those loathsome maternity outfits."

Sam offered her a smile both sympathetic and grateful. Without mentioning their financial worries, Ellen had hopefully deflected any suspicions their friends might have had. Before they'd started a family, and set up the company, Ellen and he had enjoyed shopping the NorCal malls close to where he'd worked in Marin County. When they weren't shopping, they were dining out and drinking, savoring the San Francisco nights, the downtown party atmosphere. And while Sam preferred living in Southern California, there were a few things he missed about the city they'd called home for five years.

Sam took Ellen's hand, giving it a gentle, grateful squeeze, as they ambled along the street, following Pete and Anne. Holding hands, Sam thought, was something they hadn't done in a long time. Too long. And, he knew that was on him. Lifting her hand to his lips he kissed her slender fingers. And when she looked into his eyes it was like stepping back in time, to when they first dated, when every moment was precious. When the hell had that disappeared?

*

The evening air was as mellow as the Jazz emanating from the open door of "Roo's Club."

The couples crossed the street, heading toward the club.

"Who's Roo?" Ellen wondered.

"Rupert Collins, he was semi-famous, you could say, back in the eighties, I think. Great sax player. Really gifted," Pete informed her.

Sam nodded a polite hello to the club's youthful doorman who ignored the group, with the exception of Ellen. As they walked inside, Sam noticed him checking out his wife, drawn no doubt by her choice of dress. Sub-consciously Sam touched Ellen's elbow, escorting her quickly through the entrance.

Although he hadn't commented when she was getting ready to go out, Sam had felt her cropped dress was on the daring side of skimpy. On the flip side, he admitted, she looked fantastic. Can't have it both ways, he'd told himself.

They grouped around an untended podium. A stenciled sign instructed the patrons that they should wait to be shown to a table.

"So, where is anyone?" Pete asked after only a few seconds.

Sam glanced over his shoulder at the doorman, glad to see his attention was now focused on the street.

"Isn't he a bit short to be a bouncer?" Anne asked.

Sam felt inclined to agree.

"Maybe the guy's a black belt, a Fifth Dan, or something," Pete suggested.

"Good evening," a chirpy high-toned voice welcomed them. "Table for four?"

"Booth, thanks," said Pete.

She smiled. "This way, please"

Inside the club they skirted a small, unoccupied parquet dance-floor and were led to one of the large, curving booths.

"Kinda like getting into a leather hot-tub," said Pete and he grinned.

"Brenda will be along to serve you tonight," the woman said as they slid across the well-padded seat.

Pete nudged Sam and muttered. "Sounds like a plan, eh?"

"He's terrible," Ellen said to Anne.

"You don't have to tell me. You should hear him whenever there's something on the news about another privileged guy overstepping the mark."

"My point," Pete explained. "Is that when a drunken fondle, or some off-color remark is considered as career ending as rape, then the lines are beyond blurred. Not far off, and there really will be thought crimes –"

"Can we listen to the music?" Anne asked.

Pete raised his palms and stepped off his soapbox.

On stage a paunchy tenor saxophonist was accompanied by a young woman on the alto-sax, and a superb Latino pianist who was wearing shades despite the dim lighting inside the club.

Finishing their number, the group received an enthusiastic cheer from the early evening audience.

"Give it an hour," said Pete. "Place'll be hopping."

True to Pete's predication, by nine o'clock people packed the dance floor and the music pulsed to a potent beat.

Sam felt Ellen tugging his wrist.

"Come on," Ellen urged. "Everyone's up there."

That was true, thought Sam, as he watched Pete gyrate like a spastic puppet around Anne.

Ellen finished her third glass of Merlot.

"Sam, no one's going to be watching you. They're all having too much fun. Don't you want some fun?" she asked with a heavy hint of suggestion as she got to her feet.

"Yeah, sure." Sam tried but failed to hide a sigh as he edged out of the seat.

"Oh, thanks," said Ellen. "If it's too much trouble, then don't bother."

"What?" he said. "What did I say?"

"Hey, bud," Pete slapped Sam's shoulder hard as he marched off the floor. "Wondered where you kids were at?"

He waved his hand to their waitress, and caught her attention. "'Nuther round," he mouthed and pointed to the empty glasses.

"I'm good, really," said Sam covering his glass with his hand.

"Man, you can always grab a Lyft."

Anne swayed slightly as she left the floor. "What's happening?"

She flopped down on the seat beside Sam. She blinked melodramatically and fanned her face.

"Must be stuffy in here." She turned to Ellen. "You want to get a breath of air?"

"Actually, I was hoping to dance," she stared pointedly at Sam.

"Then let's go," said Pete, taking her hand.

Ellen faltered for a moment, but then a resolute expression crossed her face. "Yes, let's."

Sam and Anne watched them merge and meld into the crowd.

Just then, the waitress arrived with their refills balanced on a round wooden tray.

"Here you all are," she said as she collected the empty glasses.

Sam nodded absently, and tried to peer through the writhing bodies to wherever Ellen and Pete had disappeared.

Anne stared at her new drink.

"I'll be back in one minute," she said as she headed in the direction of the restrooms, leaving Sam alone.

The tenor sax cut a riff, bridging the trio into their next high tempo number.

Sam caught sight of Ellen, her cheeks suffused with a healthy glow. Pete was no longer strutting his stuff, instead Ellen was circling him, brushing her body against his in a manner that looked anything but accidental to Sam.

As the rhythm intensified so did Ellen's behavior, as she draped an arm around Pete's neck, swinging in front of him, pressing close. Pete took a step away and his eyes darted over to Sam. With what looked like a forced smile, Pete extracted himself politely from Ellen's grasp and headed back to the table. Moments later Anne returned.

"You okay?" he asked as they sat down.

"Bit woozy, I think I better get some fresh air. It's awfully toasty in here."

Pete pecked her cheek.

Ellen was still on the dance floor, swinging to the beat, and watching Sam.

A man in a canary yellow shirt appeared behind her, and whispered something.

Ellen spun around startled. Sam rose to his feet.

Pete's gaze snapped from his wife to the dance floor.

"Whoa," he reached for Sam's arm, but missed.

Sam marched toward the stranger, as Ellen said something to the man in reply.

The man merely smiled and nodded, sparing a glance at her wedding band.

"... a good evening," he heard the man's bass voice.

"Who was that?" Even as he spoke, Sam knew the words sounded petulant and rather infantile.

"I have no idea. Some guy asked for a dance. And I said no," Ellen shook her head, and walked past him, heading outside to join Anne.

Sam wandered back to the table.

"Everything copacetic?" Pete asked.

"Peachy," Sam replied. "How about we get the bill?"

Chapter 6

"See what you make of this."

Thankfully, Ellen's voice sounded chirpy this morning.

Stirring, Sam squinted against the harsh daylight and turned to face her. He managed a monosyllabic grunt by way of a greeting.

"Good morning to you too," she said.

"Surprised to see you awake so early that's all."

Sam could see she was engrossed in one of her puzzle books. World's greatest crosswords, or something, he decided.

"Make of what?"

"Five letters. Here's the clue, HIJKLMNO."

She looked at him expectantly. Sam groaned, closed his eyes and let his head sink deeper into the pillow.

"You're a lot of help."

Give me a break, he thought, you're the word wizard. But he didn't say anything as he felt her shifting position, then stepping out of bed.

"I don't know why you're up on your high horse. Are you still sulking about last night, Sam?"

He offered a shrug rather than admit she was right.

"You were the one who didn't want to dance."

"That was dancing, was it?"

Ellen took a moment before replying. "I already apologized, remember? Maybe a little too much wine went to my head, I know that's not an excuse. Please, can't we forget it?"

Inwardly, Sam sighed. She was right. He knew it, and he knew he was being an asshole.

"Yes. Yes we can."

"Okay. I'm going to grab a shower."

It sounded like an invitation, but as she entered the bathroom and closed the door he heard the lock click into place.

"Shit," he whispered.

They had come here to spend time together. To mend those fences he'd trampled on over the last couple of years. And here he was screwing everything up.

Pursing his lips, he eased out of bed, and knocked lightly on the door.

"Sweetheart? I'm sorry."

"Pardon?" Ellen replied, her voice rising above the rush of the shower. "I'll be out in a few."

"It doesn't matter."

Sam turned on the TV and surfed to a local channel. He slipped out of his pajamas and pulled on a pair of shorts together with a short-sleeve shirt. He heard the shower die, and a few seconds later the ceiling fan whirred into life.

He picked up Ellen's puzzle book and carried it with him as he opened the sliding door to the patio and strolled outside.

The scent of orange blossom pervaded the air. Sitting on a wrought iron chair, Sam tried to find the page Ellen had been working on and the clue she'd read to him. He racked his brain trying to think of the answer.

He was still staring at the book when Ellen emerged, a towel wrapped around her body while she frizzed her damp hair with her fingertips. Sam offered a fragile smile, hoping for some response. Ellen stared at him for a moment, then smiled back.

"Sorry, don't think I'm much help. You okay?" he asked.

"My head feels foul," she admitted. "My fault, I know."

"Don't expect any sympathy from me."

Ellen arched an eyebrow. "Maybe I could win your sympathy, good sir?"

Deliberately fluttering her eyelashes, she scooted back into the bedroom.

Sam hopped to his feet, in pursuit, catching her by the bed, grabbing a handful of bath-towel and pulling her down onto the mattress.

"Sam," she giggled. "The door?"

He hurriedly closed the glass sliding door, and tugged the sheer drape across.

"Better?"

"Hmmm, better." Ellen let the towel slip from her body as he approached.

"Not bad, Mrs. Grady," he said, stroking her.

"Not bad? How about damn good?" She smiled, letting his fingertips caress her skin, touching her stomach then rising higher, circling her breasts.

She murmured softly beneath his touch, louder when he lowered his head, laying butterfly kisses over her neck and shoulders.

"God, that tickles."

Sam silenced her, clamping his mouth over hers, kissing her with the emotions pent up in the weeks since they'd last made love.

He teased her, enjoying her squirm helplessly, shuddering under his touch when his hands slipped lower.

"Someone might walk in," Ellen managed to breathe, straining to see over Sam's shoulders, eyes focused on the door knob. She fumbled at his shorts.

"Zipper's stuck," she said.

Rolling aside, Sam tugged at the zip.

"Don't keep a lady waiting," Ellen chuckled, watching him struggle.

Sam tugged valiantly, but the damn thing was totally stuck. He stood up and managed to rip the zip open and pull off his shorts. But by then his gaze had followed Ellen's and wandered to the door. He felt his ardor fading, conscious that someone might interrupt.

Ellen picked her towel off the carpet and wrapped it around herself. Their moment's passion a vanishing mist.

"We should probably get dressed," Ellen said.

Sam grinned lasciviously. "It was your fault, you know?"

"Oh? How do you figure that? You grabbed me."

"True, but you shouldn't have been wearing that."

"This towel?" Ellen frowned.

"That body," said Sam.

Ellen smiled, biting her lower lip. "We have to get away more often."

Sam nodded, he felt better than he could remember for a long time.

Ellen fastened her lacy bra, noticing him staring.

"I love you," he said.

"I know."

*

In his mind the man heard the steady drip of water, calling to him as he drove.

His ranch was ten miles southeast of Banning, not far from Palm Springs. His wealthy prey often visited weekend retreats in the desert, Rancho Mirage or La Quinta, playing golf or cutting deals among their clique of friends. So the ranch provided a useful base, and meant he left no paper trail behind. No hotel receipts and always paying cash in restaurants, and for groceries and gas. For the same reasons he had purchased a cabin in Mammoth Mountain, a favorite haunt for wealthy winter skiers. He'd even taken up the sport, though he didn't like the snow.

But only the desert had his special place. The dark Cathedral. Where the recently departed Charles Maitland had joined many others who believed they could do whatever they pleased with impunity. Sometimes he pondered targeting those high profile crooks and purveyors of misery you saw so often in the news, like the family behind the devastating opioid crisis which had ruined thousands of lives. Left to the courts, he doubted any of them would spend even a night behind bars, let alone the fate their sins truly merited. But the risk was too great. As it was, his workload seemed to be ever increasing. There was simply too much evil in this world.

Leaving the two-lane blacktop, the Mercedes jounced over a pot-holed track leading toward the long, low ranch. Cacti grew sporadically in the arid paddock, and the wooden fence surrounding the property needed a fresh coat of paint. He parked outside the adobe building, dawn sunlight tinting the walls a subtle shade of pink. Clouds serrated the sky with choppy waves of reds and mauves. Here he could breathe deep. The air was clean out here, not like the city. Even by the coast, the pall of pollution was ever present. Invisible and insidious.

Once inside, he cracked open the plantation shutters. Slats of sunlight spilled across the southwestern style furnishings and throw rugs. He dumped the file he'd brought from his study onto a coffee table hewn from granite.

Within the file, photographs showed a middle-aged man, with a determined jaw line and deep-set eyes. His wispy blond hair was receding, the sunlight flaring off his forehead. A perfectly ordinary guy. Not someone who would attract any attention on the street.

But someone with a secret.

The man had been saving this file. After all, Alex Casper was not a wealthy man. A police pension and his present job as a security chief at a local country club certainly did not qualify him for millionaire status.

"It's not just the money," the man said aloud. "It's justice."

And as a police officer, sworn to uphold the law, Alex Casper had erred.

It had been four years since Alex Casper retired from the Palm Springs Police Department. He'd served for fifteen years, reaching the rank of sergeant. His reason for retirement was personal. His wife had vanished one evening, and he'd devoted himself to trying to find her. The case remained open, unsolved by missing persons. Although foul play was suspected, her body had never been recovered. It was possible, the police said, that she'd just had enough with being a cop's wife and decided to walk away. But Alex knew better.

Oh, yes, thought the man, Alex knew exactly what had happened.

Sergeant Alex Casper had murdered his wife.

Luck. Plain and simple luck, had revealed the crime to the man's vigilant eyes.

Four years ago, both men had journeyed across the desert on the same cloudless night, a full moon casting its silver light across the sand.

The man had seen Alex first, and had been able to hide among the rocks near his cave. His victim's car had been parked out of sight, although not far away, near a cleft in the low ravine. The man had often considered himself overly cautious, until that night. He remembered hearing the approaching drone of a car engine and had scrambled away from the cave, climbing a dozen feet above the entrance and ducking behind a large rock moments before the other car drew up and stopped. Less than seventy feet separated the two killers.

Sergeant Casper climbed out of his car. He gazed around, although probably not expecting to see anyone in the middle of the night, in such a godforsaken place. He walked around his dilapidated PSPD cruiser and unlocked the trunk. He reached inside, and with incongruous tenderness lifted out the body. The body of his wife, her hair ruffled by the desert wind.

How the police officer had come to learn of the cave, the man did not know. Perhaps Casper, who had lived near Palm Springs all his life, had come here as a teenager, sneaking off with friends, on the edge of the desert to smoke pot. Whatever the reason, the cop had entered his sanctum, the man thought.

After Alex Casper emerged from the cave and drove away, the man had scurried down from his hiding place and entered the cave. He found the body and a suitcase partially buried under rubble, not far from the narrow passage that led to the Cathedral.

He shook his head, disgusted at the pathetic effort to conceal the body. He'd expected far more from a cop. As the corpse decayed it would attract animals, and they in turn might alert someone.

And that would never do.

So the late Mrs. Casper became the only woman to be claimed by the ink black water.

The man flipped over the photograph, a shot he'd taken a year earlier during one of his frequent trips to Palm Springs. He glanced at the brief notes scribbled on the back of the picture. The guy might be an ex-cop, but he was also a criminal. And stupid enough to have been seen hiding the body. The man wondered idly if he would be able to earn any money from Alex Casper before he killed him.

It was time they met.

*

Sam stood beside Ellen near the living room wet bar, she cradled her cell phone while she talked.

"And you're being good for grandma?" she asked.

Sam couldn't hear his son's reply, but he knew Jason would be on his best behavior.

"Here's Daddy," she said.

Sam took the receiver. "Hey, kiddo. So what did you do yesterday?"

"We watched Wall-Eeeee," Jason said, doing the voice.

In the background Sam heard Lucy chuckle and comment, "Twice."

"I hope you didn't stay up past your bedtime."

"No, Daddy," such an innocent voice. "When are you back?" he sounded plaintive.

"We'll pick you up this evening. Okay, partner?" he said, missing the little boy terribly, even more than he'd thought he would. Despite all the late nights at the office, Sam made sure to look in on Jason every night.

"Yep."

"Let me speak with grandma a second."

After a few words, he hung up. Ellen squeezed his hand. "It's good to have my old Sam back again," she told him quietly.

They loaded the Shelby's four sets of golf clubs into the back of the Explorer. Sam and Ellen would be using the old clubs, while Pete and Anne enjoyed the polished sets they'd bought each other the previous Christmas. Pete, with a nine handicap, had been playing for years.

Sam hopped behind the wheel, with Pete climbing in beside him.

As he drove out to the main road, an embarrassed silence settled over the occupants.

"I'm," Ellen broke the mood. "I don't know about anyone else, but I think I had a wee bit too much to drink last night."

Pete twisted around in his seat, and chuckled. "Yeah. But you should've seen Anne this morning, right, hon?"

"Okay, Mr. John Travolta."

They drove past the Sunday shoppers and churchgoers fresh from morning prayer.

Sam was more interested in the scenery than the crowds. The lush grass and colorful flowers stopped abruptly, and they entered the desert, only to emerge a few minutes later in another Eden.

"Take the next right," Pete commented from the passenger seat.

Sam switched lanes, and pulled through the marble pillars marking the entrance to the upscale Thirty Palms country club.

"What a dump," Sam said.

"Yeah, they should really do the place up," Pete grinned back.

They followed the driveway as it looped around a fountain with a modern sculpture that, to Sam, looked more like a Russian hammer and sickle than anything to do with golf. He pulled to a halt next to a waist-coated valet.

They carried their golf bags into the palatial clubhouse, footsteps echoing on the veined marble floor.

"Need to get you guys some shoes," Pete told them.

"I'll be all right in trainers," said Sam, thinking of the few times he'd played golf on a municipal course.

"Rules."

Sam glanced at Ellen. "Rules," he mouthed behind Pete's back. Ellen looked away, trying not to laugh. Probably get us thrown out, thought Sam. Laughing — no doubt a criminal offense at a Palm Springs golf club.

Driving the little electric cart was the most enjoyable part of the game, Sam decided after they pulled up at the fifth tee. Pete was in his element, Anne was struggling to remember all she'd learnt after months of expensive lessons with the pros. Meanwhile, Sam and Ellen were happy if their club made contact with the ball and it shot off in the vague direction of the pin. Still, it was nice to get outside and enjoy the sunshine, and at least the game was less strenuous than tennis. Maybe if it didn't take so damn long to play, he'd think about taking it up one day.

Crack! The little white ball exploded off the face of Pete's wood, arcing high into the azure sky. Sam followed the golf ball to its zenith, then lost sight of it long before it returned to earth.

"Nice shot," said Anne. She looked at Sam. "You're next."

Positioning his feet in the uncomfortable stance Pete insisted upon, Sam swung his arms, limbering up.

"That's supposed to be a practice swing," Pete told him, his voice barely masking a sigh. "Not aerobics."

"Pete," said Anne, "stop being such an old fart. We're here to have fun, not play the U.S. Open."

"Okay, okay. I just thought people might like to learn something while we go around. Obviously I was wrong."

Anne tickled his chin. "Now don't pout, Pete."

"Silence please," Sam said, still swinging his arms, even exaggerating a little for Pete's benefit.

He took a breath, moving to the ball, or addressing it, as Pete would say. Keep your eye on the ball, club smoothly back, then forward. The club swished through the air as it arced down and followed through. Perfect. Sam knew he'd done everything right, exactly as Pete had instructed. There was just one problem. The pesky ball was still sitting on the tee, unmoved by the power drive he'd aimed at it.

"Warming up," he said nonchalantly.

Frigging ball.

He composed himself and tried to remember the correct sequence. There seemed to be a million things to do in the space of a second as the club swung back, then down. He twisted his body on the follow-through, the way they did on TV. Then glanced down at the tee and the ball.

"Yeah, yeah," he said before Pete could comment.

Third time's the charm, Sam told himself. Only this time he just swung the club, ignoring Pete's suggestions, and hit the ball. Not a great shot, but at least the ball raced heavenward, disappearing into the blue. Sam glanced at Pete, whose eyes tracked the ball with military precision.

"Where'd that one go?"

Pete pointed. "In the rough."

Ellen teed off next. Unlike Sam she hit the ball the first time, giving him a cheerful grin as the ball plopped down in the middle of the fairway.

"Not bad," Pete said.

Sam couldn't wait for the game to finish. Still, at least he got to drive the cart.

*

From his bar stool, the man watched Alex Casper walk through the dining room escorted by a man he guessed was the manager. Their muted talk appeared one of self-importance and probably little substance. Perhaps a patron had been caught borrowing someone's gold-plated tees. The idea curled his lips in a wry smile.

The men hovered near a table, chatting with two couples seated there. It was one of the few occupied tables this late in the afternoon. Too late for lunch, too early for dinner.

He watched one of the golfers at the table gulp his beer. Better not be driving, mister, he thought to himself. In fact, both men had been drinking for the past half hour. Real dumb, he thought.

Annoyed with the distraction, he focused his attention on Alex Casper.

He was surprised how similar Casper looked compared to the night he'd first seen him. Evidently, guilt had not aged the man. He was probably enjoying his freedom. The man remembered the dark bruises around the murdered woman's face. Casper, you sick bastard, you'll pay for your crime.

Casper and the manager strolled away from the table and disappeared through the French doors onto the sun drenched patio.

Leaving an innocuous tip on the polished bar, the man strolled toward the French doors, following his target.

His eyes narrowed slightly as he passed the happy couples drinking and laughing at their table.

The woman in the green blouse and white slacks glanced around. And her eyes met his. Eyes of smoke that spoke of desire. Passion. Her face so beautiful, so tranquil. He offered a tentative smile and his pulse quickened when she smiled politely back, before returning to the group's conversation.

He couldn't help continuing to stare.

Her face reminded him so much of his mother.

"Ready to roll?" Pete asked, banging the empty beer glass on the table.

"Where to?" said Ellen.

"I thought we could go up the tram?"

"It's getting late, Pete," his wife said.

"I know, but it was just an idea." Then he glanced at Ellen, concerned. "Of course, if you're set on Italian?"

Ellen laughed. "I'm not set. Whatever you want to do is fine with us."

"So, why don't we eat at the restaurant up there?"

"Where?" Ellen asked.

"On top of the mountain."

Ellen glanced at Sam.

"Er, how big's this tram?" he asked, trying not to sound anxious.

"It's a cable car," Anne explained. "It's big."

"Great view. Food's pretty good too. Hell, anyone visiting P.S. ought to take a ride in the aerialway, don't you reckon, honey?" Pete said, turning to his wife.

"Only if they want to, Pete."

"That's settled then," said Pete, not waiting for a reply.

Pete and Sam laid down enough cash to cover the bill, and they started to head out.

"I need the restroom," Ellen whispered to Sam.

"Meet you out there."

Ellen nodded and went over to the barman.

The man had remained at the bar, despite his plan to follow Casper. He felt intrigued and captivated by the woman who was now walking toward him.

She beckoned to the barman.

"I was looking for the restroom."

The man stepped off the stool, placing a crisp ten-dollar bill on the bar before walking away.

He lingered in the shadow offered by the cloakroom entrance, the room itself unattended.

A dozen feet away, the door to the Women's Restroom opened, and an elderly lady stepped into the corridor. She glanced at him and he quickly bent down to adjust his shoelace. He could feel her suspicion as she walked down the corridor and back into the lounge.

Moments later the restroom door opened again. He glanced up as, this time, the woman he'd followed emerged.

Her eyes flicked past him as she approached. Her footsteps slowed and she paused, facing an antique mirror on the opposite wall.

He held his breath as he watched her reflection. Watched her studying herself as if to find some blemish or imperfection.

She tutted softly and fished inside her handbag. Pulling out a lipstick, she pouted. As she touched it to her lips, her eyes found him. She returned his gaze as she painted her lips with a tender, deliberate sensuality. When she'd finished, she circled her tongue across the slippery crimson gloss.

Finally, she turned to him.

"Hi," she said.

His pulse quickened. His voice caught in his throat.

He managed a smile, and turned his head slightly. Then he saw her eyes dart to his scar before looking away as people always did, pretending they hadn't noticed. But for once he didn't mind.

As she walked away, he breathed deeply, indulging in the heady fragrance of her perfume, as sweet as citrus.

Her smile soothed his mind.

Gradually, his good humor faded as he reminded himself there was work to be done and his thoughts turned once again to Alex Casper.

Chapter 7

Sam's fears proved only partially founded. The gondola, while crowded, mercifully was not small. He kept a fixed smile in place, his mouth dry, as everyone peered out the windows at the mountain below.

"You warm enough?" he asked Ellen, wrapping his arm around her waist.

"I'm fine." She snuggled against him. Keeping her voice low. "You sure you're okay in here?"

"Wonderful. Yeah, I'm okay."

Ellen gave his hand a comforting squeeze.

The car rocked as it passed another pylon. The abrupt judder gave way to an unnerving sway.

"When it's clear you can see the Salton Sea, that's like fifty miles or something," said Pete enthusiastically. "The country club's down there," he pointed. "Floodlights will come on later."

"Nice." Sam didn't bother looking for Pete's golf course, one of the zillion dotted around Palm Springs.

If pushed, Sam would have agreed that the sun, a blood red ball slipping behind the mountain, looked spectacular. But that didn't mean he was enjoying the ride.

He still felt trapped. And he held Ellen's hand until the tram finally pulled into the terminal.

Sam was the first out the car.

Pete slapped him on the shoulder. "See. Told you you'd love it."

Sam nodded as they strolled outside.

They walked along a path, which in winter would be lined with snowdrifts, but for now was shrouded with coarse shrubs. Pedestal-mounted binoculars allowed visitors to glimpse the panorama.

As the last sliver of sun disappeared from view, the temperature began its hasty decline. Down in the valley it would remain balmy long into the night, but at more than eight thousand feet the mountain soon became far too cold to stand outside chatting, and the two couples headed into the restaurant, Peaks.

Once inside they had to wait thirty minutes at the bar before being shown to a table.

"It's a ploy. Makes you spend more money on drinks," Pete explained when the waiter passed within earshot.

"Pete," Anne hissed, appearing to be both annoyed and amused, a little smile giving her away.

Sam glanced up from his meal, veal medallions in a rich brown sauce, and looked out the window, surprised to see it had already grown so dark. The trees outside formed twisted silhouettes, branches rustling in the swirling wind. Beyond, the city lights of the Coachella Valley were displayed in spectacular fashion.

"It's getting late," he commented. At this rate they'd be lucky to pick Jason up before eleven, and tomorrow Sam needed to be in the office early.

"Problem?" Pete asked.

Ellen must have read his thoughts and, catching Sam's eye before he replied, she gave the slightest shake of her head.

"No. Didn't realize it was quite so late, that's all."

"If you guys need to get away..." said Anne.

"We're fine," Ellen assured her.

Except, thought Sam, we probably won't be in bed until long after midnight, and then up again at five. He chopped the last strip of veal in half and chewed. Sometimes, he wished Ellen would see things from his point of view. He glanced at her and suddenly felt guilty, seeing her so happy for a change. Maybe he was the one being unreasonable. They were both enjoying the meal, and the company of friends, and all Sam could think of was getting to work the next day. Chill out, he told himself, or you'll end up with a heart attack before you're forty.

"More wine over there, Sam?" Pete asked, a bottle of Zinfandel poised above Sam's glass.

Sam hurriedly covered his glass with his hand. He swallowed the meat. "No, thanks. I'm driving."

"Good man," said Pete, pouring the wine into his glass, filling it to the rim.

"Excuse me," said Anne, her glass nearly empty.

"Sorry, sweetheart." He poured a thimbleful of wine into her glass. "Thought you'd follow Sam's example if you're behind the wheel."

"What makes you think I'm driving?" Anne asked, picking up the bottle, pouring until it was half full.

"I...er," Pete stammered eloquently. "But you always drive."

"Precisely."

"And I've drunk more than you."

Anne offered her husband a bemused smile. "What does that mean? You can drink whatever you want, and I have to act as your chauffeur?"

Pete glanced at Sam, evidently hoping for moral support. But Sam merely shrugged his shoulders.

"Thanks a lot," Pete muttered. "Okay, we'll grab an Uber and pick the car up tomorrow."

Anne chuckled softly. "Pete, I'd like to be consulted, that's all."

A moment's silence passed over their table.

"You mean you'll drive?"

"Yes, I'm certainly not letting you drive after four glasses of wine and that beer you had at lunch. But next time, you're driving."

"Deal." He picked up his glass, raising it in a silent toast to his wife.

Sam caught Ellen's twinkling eyes, and that was all he needed to set him laughing. All four people seated in the corner booth started laughing, drawing the attention of nearby patrons who wondered what could be so funny.

*

Careful. He would have to be so very careful with this one, the man told himself as he approached the rendezvous point. The former sergeant had been cautious during their brief initial meeting, not giving anything away. But Alex Casper had been sufficiently intrigued by the man's comments to agree to meet him at nine o'clock.

"I imagine it's been a while since you saw the rocks at Devil's ridge," the man had said when he'd finally caught Alex alone at the country club late in the afternoon.

"What?" Alex turned, menace glowing from his brooding eyes. Eyes that said, don't mess with me.

"We should talk, Alex."

"Yeah? Why's that?" Alex took a step forward. A big man, weighing two twenty, he'd kept in decent shape since leaving the department.

"Alex, why do you think they never found her body?" the man's voice barely a whisper. He stood in the doorway of the security office. He'd lingered until he saw the two young guys who worked under Alex Casper leave on their patrol. Even so, someone might come strolling along the corridor at any time.

"I think we should talk in private," he suggested.

"I think you should get the fuck out of here," Alex casually rested his hand on his hip, above his holstered .38, and flexed his fingers.

Don't push too hard, too soon, the man thought, eyeing the gun. But he knew he'd already gained the security man's interest. "Be at the ridge, nine o'clock tonight," he ordered, and slipped out the room.

*

Driving across the desert gave Alex Casper the chills. Christ, ever since that fateful night four years ago his life had plummeted to the depths of depression.

He'd never meant to kill Suzanne. He was sure of that in his own mind. He'd lashed out, hitting her during some dumb argument following thirty-six hours on the job at Spring Break. He'd come home tired, and pissed with the snotty-nosed attitude of visiting college kids. Thinking themselves so superior, hey, we know everything — moaning about stupid cops always hassling us. The year before he'd let his temper get the better of him, smacking one particularly obnoxious, foul-mouthed student in the face with his nightstick. The blow broke three of the boy's teeth. His father, it turned out, was some wealthy hotshot attorney from Florida, who subsequently applied enough pressure to prevent Alex's pending promotion from passing the board. Still, Alex thought, the kid's blood-soaked mouth had almost been worth it. Almost.

This time he'd taken a few deep breaths during a couple of inflammatory situations. Times when his cop's instincts knew the kids meant no real harm, although they shouldn't be drinking so much. While his guts told him to knock a few heads together. They made a few token arrests for possession and a couple of DUI's. On the last arrest they'd been outnumbered, twenty students against two cops trying to make a bust. The chants of the crowd filled his already aching head. His partner had radioed for backup. And while Alex was sorely tempted to take matters into his own hands, he didn't.

Instead, he went home.

Suzanne, usually so understanding, was waiting. Angry that he hadn't called to let her know when he was coming home. Angry that he hadn't let her know he was okay. A cop's wife, dreading the news she always feared.

"I'm here now, aren't I?" Alex said.

"Is it too much trouble to pick up the phone once in a while?"

"I'm out on the street, not a damn stockbroker," he said, with an unveiled reference to her brother. Suzanne was always comparing their lifestyle to his. So he made more money, and was home by six each evening. So what? What the hell did Lance do that was so goddamn special? Nothing, as far as Alex could see. He did deals. Deals! I'm out there saving lives, protecting people, the proverbial thin blue line, and he does fucking deals.

"I can't take it anymore," she said. "Lord knows I've tried, Alex."

"What?" he was tired, he wanted nothing more than a dozen hours uninterrupted sleep. Leave me alone, he wanted to scream.

And then she'd hit him with her news, her words striking with force of a bullet.

"I'm leaving. I want a divorce."

"No," his voice calm, colder than ice. "You're not going anywhere."

She shouldn't have pushed him. Not when his body and mind felt so vulnerable, so utterly exhausted.

He hadn't accepted her words, he refused to believe them. Until he saw her suitcase, already packed, standing in a corner of the room. Part of his hazy mind wondered why he hadn't noticed it the moment he walked in. Another part of his mind couldn't care less. All he knew was he wasn't about to lose his wife. Not for doing his job.

"I love you, but I can't —" she said, reaching out to touch his face, perhaps a final stroke of his rough cheek, before she walked away from ten years of marriage. And it had been a good marriage, hadn't it? he wondered.

Even as the unanswerable questions began spinning through his mind, he lashed out.

He struck her. The back of his hand flying upward, hitting her face. Suzanne's head snapped back and she dropped. Hitting the fireplace's stone hearth hard.

She lay there motionless.

Even as he moved toward her, sinking to his knees, he knew he'd killed her. Desperately, he breathed into her mouth. He'd used CPR successfully once before at a shooting incident, saving the life of a fellow officer.

Goddamned, why wasn't it working this time? People didn't die like this. Not this quickly, not from a punch. Suzanne was unconscious. Sure, he'd hit her hard, but he couldn't have killed her.

"Come on, Sue, wake up," he whispered into her ear, praying she would obey.

"Wake up, baby."

The home phone rang. Startled, he spun across the floor, trying to get away from the body and the accusing, shrill scream of the phone. His heart raced, his mind trying to work out... something.

Christ, he'd killed his wife. No. No. No.

Mercifully the phone stopped, the answering machine cutting in. Then he heard Lance's voice coming from the machine.

"Sis? You there?" a pause. "Nothing major. Guess I'll try you guys in the morning."

He hung up.

Alex Casper needed time to think.

Thankfully the living room drapes were closed. No one outside could have seen what happened.

Question: had Suzanne told anyone about her plans to leave him? Her brother seemed the most likely candidate, but he sounded normal on the phone moments before. No, Alex decided, she was probably planning to move out for a day or two. Perhaps she would have tried to work things out at that point. If only he hadn't... but it was too late for that. Crouched in the corner of the room, he stared at her, lying motionless on the carpet. He would give anything to see her move. Just a faint twitch of her hand, a spasm, anything.

He didn't know how long he sat, waiting, huddled in the corner, staring at his wife's body, his mind shutting down, unable to accept reality. He was a murderer, as cold-blooded as those the homicide department tracked down. And deserving the same punishment. But jail time wouldn't be the same, not for a cop. He wouldn't survive. A cop gone bad, in the worst way imaginable. The prison officers would turn a blind eye, and one time somebody would get close. A prison sentence would be as lethal as one which put him on death row and a needle in his vein.

You're a cop, use your knowledge, a voice spoke out of the nightmare turmoil that snared his mind.

A break-in, he thought. I came home and found her lying on the carpet. He could break a window from the outside, remove her jewelry, trashing the bedroom in the process. After all, a crook wouldn't know the exact location of their valuables. But she'd been dead for an hour now. What was his alibi? he wondered, in case he should become a suspect.

A kidnapping? He'd need an anonymous ransom demand, something that couldn't be traced to him. Even as the idea formed, he discarded it. Too complex, and why would anyone kidnap Suzanne? They weren't rich. Sure, Lance had some money, but not that much.

Keep it simple, he told himself.

She was packed, walking out on him. What if she'd already gone by the time he got home? What would he have done? Called her folks, to find out if she'd gone to visit either her mother or her brother. After that? Call the police.

And so he worked to that schedule as best he could.

First, he went outside, onto the street and moved his PSPD patrol car around to the rear of their house, out of sight from any prying neighbors. Usually he would have driven his own Camaro home. But technically he was still on call, and he'd retained the patrol car. The PSPD was not short of vehicles, and while a tight-ass commander would have clamped down on the practice, Chief Wallenbrook let it slide, figuring the cars were best out on the street rather than in the compound. Especially during Spring Break. It made for a more rapid deployment in case of an incident, and the Chief made a point of running the force his way.

Next, Alex lifted Suzanne's limp body from the carpet. He was relieved to see no evidence of blood. He still couldn't believe she was dead. Cradling her in his arms, he imagined she was merely asleep. He kept expecting her to murmur and stir as he carried her outside.

Silent tears trickled over his cheeks and fell onto Suzanne's face as he lowered her into the trunk. He took care not to bump her head.

He eased the trunk lid shut, barely a click, then hurried inside to collect her suitcase.

He lifted the case, surprised by how little it weighed. So light it seemed empty. A frown creased his anxious brow as the possibility flashed through his mind. He knelt, opening the two catches, and lifted the lid.

The case was empty.

He slammed it shut. Empty?

Dear Lord. Perhaps Suzanne hadn't meant to leave him. She'd been upset, and with good reason, and had wanted to scare him. Jesus, he'd killed her, and she hadn't even been thinking of leaving him. Somehow that made it worse, if anything possibly could be worse.

He couldn't breathe. He rushed to the bathroom and vomited into the sink. Heavy sobs gripped his aching chest. He hadn't meant to kill her. Please, he hadn't. He looked in the mirror at the tear-streaked face and blood-red eyes, hating the man who stared back.

Rinsing the vile taste from his mouth, he ran into their bedroom, grabbing a couple of Suzanne's favorite outfits from the closet. Underwear, panty hose, shoes, he tried not to forget anything. Makeup and perfume he put in her small travel bag, the one they'd bought for their Hawaiian vacation a couple of years ago. He'd surprised himself and thoroughly enjoyed the two weeks touring the islands. Now he wished he'd spent more time with Suzanne. He zipped the bag shut, and, along with the toiletries, he sealed away his memories of happier times.

Alex shoved her packed case onto the slippery fiberglass rear seat of the patrol car, then drove into town.

He stopped off for a beer at Mulligan's, barely sipping the cool drink, but taking the time to chat to a few fellow off-duty officers.

Within ten minutes he slipped out the back door and climbed into his car and headed out to the desert.

His best hope lay in moving quickly. Establishing a loose alibi, he figured, was better than none at all. Cops would remember seeing him at the bar. Therefore he could argue that he'd been drinking ever since he came off duty, nearly two hours ago. He would stop by Mulligan's on the way home. Another beer, perhaps a game of pool, before he said so long and headed home. The moment he arrived he planned to call Lance, worried that Suzanne was not there. If all went well, he'd make that call before midnight. Lance would insist Alex did something, launch a search for his missing sister, and Alex would oblige, contacting missing persons. After that... who knew? It was too much to think about.

"Deal with it," he said out loud, focusing on the immediate problem. He had to dispose of her body. He debated whether it mattered if the body was discovered or not. If it was never discovered then it would be nearly impossible to prove a murder had been committed. But, his conscience argued, Suzanne deserved a funeral. He owed her far more than that. That meant the body should be found, eventually. Not too soon, otherwise the time of death could be pinpointed. Maybe in a few weeks, following a tip-off from an anonymous caller. Meantime he needed to hide the body. And he knew the perfect place.

The mound of rocks rose, a silhouette before the twinkling stars above the dark horizon.

Alex drove along the dried riverbed, unable to shake off the ghost of his sin. He wanted to weep as he had so often in the days following Suzanne's death.

Alex recalled making the tip-off call, not to the police, but to a reporter. Careful to disguise his voice, he'd called from a pay phone. Suzanne had been missing for five weeks. Long enough for her disappearance to faded from the headlines. Yesterday's news. He told the reporter about a woman's body he'd stumbled across near a dry riverbed. The reporter wanted to know what he'd been doing out in the middle of the desert, but Alex hadn't bothered to answer. His heart hammering, he'd hung up and driven into town, headed for the police station.

The reporter notified the police, and two officers from Missing Persons were dispatched. Alex arrived at the station a few minutes later. The lobby grew eerily silent the moment he stepped inside. The desk sergeant had hurried over to him, pulling him to one side, passing on the news, and the location given by the anonymous caller, and reminding Alex it could be a cruel hoax.

Acting the role he'd created, Alex fled from the building, hitting the siren as he floored the car and slewed out onto the street.

Alex's car skidded to a halt beside another black and white.

"Nothing," Officer Donaghue reported succinctly as Alex threw open his car door and raced across the sand.

Alex stopped dead. His mouth dry. "What?"

"Sorry. Nothing in there but rocks and dust. Must've been some sick bastard playing a game. Sorry, man."

"What?" Alex shook his head. Keep control, he thought, they haven't looked in the right place.

Christ, her body was lying in that cave, not a hundred feet away. What sort of detectives were these guys?

"Where'd you look?"

"Searched the cave, nothing. Some signs that people, or a person, have been in there. Footprints. Nothing else."

Footprints? After five weeks? Wouldn't the wind have swept sand into the cave, obscuring his prints? Alex wondered.

And yet they hadn't found the body.

His shoulders sagged, emotionally drained after the weeks of waiting before he placed the call. He'd expected things to be resolved following the visit to the cave. Once they found the body they'd hopefully come to the conclusion that Suzanne had been killed by a vagrant. Sure, they'd investigate him, most murders were committed by people who knew the victim, usually a family member. But he had his alibi — his fellow officers. But without her body the case would remain unsolved. Even worse, he wouldn't be able to put Suzanne to rest, as she deserved. And he would never know what had happened to her body. He found her disappearance more than disturbing. It scared him.

"Hey," Donaghue touched his arm. "You okay?"

Alex nodded. "I've got to look."

There hadn't been a single day in the past four years when he'd not wondered what happened to his wife's body.

But tonight, Alex knew, he would find out.

Briefly, he wondered why the creep — who must have seen him hide the body — had waited so long before making his appearance. The man's motives had to involve blackmail. It was the only thing that, to Alex's trained mind, made any sense.

Although he was concerned about the witness, who had only now come forward, Alex also had unanswered questions. Would the man really have taken the time to move Suzanne's body, hiding her someplace where the police had never looked? And if so, why? Alex didn't know.

But he intended to discover the answer to the haunting mystery.

The stranger obviously had his own agenda for tonight's meeting, but he was about to discover how things had a way of turning around. He'd regret the moment he'd stepped into Alex's office. Instinctively, as Alex drove, his hand moved to his holster, his fingertips stroking ice blue steel.

He'd checked the weapon, ensuring it was fully loaded, a round chambered. And he was prepared to use it.

Whoever the stranger was, he'd picked the wrong guy to threaten.

Chapter 8

Sam endured the return journey in the cable car. The mountain was invisible in the darkness. He stood alone at the window and watched the valley. The streetlights and the warm glow from the houses grew ever closer as the tram drifted down for a slow-motion landing.

They left the aerial tramway and strolled across the car lot. Sam took a deep breath, smelling the balmy night air. He held Ellen's hand as they walked with the Shelbys to their cars.

"Thanks," Ellen said, air-kissing Anne's cheek when the time came to say goodbye. "We really enjoyed the weekend."

"Don't be such strangers," Anne said.

"We won't," Sam assured her.

He turned and shook Pete's hand.

"I'll have to drop by your office and see you guys in action," Pete said.

"Anytime you want to learn out how it's done," Sam teased, knowing full well that the company Pete worked for had computers fifty times more powerful than his own. Fortunately they didn't compete in the same special-effects markets. Pete was strictly upscale: movies and commercials.

Pete dropped his voice so the wives wouldn't hear. "How're things?"

"They're good. Thanks."

"Our pleasure," he hesitated then grinned. "Any time Ellen needs a dance partner, gimme a call would you?"

Sam lightly jabbed his friend's shoulder. "You'll be last on the list." He climbed into the Ford.

"Drive careful," Anne called, entwining her arm with Pete's.

They waved farewell, and the Explorer pulled out of the car lot, onto the cracked blacktop that wound back to Palm Springs.

As they drove away, Sam glanced at Ellen and caught her deep in thought.

"Penny for them," he said.

"Nothing," she smiled, her eyes tired but happy. "Thank you. That was a nice time."

"You're welcome. Yes it was," Sam said meaning every word. He rubbed his tired eyes. A couple of hours and they'd be home.

*

The man crouched in the rocks just inside the entrance to the cave and stretched out his legs to ensure his muscles didn't cramp. He was careful not to dislodge any loose debris, in case his prey had also arrived early. He lifted the compact night scope to his eye and scanned the dry riverbed.

He sipped water from his hip flask, grateful that he'd brought it on the long trek to the cave. He'd chosen to walk rather than bring his car, having done so he hoped to have the advantage of surprise on his side. Arriving early, he had scouted the area, including the cave, then climbed up to his vantage point.

He'd left the ranch at sunset. Taking a deep lungful of the arid air, tinged with the fragrance of wildflowers. Heat haze shimmered above the sand rippling the cacti, rising into the cloudless pink sky. As he walked, his shadow lengthened before becoming an insubstantial ghost as the sun dipped beyond the mountains. The temperature dipped lower, the day's heat gradually bleeding from the desert plateau. And as the sky darkened, night fell across the prehistoric landscape.

Using a compass borrowed from the earthquake kit he kept at the ranch, the man headed due south. After thirty minutes trekking across the wasteland he spotted distant pinpoints of light darting to and fro, red and white blurs as cars streaked along the highway a few miles to his right. He kept walking, enjoying the night air, and the feeling of isolation and security brought by the darkness. By eight o'clock he arrived above the rocky arroyo. He followed the dusty, meandering riverbed, the crevasse becoming shallower, less defined. Recognizing the bend ahead, which crumbled away as it progressed, boulders becoming rocks, rocks becoming scree, the man stopped and peered down. He smiled, when a couple of minutes later, he descended the precarious slope and found the entrance to his cave.

He pondered the time four years earlier when he'd watched the police officer dispose of his wife's body. Such evil, the man thought, repugnance welling in his throat, murdering a defenseless woman. Made you feel strong, did it? Made you feel like a man? Well, soon it'll be your time to suffer.

*

You messed with the wrong guy, bud, thought Alex Casper. First, he decided, he would ask a few questions, then, once satisfied with the creep's answers, he would wait to hear his demands. Blackmail. Well, go ahead, try that and you'll get a bullet in your skull for your trouble. Killing his wife had been an accident — he knew it was his fault, and he'd have to live with that knowledge. But it was still an accident, and if this guy thought he could take advantage of that, he was sadly mistaken. Killing such a person wouldn't be murder. More like pest control, thought Alex.

Despite his bravado, Alex's palms felt damp, his stomach tight with nervous anticipation as he neared the rendezvous. An adrenaline rush he'd not felt since he retired from the department pumped through his body. He was twenty minutes early, enough time to get the car out of sight, if the creep wasn't waiting for him already. Should have left earlier, he knew, but his shift at the country club hadn't finished until thirty minutes ago, and he hadn't wanted to draw attention to himself by leaving before then. Especially on a night when he might have to kill someone. He wondered if the creep knew how late he worked, and had set the meeting time accordingly. Probably, he decided.

"Damn," Alex muttered. This punk wasn't so dumb after all.

Maybe I should hear him out. Hell, even if he saw me with Suzanne, the police never found her body, and who's to say this is the person who moved her body and hid her elsewhere? Maybe I'm worrying unnecessarily, or so he tried to convince himself. After all, accusations without evidence were just so much shit in the breeze.

"Nothin' to worry about."

But his cop's instinct insisted he had plenty to worry about.

Approaching the dry riverbed, he headed due east, parking and switching off his headlights as he drew close to the meeting point. He parked in the open, having concluded surprise was probably not on his side. He climbed out, keeping the car between him and the cave entrance, his only protection. Cautious now, he waited ten minutes, listening to the shifting breeze, alert for any unnatural sounds, and letting his eyes grow accustomed to the darkness.

Nothing stirred.

He considered his next move. And marched boldly across the cracked riverbed toward the cave.

If the punk wanted to kill him he could have found less elaborate ways. At least, Alex hoped so.

Each step was an eternity. Come on, show yourself, creep, Alex mused, instinctively weaving across the open space. He had no intention of making himself an easy target. Like a goddamn chess game, he thought, trying to figure out what moves the stranger had planned, and how far ahead he might be.

Alex reached the tumbled, broken rocks, and within another minute was standing beside the mouth of the cave. Now what? He hated to expose himself still further by moving into the cave, knowing his body would be revealed, a black shadow against the starry night sky — yet what choice did he have?

He checked the time, five minutes past nine. The creep was here, he felt it in his gut.

"Hey!" Alex called out.

The only answer was a solemn echo.

He shouted again, listening intently for the slightest response. Still nothing.

Unfastening the catch securing his holster, he rested his hand on the gun butt. Keeping low, he edged inside the cave. Detecting no movement, he moved deeper into the gloom. His hand eased away from his gun and he fumbled in his jacket pocket for the small flashlight he'd brought. The lens was capped with a red filter, the light not as damaging to his night vision as white light. The pencil thin beam of bloody glow illuminated the rocks and dusty floor, tracking to the spot where he'd half buried Suzanne. He shivered despite the seventy-degree temperature.

Perhaps the man wasn't going to show, Alex thought as he turned full circle. The cave appeared empty. He flicked off the slender red beam, and was about to return to the entrance when brightness flooded the cave.

Alex squinted, raising a hand to shield his eyes, taking a step back and bumping into the cave wall. He dropped his flashlight and reached toward his gun.

"Hello." He recognized the creep's voice. He must have been inside the cave all the time, but where? Alex wondered. "I wouldn't recommend drawing your weapon, Sergeant." The man's voice was laced with scorn as he added the epithet.

"Sure." Alex held his hands limp at the side of his body. "No sudden moves," he assured the man, his mind racing. He couldn't believe he hadn't seen or heard the guy. A few years off the force and your senses dulled. The soft job working security for a wealthy country club had affected him more than he wanted to admit. Lost the edge, he realized.

"So," Alex said, keeping his voice level, in control. "I'm here like you asked. What do you want? And just who the hell are you?"

He heard the man's shoes scuff against rock, drawing closer. The bright light still aimed at Alex's eyes.

"Someone who believes the guilty should pay. Why did you do it, Sergeant?"

Alex shook his head. He'd asked himself that question a hundred times. He wished he could have those few minutes to live over. But he couldn't change the past. And he had no intention of explaining what happened to some punk.

"You want to turn that goddamn light off?" he said.

The punk laughed, a throaty cackle.

The light stayed on.

"You didn't answer my question. Why?"

"It was an accident."

"Of course," another cackle. "Of course it was. A misunderstanding, an accident. That's why you dumped her body out here."

"What the hell do you want? Money?"

"Money? Would that salve your conscience? Would that ease your guilt?" The man fell silent, as if considering his own remarks. "You should pay. Yes, I think you should. You admit you killed her. Was she armed? Was she threatening you?"

"I told you, it was an accident. I hit her. Christ, you think I wanted to kill my own wife?"

"Well, you did."

Fuck you, Alex thought, his hand edging closer to his gun. "We had an argument."

"So," said the creep, "you hit her. Not really an accident, was it?"

"Cut to the chase. How much do you want?"

"Hmm. Shall we say thirty thousand, for now."

"For now. Until next time, right?"

"Sergeant, you really aren't that important to me. You need to be punished, but you're simply not that important. I need a little cash right now to tide me over — and I don't like banks."

"This is blackmail. You're not above breaking the law, are you?"

"My, my, they did train you well at the academy, didn't they?" he laughed again.

Alex's fingers hovered an inch above his gun, his holster open. He'd managed to keep the punk distracted long enough to ease his hand into position. Draw and roll, he told himself. The punk was holding a light in one hand. Was his other hand empty, or did he have a gun? No way to know for certain. Try it now, he wondered, or do I wait for a better chance when we meet again?

"How long have I got?" Alex asked. "I ain't got thirty grand sitting in my savings account, you know."

"I'm not unreasonable. A week."

"A week? Get serious."

"Oh, I'm serious. Please believe that, Sergeant."

"One week. I'll get your money. But I've got a question."

"Yes?"

"What the fuck did you do with my wife's body?"

"Ah, that would be telling, wouldn't it. But let me assure you, before this is finished, I'll take you there."

This is already finished, Alex thought as he flexed his knees.

He drew his gun as he dived to the right.

A gunshot exploded inches from his face, the bullet striking the wall where he stood a second earlier.

The light vanished.

Alex rolled across the floor, firing four rounds with a staccato rhythm, spraying the cave where he calculated the man was standing.

Blind, he kept rolling, twisting, squeezing the trigger.

Suddenly he glimpsed a bright orange flash. His mind never registered the fact that he'd seen the end of a gun barrel firing at point blank range.

The bullet drilled a hole through Alex Casper's forehead, exploding out the back of his skull. Fragments of bone and brain and blood sprayed the floor and cave wall. Breath hissed from his lips and dampness stained his pants as his bladder emptied. Death was instantaneous.

The man stood over the corpse, fury fermenting inside his mind.

"Stupid! You stupid bastard!" he screamed, arcing his foot, slamming his boot against the dead man's skull. He kicked again, and again, stomping on the man's chest, hearing the ribs cracking.

Blood seeped from the dime-sized hole in Alex's head, pooling in his eyes. Tears of blood fell onto the floor, soaking into the dust.

"What the hell's wrong with you people?" the man demanded. First Maitland and now this moron had to play the hero. Stupid, he told the corpse.

But I'll keep my promise. I'll take you to where your wife's buried, not that you deserve to be with her. He spat in the man's unflinching, unblinking face.

He tucked away the gun used to kill the former sergeant. The weapon Maitland had used as he died. The gun he'd pried from Maitland's lifeless fingers. Now he would have to dispose of it along with Alex Casper's corpse. In a sense it was a waste, but he had strict rules about discarding the weapons he used to kill. He never used the same weapon twice.

"Real dumb," he told the dead man as he dragged the body across the floor, hauling it into the narrow seam, struggling with the man's bulk. It took twenty minutes, twice as long as usual, to navigate his way to the underground chamber he called his Cathedral. Sweat beading his forehead, he strained with a final effort and pulled Alex's body into the dome-roofed cavern.

He took a moment to search the man's pockets, pulling out a wallet, but finding little more than credit cards, a driver's license and twenty dollars in cash. Scornfully he shoved the cash back in the pocket, then rolled the body over. Continuing his search, he found a Swiss army knife and a set of car keys. These he tossed onto the floor.

"Pathetic," he commented as he dragged Alex to the abyss. "So long, Sergeant," he called as he kicked the corpse's chest with enough force to carry it over the side. A moment later, he heard the splash far below.

Despite the moment's satisfaction, he felt cheated.

With a heavy feeling of resignation, the man picked up his flashlight, Casper's keys and pocketknife, and left the chamber. An eerie darkness fell as he disappeared into the passage, the only sound the faint drip of water into the underground lake.

*

The gauge showed the gas tank was nearly empty.

"I should have filled up before we left," Sam apologized, as he left the highway and headed up the off-ramp.

"Hmm?" Ellen said dozily. "What's up?"

"Nothing. We need some gas."

A sign promising gas within one mile directed them to the right, taking them into the low desert, away from the highway. Sam flipped the headlights to full beam as the Explorer rumbled along the empty road. Within a couple of minutes he reached a fork in the road, with no indication as to the direction to the gas station.

"Great," he said, unintentionally stomping on the brake. "Sorry." He glanced left then right, peering into the night. "Any ideas?"

Ellen shrugged. "Can't be far, let's try this way. We can always turn around."

Sam nodded, pulling away and heading east.

*

Using the blade of the army knife, the man scraped congealing blood from the cave wall, brushing it into a pile in the middle of the cave, cursing the ex-cop's rash stupidity for the thousandth time. Why did he have to go for his gun? Dumb. Worse, the cave was soiled with incriminating human blood.

Standing, after half an hour spent on his hands and knees trying to remove all traces of the night's violence, the man swept his flashlight across the floor, finally satisfied that his task was complete.

Tired and burning with white-hot rage, he strode out the cave, and crossed the dry riverbed to Alex's car.

He couldn't leave the car out here, so he climbed in and started the engine. He drove across the sand, finally reaching a dirt track that led eventually to a two-lane blacktop a couple of miles from the highway. He planned to drive to the highway, dumping the vehicle on the shoulder, where he would wipe the steering wheel, the door handle and any switches he might have touched. He would then have to trek across the sand to his ranch. He calculated he would be home long after midnight.

The winding road leading to the highway was deserted, as he'd expected this late at night. Even so he obeyed the posted speed limit and kept a wary eye open for a wayward police car patrolling the boondocks.

*

Sam blinked his tired eyes. They'd driven well over a mile from the fork, and seen no sign of habitation, let alone a gas station.

"I don't think this can be right," he said, easing off the gas and pulling onto the sand-shrouded shoulder. "Have we got any water left, honey?"

"There's that bottle we brought with us on Friday."

"That's fine."

"Sam, it's been sitting in a hundred-degrees all weekend. It'll taste awful."

"It'll be fine, you want me to get it?"

"No, I can manage," she said, reaching back between the front seats, groping for the plastic bottle. "Of course, some light back here would be helpful."

With a grin, Sam flicked on the dome light and watched his wife.

"What's so funny?" came her muffled voice.

"Nothing. You sure you don't want some help?"

"Positive."

He could hear her cursing beneath her breath.

"Got it!" she exclaimed so loudly that Sam startled.

"What?"

She wormed her way back between the seats, and held up her puzzle book.

"Where's the water?," Sam said, wondering what had gotten into his wife's mind.

"That's the answer." Ellen opened her book, flipping through the pages to one of the myriad crosswords. "HIJKLMNO, remember?"

Sam shook his head, shifting the car into drive. "I'll grab a soda at the gas station."

"H to O. H two O, that's water, that's the answer. Thanks."

Sam shook his head and eased the car back onto the road, making a U-turn.

Keeping to a steady forty miles an hour, the man drove Alex's car, his mind in turmoil after the events of the last few days. Everything had gone wrong. It simply wasn't fair, he decided as he slowed for a tight bend.

The man hit the brakes and the horn at the same time. He swerved to avoid the Ford that was stupidly blocking the road. As he shot past the car, he glimpsed the two occupants illuminated by their dome light. He saw the driver raise his middle finger and mouth some obscenity. And he saw the woman. Her startled eyes wide with shock and fear. And in that moment he recognized her. The beautiful woman he'd seen at the country club earlier that day.

In the middle of his U-turn Sam noticed the headlights out the corner of his eye. He hit the brakes. The tires squealed in protest despite their slow speed. And the Explorer jolted to a halt.

"Dickhead!" Sam yelled at the driver as the car swerved around them.

He spun to face Ellen. "Are you all right?"

"Yes."

"You believe that jerk?" he asked.

"Sam," Ellen scolded when he flipped the other driver the bird. "What if he sees you."

"So? The guy's an idiot! He's got to be doing sixty!"

Angry with himself, for not taking more care, Sam eased off the brake. His leg trembled as he touched the gas pedal. His heart pounded double time.

"That guy could've hit us."

"But he didn't," Ellen pointed out.

Sam took a couple of deep breaths and drove down the road, heading in the same direction as the other car.

"People like that shouldn't be allowed on the road," he said.

"Sam, calm down."

Forcing himself to relax, Sam forced a tight lipped grin. "Well, you know, they shouldn't."

"Sam," she said firmly.

Sam raised a hand in submission. "Okay, okay, I'm calm."

A tightness gripped the man's chest, squeezing his heart and lungs. He saw his fingers gripping the wheel, his knuckles white as china, as if to choke the life from the inanimate object. Who the hell did that guy think he was? Put your car in the middle of the road, then mouth off at me, as if it was my fault? People like that had to be taught a lesson.

The man coasted to a stop.

He watched the rearview mirror. It didn't take long before a pair of headlights swung into view less than a hundred yards behind.

Chapter 9

"Sam," was all Ellen needed to say.

One glance at her face revealed her dread. "What does this guy think he's doing?" said Sam, trying to keep the fear out of his own voice. Suddenly his throat felt as dry as the desert.

He lifted off the gas, the Ford gradually slowing, but still rolling closer to the car parked in the middle of the road.

What the hell is the guy's problem? Sam wondered.

Sam flashed his lights, the powerful beam stretching along the tarmac, bright on the light blue Oldsmobile, shining off the chrome rear bumper.

"Come on," Sam muttered.

The brake lights on the Olds flared.

Sam tapped his brake pedal, reluctant to draw any closer, the other car only forty feet ahead now.

The Oldsmobile edged forward.

Sam inched along, maintaining the distance between the two vehicles.

The two cars crawled along the road.

Sam glanced at his speedometer. The needle was fluttering around ten miles per hour.

"This is ridiculous."

"I don't like this, Sam. He must be drunk," Ellen said.

"It's okay." He reached out, and lightly squeezed her hand, hoping that it really was okay, but fearing the worst. What if the guy had a gun?

Smart move, Sam, he thought, remembering jerking his finger at the guy. Why not really piss the guy off?

Ahead the brake lights glowed momentarily.

Again Sam touched the brakes.

He fumbled for his cell phone. It was switched on, but unable to get a signal out here in the middle of nowhere.

"Dammit."

"Let's just turn around," Ellen suggested.

"What? What if he follows us?" His eyes flitted to the gas gauge, the needle barely hovering above empty. Not much choice, they desperately needed to find that gas station. But they hadn't even reached the fork in the road where they'd taken a wrong turn. A very wrong turn as it transpired, he thought.

Sam reached a decision and gritted his teeth.

"Hold on."

"What?"

Sam shifted down into first gear and floored the gas. The heavy duty tires spun briefly then gripped the road surface, launching the Explorer with surprising agility and a heavy dose of torque-steer. Sam yanked the wheel, darting across the yellow striped median, racing to overtake the Oldsmobile. He gripped the wheel with both hands as he felt the back of the car snake. The engine screamed in protest as it hit the tachometer's redline, but he didn't dare let go of the writhing wheel and shift out of first.

He thought for a moment he'd make it, shoot straight past the guy, and keep on driving until he found the gas station. And the moment he got there Sam planned to call the police.

But he never had the chance.

The driver must have been watching his mirrors intently, anticipating such an attempt, because the Oldsmobile accelerated in a tire-smoking maneuver that carried it across the median, blocking Sam's escape.

Ellen screamed!

Sam hit the brake and dove back into the right lane.

He heard Ellen's rapid breathing beside him. When he turned to face her, he saw the fear in her eyes transformed to anger. Anger directed at him.

"What?" he said defensively.

"That was intelligent."

Sam shrugged. "We can't just sit here. We're almost out of gas."

Stalemate. The Oldsmobile waited patiently a dozen yards ahead. "This prick obviously likes games."

"I don't think this is funny," she said.

"No? Nor do I."

The man laughed, rocking gently in his seat, eyes glued to his mirror.

"Not feeling so clever now, eh?" he said to the reflected headlights in his mirror.

He remembered seeing the guy drinking at the country club. Probably he'd downed a few more at dinner, then insisted on driving.

For a moment the man wished he'd kept Maitland's .22, even if it had broken his rule. He imagined approaching the car, standing alongside the driver's window, then pointing the gun at the man's head and pulling the trigger.

But then he would have to kill the woman too. He could not afford to leave an eyewitness. And yet, he knew, he desperately didn't want to kill her.

Besides, she had spoken to him. Her words had surely meant something. There hadn't been time for her to say anything more. Did she feel the connection? Did she know they were meant to be together? The two of them.

The driver, her husband or boyfriend or whatever he might be, would have to die.

A dull ache began to blossom inside the man's head.

He squeezed his eyes tight, trying to ignore the burgeoning pain, his thoughts losing focus.

He couldn't just drive away. The drunk at the wheel a few yards behind had become his responsibility.

I must to do something, he realized.

So far he'd been lucky and no other vehicle had driven down the road, but now he was engaged in a situation which broke all his rules. Foolishly, he was drawing attention to himself.

He couldn't think it through. His head was throbbing behind his right eye, the start of a migraine attack. The pressure continued to build, a stabbing pain beating in time with his pulse. He massaged the side of his head, but it didn't help. Needles of light flickered across his vision, distracting him from the bright headlights in the mirror. He swiped his sleeve across his eyes as if he could wipe away the image like a piece of grit. He stared at the headlights desperate to do something before the pain became unbearable and he risked passing out.

Sam and Ellen exchanged an apprehensive glance. Sam was tempted to try the same maneuver again. Perhaps if he'd been alone he would have done so. But he was supposed to protect her, not put her in even greater danger with some insane driving stunt that could kill them both.

What did the guy want? Was he angry because of Sam flipped him off? Did he want an apology? Sam felt he was a reasonable man, he'd apologize if it meant they could continue on their way and put a stop to this childish game. He'd even agree not to call the police, and keep his promise.

He debated turning off the engine to save fuel. If we sit here for another ten minutes, we'll be out of gas, he thought. He rested his hands on the ignition switch, then turned the key, and felt the engine die. The headlights dimmed a little, but he kept them turned on. The battery would last a reasonable time. He kept his hand on the ignition key, ready for action.

For five, long minutes nothing happened. The silence inside the car grew palpable. Tense.

"Sam," Ellen finally whispered.

"Honey?"

"I'm scared."

Sam nodded. "I know. So am I," he admitted, hoping he hadn't said the wrong thing.

"What are we going to do?"

Sam shook his head, he didn't have any idea. He just hoped another car would come along soon. Preferably one with a chunky red and blue light-bar fixed to the roof. That would end the problem real fast. The Oldsmobile would most likely take off, and Sam would be more than happy to give the cop the license plate and a description.

But the longer they waited the more anxious he felt. Even worse, Ellen was feeling the same way. He had to put an end to this stupidity. The question was how?

At that moment the door of the Oldsmobile opened.

A lanky man dressed in black climbed out of the car. He lurched forward, grabbing the car door to steady himself. He stared into the headlights.

Ellen yelped.

The man took another unsteady step away from his car, toward them.

Sam gripped the ignition key and twisted it.

Nothing.

His heart stammered in panic. He turned the key again. Still nothing.

"Sam! Let's go!"

"Come on, come on!" he urged the recalcitrant car.

Through the windshield Sam watched the man stagger closer, his left hand rising, gripping the side of his head.

Please let there be some gas left in the tank. There had to be.

He turned the key. The engine was dead. Shit!

He glanced down, suddenly noticing the gear selector was pointing to drive. He grabbed the column-mounted stick and shifted into neutral, twisting the key.

The engine fired, and Sam felt his shoulders sag with relief. He glanced out the windshield. The man was less than twenty feet away.

"We're out of here," Sam said.

He pressed his foot to the floor –

The car shuddered and the engine missed a beat and stalled.

"No," his voice cracked.

Relentless, the man outside lurched toward them. Only a dozen feet away.

"God," Ellen breathed. "I saw him before..."

Oblivious to Ellen, Sam fumbled with the key, praying.

Bang!

Sam jerked up to see the man slam his hands down on the Explorer's hood.

Sam spun to his left, hitting the door lock, hearing the reassuring clunk as the central locking did its job.

The man yelled, his eyes wild, his fury muted by the glass. He glared at Sam.

Something silver flashed in the man's hand, and they heard a high-pitched screech as he scored a penknife across the hood, gouging deep into the paint.

"Son of a bitch," Sam said, giving the key a vicious twist.

The engine roared. The most beautiful sound Sam had heard in a long time.

The man's scarred face looked up abruptly, and his eyes met Sam's.

"Things look a bit different now, eh, buddy?" said Sam.

He revved the engine.

The man took a hasty, startled step away from the damaged hood.

Sam dropped the stick into drive.

The Ford jumped forward, taking Sam by surprise. Sam expected the man to leap aside. But he stood, frozen in time. His eyes betrayed no hint of fear. Instead they reflected a manic determination.

Sam was only vaguely aware of Ellen's scream, on the periphery of his concentration, as he plunged the brake to the floor. They stopped scant inches before hitting the man.

"This guy's crazy," Sam muttered.

He notched open his window.

"Hey! You. You want to move out the way, or you want to get hit?"

"Let the lady drive." The man's voice carried an unnatural stoic calm.

Didn't the guy realize he'd almost been run over?

Sam glanced at Ellen, confused. "What?"

"You shouldn't drive," the man said.

"Yeah, right." Sam revved the engine again, but the man held his ground. "Screw you, pal."

"I'm warning you." The man's rage carried over the high revving engine.

Warning me? Fine. Sam let the engine return to idle, then dropped it into gear and eased forward.

The man laid his hands on the hood again as it nudged against him.

"Sam," Ellen said, startled.

"He'll move once he realizes I'm not stopping," Sam said, praying he was right.

The man took a single step back.

And, at the moment when Sam's nerve failed and he was about to press the brake, the man tumbled aside.

Sam accidentally floored the gas.

The man screamed. An ear-piercing roar of agony that rose above the engine as the front fender struck his knee.

Sam watched as the menacing figure disappeared beneath the front wheel. Sam wrenched the wheel sharply, trying to avoid the falling man, but his reactions were too slow.

Sam pivoted in his seat, looking back.

He stared at their tormentor, the man lying motionless, face down on the asphalt.

"Oh, Jesus. Jesus," Sam breathed.

His hands shook uncontrollably.

He can't be dead, thought Sam, unable to believe he might have just killed the man. He can't be dead. His bladder felt tight, his guts twisted in stark fear.

"Sam?" Ellen repeated, her voice penetrating the terror that cloaked him. He felt her touch his hand and turned to face her, his jaw slack.

"What happened?" he whispered.

"I don't know. We should see if he's..." her voice melted away. Strangely, Sam could see her lips moving, forming words his mind refused to acknowledge.

Only when he saw her open her door did the dark shroud begin to lift.

"Wait!" he yelled.

Ellen glanced back. "It was an accident. Maybe he's hurt."

"Maybe he's... maybe..."

Ellen bit her lower lip, uncertain. "We have to do something, Sam. We can't just leave him."

Sam nodded. But his body refused to move. If they left the man where he was, and later the police discovered whose car had been involved, well, that was hit and run. And if the man was dead? That was murder, wasn't it? That meant prison. Jesus. He shook his head, trying to clear his mind. He didn't want to think about it.

Get out the car, he told himself, and check if he's still breathing. Wait!

What if that was what the man was waiting for? What if he wasn't really hurt? After all, he had a knife. Sam glanced in the door mirror. The dark figure hadn't stirred.

They had to do something. Sam's heart was pounding like a giant drum. He didn't know what to do. But the longer they waited, the greater the chance someone would drive along this deserted stretch of road and discover what had happened.

Someone comes along now, but not in the last twenty minutes when we needed help. That would be typical.

He didn't notice Ellen slip out her door, not until he saw her shape moving in the red glow of the taillights, moving toward the body.

"Stop," he screamed, throwing open his own door. He raced toward her, fighting visions of the man reaching up, thrusting his knife deep into Ellen's chest as she bent over to help him.

Ellen jerked around as Sam grabbed her shoulders, standing between her and the prone figure cloaked in black.

The man's left leg was broken, twisted at a sickening angle. His arms pinned under his body meant there was no way to see if he still clutched the knife, waiting to strike. Cautiously, Sam took a step toward the body. He felt a clash of emotions. He prayed the man wasn't dead, but at the same time dreaded what might happen if he was alive. Again he pictured the flashing blade, this time seeing it stab between his ribs, puncturing his heart.

He knelt on one knee and prodded the man's leg. It flopped limply to the side.

The man made no sound of protest or pain.

"Hey," Sam said, poking the man again with his finger.

Still no reaction.

Sam tasted bile rising from his stomach, filling his throat. The man had to be dead. And he'd killed him.

"Is he...?" Ellen's frightened voice faltered.

Sam's breath came in unsteady rasps. Suddenly he turned away from the body and vomited. Bitterness burned his throat, leaving a vile aftertaste as he finished heaving his guts onto the roadside.

"What are we going to do?" Ellen sounded a million miles away, detached from the darkness Sam found himself drowning below.

Her question echoed the one thought spinning through his mind.

What could they do?

Call the police? A chill hand clutched his heart, the prospect filling him with icy dread. There was no way he was going to call the police.

Run.

The word rose from his subconscious, filling his thoughts. They had to get away. They had to get home. Fast.

He stood suddenly, causing Ellen to stagger back in surprise. He took her hand, pulling her away from the body.

"Come on!"

He tugged Ellen again, and she stumbled. He grabbed her forearm, helping her regain her balance as they ran to the car.

Run.

He threw open the door and dove inside. Ellen climbed in beside him as he started the engine and accelerated, barely giving her time to close the door.

He glanced in the rearview mirror. The man's outline fading, black against the black of the road, rapidly disappearing from sight. Yet Sam could still see the man's face. He saw the stranger's anger turning to shock as the car struck him. The expression on the dying man's face sent a shiver over Sam's flesh. Their eyes had met. And Sam would never forget those dark, empty eyes.

"Sam, we can't just leave him. What if he's alive?"

"He's not."

"But we didn't check, maybe he's unconscious."

"What did you want me to do? Wait around until someone else showed up? Jesus, Ellen, he's dead."

He blinked away his tears.

Maybe Ellen was right, but what if the police had found them there? He shivered.

"What if you're wrong? What if he is alive?" she persisted.

Sam sighed. "All right. We'll call for an ambulance from the gas station, okay?"

He glanced at her, relieved to see her nod in reluctant agreement.

They rounded a bend, reaching the fork in the road. The fork where they'd taken a wrong turn minutes earlier. Was it really such a short time ago? That couldn't be right. Sam felt lightheaded, his mind swimming. He had to concentrate. He glanced at the fuel gauge. Where the hell was the gas station?

"Damn," he cursed under his breath.

He wanted nothing more than to head back to the highway, and home. He stared at the gauge, as if he could will the tank to become full.

"Sam?"

He was about to reply when their car filled with light. Headlights. A van from the highway slowed at the fork, its lights shining into Sam's eyes, forcing him to squint.

Sam hoped the van driver was looking for the station, that he would turn left.

Not wanting to appear suspicious, Sam drove across the intersection, praying the van would follow his lead.

He gazed at the mirror. The van remained stationary. Sam slowed as he approached a sweeping bend, desperate to see which direction the van would head. But all too soon the van's lights disappeared from view.

A moment later the gas station appeared.

"Can you fill her up?" Sam told Ellen as he pulled into the old 76 station. The building was a decrepit lapboard structure, the orange globe shattered and no longer illuminated. Beneath the globe stood four tired pumps, one already occupied by a red sports car. Sam pulled in behind the car, at a self-serve pump. He licked his dry lips.

"I'll find a phone, if they even have one," he said and climbed out.

Sam glanced around for a pay phone. Not seeing one, he headed to the restrooms around the rear of the wooden building. There he found an old-fashioned phone, with a battered rotary dial, fixed to the wall. He reached for the black receiver, then hesitated. He fumbled in his pocket for a handkerchief. He'd seen enough movies, and his brain was still functioning well enough to know that he didn't want to leave his fingerprints as he dialed 911.

The operator came on the line, and he blurted out. "There's a man, he's been run over."

"Where are you, sir?"

Sam looked around, uncertain. "I don't know, off the one eleven." He hurriedly described the gas station and where he'd seen the body. The woman asked his name and he hung up.

Shoving his handkerchief in his pocket, he jogged around the building and stopped. The van pulled in beside his car.

Sam slowed his pace, trying to act casual, and strolled back to the car. Ellen was gone.

He froze.

Then turned, and saw her. Ellen waved to him as she walked away from the booth, having paid for the gas she'd pumped. Evidently this wasn't a high-crime area, thought Sam. Here they let you pump, then pay. Little crime. Except for the murder he'd just committed.

He climbed into the car, trying to ignore the van parked behind, hoping they'd come here directly and not made the same mistake he had. Praying they hadn't stumbled across the body.

Hurry up, he beckoned through the window to Ellen. She climbed in beside him.

"Did you call them?"

He nodded, yes.

Her shoulders relaxed slightly, a little of the tension easing from around her eyes. He started the engine, pulling around the red car, and back onto the road.

"Maybe we should go back there and wait. We could always say we went to get help."

"What?" Sam stared at her in disbelief. "Christ, Ellen. I ran that guy over."

"But it was an accident. They'd have to understand that."

"Why? We knocked him down."

"But... He attacked us."

Sam shook his head. "Forget it."

His heart hammered. Faster, the sound again blocking into his ears. He found he couldn't catch his breath. Jesus, he thought, I'm having a heart attack. He tried to remain calm, starting to ease off the gas.

Slowly the scary sensation passed, leaving him trembling.

He gripped the wheel and fixed his eyes straight ahead, not daring to look a Ellen.

A few moments later they reached the highway and headed west. Neither spoke during the ride back to Riverside, where they picked up Jason, then headed home.

Hours later, while he lay awake in bed, Sam's nightmare began.

Chapter 10

Officer William T. Hilliard responded to the call that came over his radio. He was driving along the highway, about five miles from the Old Cabazon road.

WT hit the siren and lights and accelerated past a truck, cutting in front of it and onto the shoulder. He sped along the shoulder at seventy, swooping up the off-ramp and onto the cracked blacktop.

If he'd arrived five minutes sooner, he would have seen a dark green Ford Explorer rushing in the opposite direction.

Instead, the only car he saw was an Oldsmobile heading sedately toward the highway.

WT took the corner at the fork a little fast, turning right, crossing onto the opposite side of the road. Glad, indeed, that there were no other cars around. He raced along the blacktop for two miles without seeing anything out of the ordinary. Finally, he pulled over and typed onto the Mobile Data Terminal, and lifted his radio-microphone.

"Two-five-niner. You want to run that location by me again?"

The dispatch officer reviewed the report that had been received.

"That's what I thought." WT pulled off the road. "Well, I must've gone twice that far, and I ain't seen no dead body."

He wondered if it might have been kids making a prank call, perhaps hiding in the brush, waiting to see a police car go speeding past, and having a good laugh. But the report didn't sound like a hoax, and dispatch said the caller was an adult male.

"Maybe be the guy'd been drinking, seeing things," he wondered, releasing the mike switch.

"Could be," crackled a disembodied voice.

"I'll keep heading down here, another couple of miles. "

"Ten four."

WT rubbed his chin, something told him he wouldn't find a body lying in the middle of the road. Told him there wasn't anything to find, but it didn't feel right.

Most likely, he reasoned, the caller had seen some animal, a wild dog or some other road kill. The night could play strange tricks on your eyes. And between the time the caller saw something and phoned it in, and WT's arrival, a scavenger could easily have come along and carried it away. Who knew?

Even so, WT judiciously drove another two miles, and a little beyond, just to make certain. Finally, he turned around and headed back in the direction of the old 76 station.

If he hadn't been driving slowly, paying greater than normal attention to the road, he wouldn't have seen the flash of metal in his headlights, and he certainly wouldn't have stopped to investigate. He was a mile from the fork, pretty much the location of the supposed victim. He climbed out and stepped into the beam thrown by his headlights. Pulling on a glove as he bent down, he picked up the metal object. A penknife. Holding it carefully, he examined the red-handled, Swiss army knife, the blade open. The blade itself was marked with dark shavings. He rubbed a little on his palm, sniffing it, but not recognizing it as a drug. It looked more like paint. Climbing back into the car, he dropped it into an evidence bag, though evidence of what, he wasn't sure.

It always amazed WT how such out-of-the-way businesses kept going. Plenty of modern gas stations lined the highway, with their gaudy neon signs lighting up the desert at night. But he kind of liked the ramshackle building. It reminded him of the places he'd seen in Texas when he was growing up, riding along with his father. An occasional treat, cruising the quiet streets of Woodville.

His car kicked up a cloud of dust as he parked away from the empty pumps. He strolled around the building, noticing the ancient phone, and then ambled inside.

The young man behind the counter watched him.

"Er, help you, Officer?"

"I don't know, son," WT said, idly wondering if the youngster had been up to something. "Use this phone tonight?"

The kid glanced to his right, frowning. "No. Not me. Why?"

WT followed the boy's gaze, seeing a phone on the counter, nearly concealed behind a display of candy.

"How 'bout the one outside?"

The boy shook his head. "No, sir."

"You see anyone use the phone, 'round ten-thirty?"

The kid thought for a moment. "No, I didn't."

"Well, somebody did."

"Sorry."

"You got any records? Of the cars that stopped for gas tonight?"

"Don't really keep any records."

"How about credit card receipts?"

The kid shrugged. "I don't know if I'm supposed to let anyone see them. Mr. Weisman said they were confidential."

"You seem a decent kid, but I'm already investigating one person who wasted our time tonight. You don't want to get added to that list, do you?"

The boy hurried away and returned with a handful of crumpled credit card receipts.

"Six?" said WT as he flicked through them. "That all?"

"'Cept a couple of people paid cash."

Cash. WT pulled out his notebook and jotted down the names on the receipts. If a body happened to show up, then he'd be sure to contact them. Otherwise, well, he wasn't about to spend hours trying to track down someone who had most likely made an honest mistake.

"Thanks," WT said, heading outside.

*

His leg throbbed. His ankle was swollen, broken. He remembered straining to move his aching head and look up as the man and woman left him for dead. He'd heard their engine start, and he'd turned his head enough to glimpse the license plate before the car vanished into the night. He'd repeated the number in his mind, a mantra, as he struggled to crawl toward the Oldsmobile.

His left leg had collapsed beneath him, sending waves of pain and nausea through his injured body. He clawed at the asphalt, dragging himself toward Alex Casper's car.

His mind seethed as he continued his silent chant. He would not forget that number. He'd find the driver. And make him pay.

Yes, thought the man, he would pay dearly. He would learn lessons about suffering, lessons he could never have imagined.

Why hadn't the fool let the woman drive? Everything would have been so much simpler.

He winced as his left foot scraped and dragged along the ground.

The five minutes it took to limp and crawl to the car felt eternal. He knew his ankle was badly broken. His foot had twisted viciously as the fender struck his leg. But he'd known pain before. However, that did nothing to ease the agony that lanced through his leg each time his foot scraped the ground.

Finally he reached the car. He'd left the door unlocked, the keys in the ignition. Groaning, he hauled himself into the driver's seat. Gritting his teeth, he swung his leg inside. And, with exaggerated patience, he eased his foot out of his shoe, probing the tender flesh. In the dim illumination cast by the dome light, he saw the swelling had already darkened, heavy with blood.

He started the engine and drove away, all the while reciting the license plate.

He reached the fork without passing another vehicle, and headed to the freeway. Despite the unexpected confrontation, he still had other problems to deal with. More immediate problems. He had to dump Casper's car, and then he had to get back home.

His heart leapt as a police car, lights flashing, raced by in the opposite direction. He watched it disappear in the mirror.

Minutes later, he was in the acceleration lane of the highway, melding with the late-night traffic. Cars and trucks hurtled along the three westbound lanes, headed who knew where. Sunday nights were as busy as the Friday exodus, the rush to escape the city. Madness, the man thought. He kept a close watch on the mileage, pulling onto the shoulder after three and a half miles, which he estimated to be the closest the highway came to his ranch. But he was still two miles from home. Two miles of desert between him and sanctuary. Two agonizing miles which stretched before him.

As he'd done so often before, he wiped clean those places inside the car he'd touched, his movements more instinct than rational. Once finished, he studied the traffic flowing past, waiting for a lull. Then he climbed out, wiping the door handle, and hobbled into the darkness.

Thorny spikes snagged his clothing as he pushed his way through the brush along the highway. He tugged his sleeve, ripping the cloth. A thick, wizened stem blocked his path. He tried holding it aside while he squeezed by, but his strength was failing, his injury sapping his body's reserves. He fumbled in his pocket for the penknife, deciding it would be easier to hack through the branch. He frowned, and reached into his other pocket, then glanced back in the direction of the car. Where the hell was the knife? He cursed himself, realizing it must have fallen free when he'd been knocked down. Not that there was anything he could do about it now. Still, it was a stupid mistake, and he'd been making too many of those recently.

He had to keep going. Thorns clawed his flesh as he struggled through.

Sand shifted beneath his unsteady footsteps. He tried to put a little weight on his damaged ankle, and was rewarded by a bolt of pain so fierce it threatened to overwhelm him. He couldn't afford to pass out. He shook his head, breathing deep, feeling the wooziness ebb.

Only two miles, he told himself. Trying to believe he would make it. He limped forward, dragging his damaged leg through the sand, his arms swinging as he tried to keep his balance. One plodding step at a time he moved across the silent sands.

*

The monochrome UFO loomed above the White House, a flare of jets and gases ignited as it floated toward the lawn.

"I wonder what they'll look like," mused a bewildered scientist, his hands thrust deep into his lab coat pockets.

Sam blinked. He sat huddled on the couch, shaking, but not from the cold. He stared at the black-and-white B-movie playing on TV, unsure how much time had passed since he'd crept out of bed and downstairs, unable to sleep.

He couldn't get the man's startled face out of his mind. The man's dark, foreboding eyes fixated on Sam. Sam's heart spasmed each time he saw the stranger stumble and disappear beneath the car. He could scarcely remember the drive back from Palm Springs. His eyes had flitted continually to the rearview mirror. One moment wondering if the police were on his tail, the next wondering if perhaps the stranger was still alive, and in pursuit. Perhaps the Oldsmobile would suddenly draw alongside and the driver would stare at Sam with the eyes of the dead.

Kneeling on the road, staring down at the motionless figure, Sam had felt certain the man was indeed dead. But he was no longer so sure.

And that was the most terrible feeling. Not knowing. The man hadn't moved, but perhaps Ellen had been right, maybe he was unconscious. Sam knew he should have taken the time to find out. Except panic had overridden his common sense in those terrifying minutes. The sensible thing, after making the phone call, would have been to return and wait for the police. Maybe they would have believed the truth. The stranger had attacked them, and Sam hadn't meant to knock the man down, it had been an accident. Instead, he'd run. Now the police would be looking for him. He wondered about the gas station, the kid in the booth, the van and the sports car. What if they read about the incident in the local paper, the police appealing for witnesses, would they remember seeing him?

Sam shivered and drew his legs up, his chin resting on his knees. Goose pimples touched his forearms. He glanced at the DVR, its LED clock glowing 3:09am. He felt wrecked.

"Sam?" Ellen's voice whispered. He heard her soft footsteps on the curving staircase, descending.

Ellen appeared in the doorway dressed in a vaporous negligee. Moonlight limned her figure. "What are you doing?" she kept her voice low.

Sam shrugged.

Ellen moved into the room, glanced at the old movie, and flicked off the TV.

"Sam?"

"God, I don't know."

Ellen nodded.

"I keep thinking I should have done something else," Sam said, his eyes wide, pleading for something Ellen couldn't give.

Peace.

Ellen stroked his arm.

"What am I going to do?" he asked. "What if that guy's dead? If I killed him..."

"It was an accident," he heard her catch her breath, trying not to cry.

He took her hand in his, and squeezed gently.

"Maybe he's all right," she said.

Sam shook his head. How he'd prayed that was so.

"I'll call Anne, first thing in the morning," Ellen said.

"What?" he said, startled.

"I'll ask her to pick up a local paper for us."

"What? Oh, great. Tell her to let us know if she comes across any hit and run victims. 'Oh, no reason, we were just curious'," he mimicked.

"That's not funny. I'll tell her we want to check out the property prices, or something."

"Christ, if there's anything it'll be online." Sam took a breath, then shrugged with resignation. What did it matter?

"Then what's your plan?" she asked. "Sit up all night, every night, waiting for the police to knock on the door, or the phone to ring? I saw the way you jumped when Mom called to make sure we arrived home safely."

Sam couldn't deny that. The phone had rung about ten minutes after they walked through the door. Ellen was putting Jason to bed, and Sam had been in the kitchen, fixing a coffee. He'd spun to face the phone, his cup slipping from his trembling fingers and smashing on the floor. He'd stared at the phone, his mind racing. The police. Somehow they'd already found out who killed the man they'd discovered sprawled on the road. As the phone shrilled again, Ellen had walked in, frowning at him as he stared, transfixed. The answering machine had picked up on the fourth cry, and they heard Lucy's voice.

"Sam?" He was suddenly aware of Ellen rocking him, talking. "You scared me. You looked like you were in some sort of trance."

"I'll be okay," he said, not sure if he was trying to convince Ellen or himself.

"Come to bed. You need to get some sleep."

He nodded and followed her back upstairs. Although he knew he wouldn't get a wink of sleep tonight.

*

Darkness.

The man blinked, his eyes felt as if they'd been scraped and scoured by sandpaper. He managed to blink away the grit, and was shocked to discover he was lying on his back, looking up at a veil of stars. A gibbous moon shone far overhead. He glanced at the luminous hands on his watch. It was past three o'clock. That couldn't be right. He remembered lurching forward, the jarring pain piercing his ankle, then... Then nothing.

He must have been unconscious for three hours. He glanced at his legs, hidden beneath a thin gauze of sand. Sand swept across his body by the wind. He struggled to sit up, feeling faint and sick. He had to get home before sunrise. He didn't know how soon Casper's car would be found. Perhaps it had already been discovered. In which case the police, especially once they realized the owner was an ex-cop, would begin their investigation in earnest. And perhaps that would lead them to the cave, where four years earlier they'd searched for Alex Casper's missing wife.

Meeting Casper at the cave, the man realized now, had been a big mistake. A mistake compounded by Casper's stupidity when he drew his gun.

"Why?" The man's voice sounded hoarse as he wondered aloud what made men such fools. Surely Casper had known he didn't stand a chance.

The man struggled to get to his feet. His left leg felt numb, until he accidentally put a little pressure on his ankle. White hot fire seared his nerves. The desert plateau swayed before his eyes, and he collapsed to the ground once more.

Rolling onto his stomach, he began to crawl, snaking his way painfully through the sand.

He labored for each breath, sucking air through gritted teeth. His lips felt dry, chapped by the cool night, his mouth and throat caked dry with dust, making him cough and wheeze. But in his heart he felt elation, as he groped his way across a dirt track. Ahead lay his sprawling ranch. The sky over the terracotta tiled roof was tinged with dawn light. It had taken him over three hours to crawl home. A lifetime of pain spent clutching a tenuous consciousness, knowing if he passed out again he wouldn't wake until daylight. And he couldn't risk being found in such a condition. There would be too many unanswerable questions.

He struggled to the fence, using it to lever himself up, then made his way to the tiled porch. His foot slid on the cold Mexican pavers. His hand, shaking from exhaustion, clutched the doorknob and turned it. He leant against the door, feeling it swing open, and he stumbled inside, and toppled over.

As he fell, his head struck the edge of a marble column, upon which stood an intricately engraved glass vase. The vase wobbled and tumbled from its stand, smashing on the floor beside him. He neither heard the sound nor cared.

Chapter 11

The alarm buzzed.

Sam's eyes shot open, his body flinched, and he realized it was already morning. At some point during the night he must have drifted into a troubled slumber. He couldn't remember the demons which had haunted him through the night.

Ellen murmured something.

"Honey?" he whispered.

But her eyes remained closed, her breathing deep and steady.

Trying to move without disturbing her, Sam eased out of bed and disappeared into the bathroom.

The ceiling fan whirred as he flicked on the light and shut the door. He glanced at his ragged reflection. His eyes bloodshot, stubble shadowing his chin, his hair disheveled.

"You look like I feel," his voice sounded strained as he spoke aloud to the person in the mirror.

Half closing his eyes, he felt his way inside the shower and turned on the faucet. A blast of cold water struck him. He didn't flinch.

Downstairs, he glanced at the line of breakfast cereal packets in the kitchen cabinet. His stomach churned, the prospect of eating anything made him nauseous. He closed the cupboard door, and settled for a glass of orange juice. The acid hitting his empty stomach wasn't a clever idea either. He heard Ellen moving around, going in to Jason's room, and heard their indistinct voices.

At seven-thirty he trudged upstairs to say goodbye.

"I'll probably be late home," he said, leaning against the doorjamb.

Ellen nodded, helping Jason to put on his tiny sweatshirt.

"Bye, bud," he said, walking over to Jason, giving the boy's shoulder a squeeze. "You take care."

Jason looked up with wide, happy eyes that broke Sam's heart. Sam glanced at Ellen, wanting to say something, but there was nothing to say.

A horn blared! Brakes squealed!

Jolted from his reverie, Sam focused on the road and saw another driver waving furiously at him. He'd turned right on a red light, not thinking to check the oncoming traffic.

Concentrate, Sam, he admonished himself, and waved an apology to the middle-aged businessman in his Jaguar.

The man scowled, then pulled ahead.

What's happening to me? Sam wondered. It felt as if his mind was falling apart and taking his body along for the ride. He was exhausted, mentally and physically. And all because of one stupid mistake. If he'd kept calm the previous night. If he hadn't panicked, maybe the scar-faced man would have simply walked back to his car, climbed inside, and driven away.

"It wasn't my fault," Sam protested.

He hadn't wanted any trouble, all he'd wanted was to buy some gas and get home.

*

Andrew Bernard had deliberately switched his cell phone to Airplane Mode when he left his Lemon Heights home.

He'd driven most of the way, through stop-and-go traffic, to his practice before he realized he hadn't kissed Stephanie good-bye. He wasn't sure why, but that fact only served to deepen his self-loathing. Indeed, ever since the stranger had stepped foot on his boat, the only thing Bernard could think about was how foolish he'd been over the last eighteen months.

He pictured pulling into the underground car park, and seeing Celia Provenzano's car parked there. Christ, he thought, there was no way he could face her today. He needed time to think.

Activating his phone, he called his practice.

His receptionist, Beatriz, answered in her usual, quiet manner, and he made his excuse.

"I should call everyone for today?"

"Yes, please," he coughed deliberately. "I think Mrs. Vanderhorn is the only OP scheduled. Try and move her to the end of the week. She'll complain but she knows we'll suck ten pounds out of her and make her look wonderful again."

"If there are any problems -"

"Then call Simon, will you?" Bernard snapped.

"Yes."

"Sorry. Look, thanks. I need to shake this thing off. I should be in tomorrow," he broke the connection.

Leaving the freeway, Bernard took a winding road around Newport's scenic Back Bay, the estuary leading to the harbor and from there to the ocean.

Ten minutes later he unlocked the cabin door, and entered the cockpit of his boat. He locked the door behind him and went down a short flight of steps into the galley and poured himself a large Scotch.

Sipping his drink, Bernard wondered where on earth he could turn to raise the amount of money the stranger had suggested.

Bernard snorted. Suggested? Demanded was more like it. With those damned, and damning, pictures the man could ruin his marriage or his business. His whole life was screwed and there was nothing he could do. Except pay. "Christ," he muttered.

He flopped down on the low couch, scarcely noticing as the drink sloshed and spilled onto his pants.

Rolling the glass tumbler between his hands, he offered up a silent prayer for his own salvation.

Tears brimmed in his eyes, and he couldn't help but cry. He'd been so stupid, but should he have to pay such a heavy price? A million dollars? It was absurd. There was no way he could hope to raise that amount of cash.

Bernard knocked back the remaining Scotch and marched over to cupboard for a refill. Tears fell from his cheeks, and he gripped the counter top.

Unbidden, the image of Stephanie cradling the telephone came into sharp focus. He pictured how she'd stood when he'd left on Friday afternoon. Friday, it seemed such a long time ago. Like another life. I'm sorry, he thought, the words sounding so hollow and worthless.

He kept pouring until the glass was filled to the brim and the bottle all but empty.

As the effects of the alcohol seeped into his mind, he realized he did have a choice. It would be so easy, he mused; some drink, some pills, and he could sail away from everything across an eternal ocean. Would that be worse than staying and enduring what was surely to come? Perhaps there was a way out after all, he decided.

*

Sam pulled into a space behind his office. His sweaty shirt stuck to the leather upholstery as he climbed out.

Feeling self-conscious, he headed in through the glass door.

Kathy greeted him from behind her desk with a cheery Monday morning smile filled with youthful enthusiasm.

"So, did you two have a good time?" she bubbled.

"What? Yes, thanks. It was great."

Her smile faltered. "Is everything okay, Sam?"

Sam put on a brave smile. "Couldn't be better. We got back kind of late. Rough night," he explained.

Kathy nodded. "Looks like you could do with some coffee."

"Black, and strong," he said, strolling into his office.

He closed the door and slumped into his chair.

An untidy stack of unpaid bills and unanswered correspondence littered his desk. He knew he should be delving into the paperwork, but he couldn't concentrate on anything. His mind kept wandering. Had the man's body been found? What were the police were doing to track down the person responsible – his killer?

Kathy knocked lightly on the door as she opened it, carrying a steaming cup of coffee.

"This'll help," she said, clearing a space on the desk so she could put the china cup down.

"Thanks, Kathy."

Her eyes studied him for a moment, still concerned, but she didn't say anything. She simply nodded and returned to reception, pulling his door closed as she left.

The coffee tasted like liquid tar. His empty stomach grumbled once more in protest, but at least the caffeine quickly took effect.

Sam could feel his head clearing, and he began to sort through the mass of papers he hadn't had time to deal with over the last two weeks. The recent presentation had taken every available minute. He glanced at a phone bill he'd printed out as a reminder a few days ago, cursing when he realized he was already late making the payment. He logged onto the bank's website and entered the payment, hoping the handful of customers who owed him money would soon pay up.

He'd barely started on his emails when Martin strolled into Sam's office.

Martin chewed on his gum. "You don't look so hot, boss."

"Thanks, Marty. And how was your weekend?"

Martin blew a bubble, popped it. "Cheryl wanted to go shopping," he groaned.

Sam smiled. "Sounds like things are getting serious with you two."

"Yeah." He didn't sound too happy about the prospect. "I guess. I mean, she's nice and all, but she's getting a bit heavy with 'our relationship.'"

"Ah, you'll be in the jewelers before you know it," Sam teased.

Martin blanched and blew another bubble. "So what time's big John getting here?" he asked.

Sam frowned. Oh, shit! God, how could he have forgotten? John Terrance was coming over to preview the racing car animation Martin had been working on.

"Ten," he said numbly.

"Guess I'd better fix up the demo room."

"Yeah, sure. Thanks."

I should have worn a suit, Sam thought. He was dressed in slacks and an old paisley shirt, with a button missing near his midriff. Not exactly power dressed.

They'd be here within the next few minutes. He didn't have time to rush home and change. But perhaps Ellen could dash over with his suit.

He grabbed the phone and dialed. The line went straight to voicemail.

"Great," he muttered, hanging up. No point leaving a message at this late stage.

He scurried out of his office and into the restroom. Inside, he glanced at his drawn features and ran his fingers through his lank hair, and wondered how he could have forgotten such an important meeting. A meeting he had to face after a sleepless night.

After he'd killed a man.

He shuddered and splashed cold water onto his face, and dipped his head under the faucet to rinse his mouth clean. Grabbing a fistful of paper towels, Sam dried his face, then hurried into the demo room.

"What a mess," he said, glancing at the empty boxes littering the floor. Pens and notebooks covered the sleek gray and white computer furniture.

"I just tidied up," Martin retorted.

"You'll make someone a wonderful wife," Sam said as he swept his arm along the desk, scooping everything into a small cardboard box. Hurrying into the corridor, Sam shoved the box into a crammed cupboard.

At that moment he heard an unmistakable baritone voice in reception. John Terrance had arrived ten minutes early.

Sam ran back to the demo room.

"Look sharp," he told Martin.

Martin didn't glance around. He logged onto the computer system.

"No problem," said Martin.

Sam gathered up the remaining garbage and looked around for somewhere to dump it.

"Sam?" Kathy called. "Mr. Terrance is here."

"Be right there."

Sam nudged the restroom door open and dumped everything inside.

He hurried down the passage, slowing to a brisk stroll as he entered the reception area.

Burly John Terrance filled one of the maroon armchairs, another colleague stood nearby, staring out the window.

"Sorry to keep you waiting, John."

John stood, like a giant roused from his slumber, and shook hands.

Sam felt as if his fingers had been squeezed through a vice, but he managed to grit his teeth and smile.

"Don't reckon you've met Calvin before?"

Calvin stepped forward. "Hi," he gave a perfunctory hand shake.

"Calvin's my number one driver," he said referring to his racing team, not a chauffeur.

"Good to meet you," Sam said.

"So, we going to see this thing, or what?" Calvin asked.

"This way."

Having introduced Martin, Sam explained what they'd done and how they'd done it. At the same time he was trying to hint that things could still be changed, albeit at a price.

Using the mouse, Sam recalled a wireframe model from the drive. On the screen, a racing car appeared drawn with two thousand thin lines and arcs.

Sam glanced at Calvin. "We always start with a wireframe, and create the model."

Calvin merely grunted and kicked back in his chair. Sam ran the thirty second presentation. As the racing car passed by, its inner workings were exposed. The engine, pistons firing, the chassis flexing, the suspension riding the road surface.

Sam selected a quick render feature, and let the computer paint a simplified sketch of the vehicle, but at least you could tell which bits were at the front. Something he always found difficult with intangible wire-frames.

"We can do a fast shade. Make sure it looks right before we render everything."

The car raced once more around the track, its dark red body-work dissolving, becoming translucent. The viewpoint traveled with the sleek vehicle, hurtling down the straight, giving the viewer a few seconds to admire its mechanics.

Impressive. Sam liked the way Martin had put this one together, it looked the equal of the cars in that Ron Howard movie, *Rush*. A blend of live action and CG elements which Sam had particularly admired.

"That it?" Calvin said not hiding his scorn.

"That's before it's rendered."

The driver glanced at his boss. "Lookit, I gotta check out a whole new setup at the track this morning."

Sam nodded, trying not to show his frustration. Why had the driver bothered to come if he wasn't going to shut up for five minutes?

"Won't take a minute," Sam assured him.

Calvin groaned.

"You carry on, there's no rush," John Terrance said to Sam.

Sam started the 'final' rendering. The display faded from black and replayed the high definition animation Martin had created on the computer over the weekend.

A grin spread across John's face. "Well, how about that? What d'you say, Cal?"

Calvin pursed his lips, then finally nodded. "Yeah, pretty dang cool. How do you make it change like that, kinda like glass?"

"Got to have our secrets," Sam said, giving Martin a hearty slap on the shoulder. "Right?"

"Yep."

"Can I see it again?" Calvin asked.

"I'll put it on Vimeo and email the password, if it's got your approval? And I'll shoot the link to the guys over to QV post," he said, referring to the company that was producing the rest of the JT Racing production video.

"Sam, it looks great." John offered his hand once more.

Hiding his reluctance to have all sensation wrung from his fingers, Sam returned John's firm grip.

"Nice doing business with you. I'll get my accountant to move your money through."

"Thanks, that'd be really appreciated," Sam said as they ambled back to reception.

Sam held open the door. He watched the two men cross the crowded car lot to a gleaming fly-yellow Ferrari TDF. Somehow John squeezed his bulk behind the wheel.

"That was quick. How'd it go?" Kathy asked as Sam let the door swing shut.

He gave her the thumbs-up and headed back to his room.

Sam sank into his chair, drained.

He glanced at the phone, wondering when it would ring.

Wondering who would call.

Chapter 12

The highway patrol cruiser pulled onto the shoulder. As the vehicle stopped the blue and white lights started to flash. An eighteen-wheeler thundered past, and Officer Eva McGraw felt the strong flap of wind rush past as she opened her door. Thanks, she thought, eyeing the truck from behind her expensive Oakley A-wire shades.

McGraw circled the abandoned Oldsmobile. From the MDT in her car, she knew the owner of record but there was no sign of him, or anyone else in the vicinity of the vehicle. Glancing through the window she didn't see any keys, but the car had been left unlocked. It had been reported a while earlier, but the shift change, after a busy night, hadn't left an opportunity to follow up until now.

Her Sergeant's voice came over her radio.

"Guy's an ex-cop. PSPD are sending a car," he paused. "Truck's on its way too."

Eva recalled the name she'd read on the computer. "Alex Casper."

"Yeah... They've tried to reach him. No sign of him at home or his employment either apparently."

McGraw frowned, wondering what the owner might be up to. Probably some domestic tiff, she figured. Or money trouble. Or some genuine, innocent reason for wanting to disappear for a while - eight times out of ten it was the latter and not foul play.

She shifted focus. Why would an ex-cop abandon his vehicle on the side of a freeway. Why would he want to disappear? As thoughts began to race into her mind, she continued around to the trunk, suddenly wary. Subconsciously, her hand went to her gun, and she drew the weapon as she started to unlatch the trunk.

A horn startled her and she leapt back from the car as a tow truck pulled onto the shoulder some distance ahead. "Asshole," she cussed under her breath.

The truck beeped incessantly as it reversed toward the car.

It was a flatbed, with Tucker's Repair Service airbrushed across the doors.

"Yo. What you got?" the beefy driver leaned out of the cab and grinned at McGraw.

"Probably kids, joyriding, got fed up and dumped it out here," she replied, returning her attention to the trunk.

"Damn kids," the trucker grumbled as he jumped down and unlocked the winch.

McGraw glanced up as he hauled out a length of chain and strolled toward the front of the Olds. Then she focused on her task and popped the trunk.

Clean and empty.

Joyriders, McGraw thought, were certainly a possible explanation. They could have stolen the car off the street, or right out of the guy's driveway. Only trouble was, that didn't explain why Mr. Alex Casper was nowhere to be found.

As the truck driver hooked the chain onto the front wheel, a PSPD patrol car pulled in behind McGraw's CHP cruiser.

A young officer stepped out. She recognized him, though it took a moment to remember his name.

"Hi, WT?" she said, stepping away from the Oldsmobile.

He smiled. A nice, country-boy smile, as he approached, his eyes locked on the ex-cop's vehicle.

"Yo," the truck driver said as he appeared from beyond the hood. "Which of you's department's paying for this?"

McGraw suppressed a grin. "It's not an A.V.A," she said, referring to the Abandoned Vehicle Abatement program that paid for the removal of derelict vehicles from public roads and freeways. The Oldsmobile hardly qualified as a derelict. "Guess it's all yours," she said to the Officer.

WT didn't reply. Instead, he opened the passenger door, using a cloth, and peered inside.

"What are you thinking happened to him?" McGraw wondered aloud.

WT reappeared. "No signs of a struggle or nothing."

McGraw was about to ask another question when her radio interrupted. A large armchair had fallen from the back of a pickup and had been promptly demolished by a mini-van. No injuries were reported, but there was debris across all the lanes, and the woman in the van was in distress. Fortunately, both her children were unharmed. The incident was less than a mile away. She needed to roll.

Chapter 13

"It's no problem," her friend, Judy, assured Ellen Grady.

"You're sure?" Ellen glanced along the hallway to the living room, where Jason was sitting on the carpet with Carter, Judy's two and a half year old.

"He'll be fine, Ellen."

Having already said goodbye to her son, Ellen backed out the door and strolled across the lawn to the Explorer parked at the curb.

It took longer than the usual ten minutes to drive around Newport's Back Bay, thanks to a construction detour on Bristol Street, which was always busy, and frequently under repair.

The sun, reaching its zenith, shimmered off the waters of the bay, the marshland a sanctuary for wildlife surrounded by suburbia. A heron took flight from the water's edge and flapped its ponderous wings, feather tips skimming the water.

The road rose, the bay vanishing behind a swarm of bluff houses that lined its eastern shores, and a mile later Ellen turned left, heading for the library on the outskirts of the upscale shopping mall. Although she felt guilty to admit it, she thoroughly enjoyed her trips to Fashion Island, despite Sam jokingly referring to the place as either Fascist, or more often, Fantasy Island. Seldom had she found anywhere quite so relaxing. Ambling in and out the pricey designer boutiques and high end department stores, with no need to hurry, she would stroll in the sunshine with Jason tagging along beside her.

But today she wasn't window shopping. She skirted the mall and turned onto Avocado and pulled into the parking structure near the public library, the building an eclectic mix of angles, concrete and glass. While the roof above the adjoining civic center always reminded her of waves about to break ashore.

Sam had been right: it would be ridiculous to call Anne. All the same, Ellen desperately needed to find out what happened to the man they'd struck down. She had to know if he'd been killed. And the library was the only place she could think of that might have a Palm Springs newspaper – there had been no such reports online.

As she strode toward the sliding glass doors, a roar thundered in the sky, growing louder, and the familiar shiny dragonfly shape passed overhead. The police helicopter descended, circling Fashion Island, headed for the nearby police station. The sight of it chilled her. The police, she thought, were everywhere. And if that man was dead, surely it was only a matter of time before some small clue, some key piece of evidence, linked her and Sam to the crime.

Her pace quickened. She felt relieved to step into the pleasant cool and quiet atmosphere, displaced from the world outside. The book-lined shelves exuded tranquility. Even so, Ellen felt the urgency behind her quest, and hurried to the information desk.

"Could you tell me where today's newspapers are?" she asked the redheaded librarian.

"All the way down the aisle, after the magazines. Are you looking for anything in particular?"

"No," Ellen said, moving away.

Five minutes later she picked up the morning edition of *The Desert Sun* and carried it over to a small, empty desk beside a narrow window. Sitting down she started to scour the pages.

*

Sam felt drained, his body numb and his brain leaden. He couldn't get the stranger's face out of his mind. He'd spent the rest of the day, once JT racing left, hiding in his office. Kathy had stopped pestering him after he'd yelled at her to quit annoying him. And that had merely added to his immeasurable feeling of guilt.

If only I hadn't tried to get past him, Sam thought.

If only I'd done something else.

If only...

Those two words had throbbed inside his skull all the way home from Palm Springs and all through the night. He squeezed his eyes tight until he could see yellow swirls behind his eyelids. He would do anything to change what had happened.

The phone shrilled.

His heart leapt. Every time the phone rang, he felt on the verge of a heart attack. He dreaded to think what his blood pressure was doing. Despite himself, a wry smile twisted his lips. His doctor would be unimpressed, especially after his poor performance at his last physical.

The phone kept ringing.

"What?" he snapped, lifting the receiver.

"Mr. LaCrosse is on the line for you," Kathy said, her voice discordant, upset. "Shall I put him through?"

"Please, and Kathy, I'm—" he began, but heard the line click. "Hello, Mr. LaCrosse."

"Sam, wanted you to know that our lawyers are pretty much finished drawing up the contract. Do you want it sent to your people, or should I have them email to you direct."

"Could you send it here?" Sam said, choosing not to mention that he didn't have any *people*. "I'll pass it on."

"Can do. And I'm waiting on the schedule you promised."

"It'll be going out today, tonight by the latest."

"Good enough."

And with that the line clicked dead.

His muscles cramped and aching, Sam stood and walked over to the door. Putting his head outside, he cleared his throat. "Kath?"

Pouting, Kathy glanced up from her computer.

"I'm sorry," he said. "It's just a lot of things, you know? Anyway, I'm really sorry for being a jerk."

Her pout gradually slipped away and her smile returned.

"I wouldn't say jerk… asshole maybe."

To his surprise Sam found himself grinning back. "Fair comment."

Kathy nodded, and returned to her work.

If only everything else was remotely that simple, thought Sam.

If only he could say sorry to the man he'd killed, and somehow that would bring him back to life.

If only.

*

The cold Mexican pavers seeped through the crippled man's clothes, chilling his flesh. He awoke trembling, unsure how long he'd lain on the floor. He'd wavered in and out of consciousness, unaware of the passage of time.

Motes of dust danced in the prismatic shaft of light that fell through a glass diamond in the front door. The beveled edges cut in the glass fanned the rainbow light over his injured leg.

His head ached, his ankle felt as if it had been shattered. He rolled onto his side and tried to stand. Nausea swept over him, and he sank back down to the floor.

Mustering what little strength he had, he crawled through the dining room and into the kitchen, finally pulling himself upright. He opened a bottle of spring water, putting it to his parched lips and swallowed too hard. He choked, water exploding from his mouth.

"Slow," he told himself, sipping from the bottle.

He drained two bottles before slaking his thirst. He no longer felt so lightheaded, although when he tried to walk, his leg buckled. He needed medical help. But he wasn't about to go to any hospital, and the only doctor he trusted was a hundred miles away. And he only trusted Felix because the man would do anything for money, including keeping his mouth shut, having had his medical license abruptly revoked a few years ago. Of course, Felix had no idea that the man had pulled the long strings to make that happen. Just like a master puppeteer.

The man grimaced and glanced at the time, surprised to discover he had been unconscious for over fifteen hours. Along with that realization, he felt a pang of hunger. He needed to eat before undertaking the long drive back to the coast, where he could contact his private doctor.

In the refrigerator he found a stale beef sandwich. And while he chewed on the tough bread he began to plan. Plotting his revenge against the driver who had dared confront him.

He hadn't forgotten the vehicle's license plate.

Picking up his car keys, he downed another can of Coke and limped from the room toward the garage.

He reversed his luxurious Mercedes onto the driveway and pressed the smart remote control, closing the garage door and simultaneously arming the sophisticated security system. Turning the car around, he accelerated past the dark shapes of cacti and sped along the potholed track.

Twice on the agonizing journey to his home in the OC his head had started to pound, pressure pulsing behind his eyes, and he feared another attack would engulf his senses. Yet, he'd been spared.

Finally he pulled up outside the security gate. The guard acknowledged his arrival with a terse nod as the iron gate trundled aside.

The Mercedes entered the secured enclave, and drove along the tree-lined avenue, passing mansions of every architectural style, from Frank Lloyd Wright copies to French chateaux to New England colonial to Spanish villas. He pulled into his sweeping semicircular driveway, parking close to the main door.

Hobbling inside, the man locked the door, and collapsed onto the sofa. He reached for the cordless phone and dialed.

"Felix," the voice sounded drowsy.

"Good evening, Doctor," the final word laced with scorn.

Suspicion crept into the doctor's voice. "Who is this?"

"Don't you remember me?"

"Listen, I've had a long day. Who is this? How'd you get this number? This is unlisted, you know."

"I know."

The doctor paused. "Purdit?"

Yes, that was the name he'd used back then.

"I've had a long day, Doctor. A real bitch of a day, you might say. And I find myself rather urgently in need of your services."

Felix hesitated. "I'm not sure. This is most," he hesitated. "Unorthodox."

"Unorthodox? An arrangement for some private treatment? I need your help." He kept his rising temper hidden. He suspected the doctor was angling for more money. "And you know I'm willing to pay well for it."

"Yes. Of course, of course."

The jowly-faced doctor knelt beside the sofa and probed the man's ankle.

"I really need X-rays to make a full diagnosis."

The man shook his head. "You know the rules, Doctor. Just you and me."

"How on earth did you do this, anyway?" The bruised skin had discolored, becoming black, swollen.

"Just fix me up and give me something for the pain."

"I can give you an injection of morphine," he offered, reaching in to his medical bag.

"For five thousand dollars, I should think so."

Felix pulled out a syringe and ampoule. He pierced the seal with the syringe.

The crippled man's enigmatic face watched as the doctor slid the long needle into his flesh, sinking it deep before injecting the painkiller. As the drug took effect, a tingling sensation faded to a pleasant numbness.

Felix set a temporary cast.

"You'll need to stay off your feet for a few days at a minimum."

The man nodded, although he had no intention of following the doctor's advice. He had things to do. All he needed from the ex-physician was something to numb the distracting pain, freeing him to concentrate on his plans.

Felix disposed of the used syringe in a plastic bag labeled Hazardous Medical Waste, which he duly returned to his case.

"Give me the rest," the man said.

"I... I shouldn't leave any of this with you."

"Spare me the concerned lecture. Our deal's simple. You give me enough morphine to keep the pain away. And I let you walk out of here with all that cash in your pocket."

Reluctantly, Felix pulled out a packet of syringes and two brown glass bottles.

"I was thinking." He licked his fat upper lip, not looking at the man. "Maybe this is worth more?"

Felix laid the syringes on the table and edged away.

The man's jaw formed a hard ridge.

"I thought," Felix continued hastily, his voice stumbling. "I thought, ten thousand. That would be fair. I'm the one taking all the risk these days. I have to source the drugs on the black market and-"

Suddenly the man lifted his head and laughed, a hoarse, discordant laugh.

"Doc, you've got balls," his laughter subsided, his face became severe, eyes cold with lethal sincerity. "I'm sure you'd prefer to keep them." His eyes flicked to the dining room table. "Your money's on the table."

The doctor hurried across the room and opened the manila envelope he found there. Inside was a wad of hundred dollar bills.

"Five thousand, tax free," said the man, easing his legs off the edge of the sofa and sitting up. "I suggest you take it."

Felix's plump cheeks forced a smile. Then he greedily stuffed the money into his medical case and snapped the catch shut. He paused.

"You can go," the man said, dismissing the doctor with a vague wave of his hand.

Moments later he heard the front door open, then a solid clap as it banged shut.

Felix had served him well, but the ex-doctor was becoming a little too greedy. Perhaps he should suffer a tragic accident, although that would be a waste. He pondered the conundrum for a moment and decided there might be a better way to persuade the doctor to remain loyal. After all, Felix did have a wife and a teenage daughter, and family always made people vulnerable.

The man smiled, satisfied he would not have any more problems with the prematurely retired physician.

Besides, he had more important things to consider.

Closing his tired eyes he recalled the woman's beautiful face. He pictured her in the country club restaurant. And later, glimpsed in the flash of headlights when he'd passed their car as it straddled the road.

And he remembered the driver who had left him for dead.

"Why didn't you stop him?" he asked the woman, seeing her sensual visage in his mind. "Why?"

Didn't she realize that made her an accomplice?

Yet he could never imagine punishing her.

Then, unbidden, another woman's face swam into focus. A woman, silver haired and old beyond her years, whose hard life had left its ravages in the creases around her lackluster, unblinking gray eyes. He always remembered his mother this way. The way she looked when she'd been taken from him. Despite everything he'd done to save her; despite murdering his foul father. She had been killed two years later. Stolen from him.

He pushed her image away. He needed to focus.

A different face crystallized in his mind. A man's face seen beyond two dazzling lights. The unknown driver who had dared to confront him. Who had tried to kill him. Who would pay dearly.

*

Bleary-eyed, Sam lifted the phone, and pressed the speed dial and called home.

"Sam?" Ellen said, the moment she answered.

"Yeah. Look, this is taking longer than I thought. I don't think I'm gonna get back for another hour at least."

"Sam, it's nine o'clock."

"What can I say? This has to be on its way by tomorrow."

"Okay."

Sam frowned, disturbed by Ellen's acquiescence. "Everything all right back there? Is Jason okay?"

"We're fine. And I've got some news for you."

Sam's heart felt like it skipped a beat.

"What?"

"I went to the library, and looked in the paper. There was nothing about any road accident. No mention of someone being found."

"You're sure?"

"Positive, Sam."

Sam was hesitant to make any rash conclusion. "I guess that's good. Maybe the police are keeping it out of the papers. I wished you'd called earlier."

"I tried, but you were on the phone, or in some meeting."

"Kathy would've put you through if you'd told her it was urgent."

"Well, *sorry*."

Silence hung between them, a palpable void that separated them.

Finally, Sam could stand it no longer. "No. I'm the one who's sorry. Thanks for doing that."

"Do you think it means that man was all right? That's he's still alive?"

"I don't know. God, I hope so."

"Though, why wouldn't he have gone to the police?"

"I don't know, but he threatened us. It's his word against ours, maybe."

After promising to be home as soon as he could, Sam sank into his chair. He tried to relax. His fervent prayers had been partially answered. There was a chance the stranger was still alive. If the police had found a body following Sam's call from the gas station, then surely it would have been reported in the paper. Sam decided to drop by the library himself tomorrow morning and check Tuesday's edition. If he found nothing, then maybe, just maybe, everything would be okay.

Chapter 14

A tiny voice gasped.

Sam stirred. It seemed only moments ago, after a restless hour spent tossing beneath the sheet, that he had finally fallen into a troubled sleep. Haunted and tormented by the scarred man on the lonely, dark road. The road itself seemingly alive, the blacktop rippling like insidious water.

Sam shuddered, his eyes opening, suddenly alert. His pulse pounding in his ears.

"Daddy," the voice whispered.

Sam forced a smile, seeing his son in the dim light which filtered from a street lamp beyond the drapes.

"You okay, buddy?" Sam whispered back, glancing at Ellen, and making sure his sudden movement hadn't woken her. The last few days had taken a toll on her as much as on himself. They were both exhausted, irritable. And the evening had degenerated into another fight about nothing. Naturally, Jason had sensed something was wrong.

"Bad dream," Jason said.

Sam nodded. He knew the feeling.

"You need the bathroom?" Sam asked. In the past, a nightmare had rarely been nothing more than Jason waking up, needing to use the bathroom.

This time Jason shook his head, his eyes wide and fearful.

Taking the small boy's hand in his, Sam led Jason back to his bedroom. Jason plopped down on the racing car bed.

"So, what was it about?" he asked, concerned by the increasing frequency of Jason's dark dreams.

"Big rat," Jason said. "It hiding under there," he pointed down.

Sam nodded, sliding off the bed, onto his knees. He lifted the sheet at the foot of the bed and peered underneath.

He emerged. "Nothing there now. Safe and sound. What say we tuck you in?"

Jason shook his head firmly.

"Come on, Jason. It's really late."

But Jason refused to lie down.

"There's nothing there," Sam assured the child. "Honest."

"Is."

Sam sighed. "Jason, I'm tired. I need to be up early tomorrow. Settle down."

Sulking, Jason sank into bed, allowing the cotton sheet to be pulled over his shoulders. When Sam leaned over to kiss his son good night, the little boy rolled onto his side, facing the wall.

A lump rose in Sam's throat as he kissed the top of Jason's head.

"Good night. I love you," he added, hoping for a reply.

Jason said nothing.

Sam paused before he left the room, glancing at Jason, but the boy refused to look up. Sam felt lost, his world falling apart. And whatever he tried to do to fix it failed.

Ellen stirred as he climbed in to bed.

"Was that Jason?"

"He's okay," Sam replied.

Ellen muttered something, he didn't catch.

"What?"

"Nothing."

"I want to know."

"Go to sleep, Sam. I want to be up early," she said, echoing his words to their little boy.

Sam hesitated, then reached out, his hands stroking her shoulder, massaging her neck.

"I love you, hon," he said.

"I love you too, Sam. But that doesn't make everything all right. I need to see you, and so does Jason. We need to spend more time together, not less."

"I'm trying. Hey, we went to Palm Springs, I thought that was what you wanted."

"I want things to be like they were. I know how important the business is to you, I can accept -"

"To us."

"No, Sam. To you," he could feel her shoulders trembling, and knew she was crying. Silent tears, hoping he wouldn't realize. And that wrenched his heart.

"You're right," he said.

"Couldn't you finish early? Just once in a while, come home and spend some time with Jason? He misses you."

Tears filmed Sam's eyes.

He nodded, promising himself that things would change. They had to. If that creep on the road was indeed alive, if Sam had been given a reprieve, then he swore he would make things right with his family. A second chance.

As he lay down beside Ellen, he saw a shadow in the doorway, and glimpsed Jason disappearing back to his room. He wondered how much the young boy had overheard.

"I will," Sam whispered to Ellen as he rubbed her back. "I promise."

Whatever it took.

*

Sam reached work by seven o'clock on Wednesday morning, having been unable to get back to sleep after Jason's nightmare. Inside his office he slung open the filing cabinet, pulling out the personnel files. It was fast approaching the end of the month, payday.

Before starting the payroll run on the computer, he tried to log on to the bank's website only to find the internet was down.

"Great," he muttered.

While he rebooted the cable modem, he picked up the phone and dialed the bank's automated service. He punched in the account number for Grade-A FX, followed by the last four digits of the company's federal ID number. A computer-generated voice informed him that the checking account held a little under fifteen thousand. He requested a review of those checks that had not yet cleared, relieved to find his calculated balance matched the bank's computer, and hung up.

By the time he'd finished the call his internet connection was restored.

He logged into the payroll service. Luckily there were no changes this month, and he had everything transmitted by the time he heard Kathy stroll in.

"You're the early bird today," she chirped.

"You seem very cheerful," he said.

"That's because I know what you've been doing," she smiled.

Sam frowned. "What?"

"Payroll? Haven't you?"

He laughed. "Such a mercenary bunch."

"That's right," she paused, then added, "Well, since you're paying us this month, I suppose I should get that report finished for you."

"No peace for the wicked, eh?" Sam muttered, gathering up a folder of outstanding invoices. "Better hold my calls for a while," he told Kathy as he disappeared into his office. "See if I can dig up some money to keep the lights on."

He'd made a couple of calls and gotten the brush off from the one credit controller he'd managed to get on the line. She'd politely informed him that they were now paying on sixty days instead of thirty. Sam accepted the fact and held his tongue. It was getting ever more difficult to keep a small business afloat, especially in California.

He was about to make his next call when the phone rang.

"Kathy," he said heavily.

"Sorry, I know you said hold your calls, but there's a Sergeant Creswell on the line. From the police."

Police? Oh, shit. Shit!

Sam stammered, lost for words, his mind numb. "What?"

"Er, do you want me to ask him what it's about?"

"Yes," Sam hesitated. "No, wait. I'll talk to him."

What choice do I have? he thought, wondering if it was usual for the police to phone their prime suspect. Feverishly, he imagined a wail of sirens as squad cars lined up outside the office. Maybe a SWAT team gunning for him. Calm down, he thought, just calm down. Breathe.

"Sam Grady," Sam answered the phone.

"Sam, good morning," said a jovial voice. "Sergeant Jake Creswell here."

Sam's heart beat faster. "Yes?"

"Police Officers' Benevolent Association," Creswell added.

But Sam wasn't listening. How had they found him? Was the man dead or injured? He wanted to ask, but he didn't dare admit, or say anything. One thought ruled his mind, get a lawyer.

"What's wrong?" he mumbled.

"Oh, nothing serious."

Sam swallowed.

The sergeant continued. "We just got ourselves a little problem."

"Can I help?" Sam asked, bewildered by the tone of the conversation.

"Knew you'd understand. You see the Association sent you over a package last week-"

"Package?" Sam interrupted. "I don't understand, last week?"

"For your donation, sir. Wanted to thank you again for that, and get this confusion sorted out."

"Who are you? A charity? You're not the police?"

"Police Association, sir. Collecting on behalf of the retired officers."

Sam shoulder's sagged with relief. Thank God.

After he'd pledged fifty bucks solely to get rid of the guy, Sam collapsed back in his chair.

Jesus, he thought. If that had been a different call – a call to say the police had found a body, and they wanted to talk to him... His mind trailed off, unable to comprehend what such a catastrophic event would really mean. His family, his business, everything he cared about would be wiped away in that moment.

Shaking, he picked up the phone and dialed the landline at home.

But he hung up before Ellen answered.

There was nothing to say.

He let the phone drop back into its cradle, and he sat with no desire to do anything. He punched the Do Not Disturb button on his phone.

"Sam?" Kathy stared at him from the open doorway.

"What?" he roused from a numb reverie.

"I said, Ellen's on the line. She sounded worried."

"Shit," he grabbed the phone, and noticed Kathy's look of surprise. "My bad."

"Sam?" Ellen asked. "You called a minute ago. Are you okay?"

"Yes. I just wanted to, I don't know..."

"God, Sam. I picked up and you could have said something."

"Yeah, I wasn't thinking straight. Sorry." He felt like he was forever apologizing. "Look, do you want to grab a coffee or something?"

"Why?" Suspicion suddenly overrode the fear that had been in her voice. "What's wrong? Did something happen?"

"No, nothing. I just wanted to see you. To talk. Please."

His breath caught when she didn't reply at once. Finally she spoke. "Of course, Sam."

*

Armed with their Starbucks, Sam and Ellen strolled across the strip mall beneath the shade of thirty-foot tall palms and wandered into a small area of parkland.

"It's not the business, is it?" she remarked as if reading his thoughts and said. "It's him."

"I can't get what happened out of my head," Sam admitted. "I can't think. I can't even sleep. I just see that godforsaken road when I close my eyes."

"But there's been nothing in the papers. He must be all right."

"What if he's not? What if I killed him? Maybe the police aren't releasing any details until they find out who did it. What if they're looking for me, for us right now?"

Concern darkened her liquid gray eyes. "Sam, don't do this to yourself. You'll end up making yourself sick."

"Me? I haven't got time to be sick," he said, as they passed an elderly couple strolling together, arms linked.

He turned to Ellen.

"A joke. I was kidding. I'll take care, I promise. And I'll be home early tonight. Okay?"

Ellen nodded, but he saw the doubt in her eyes.

She's right, thought Sam. If I keep this up I'll drive myself literally insane or into an early grave.

"I should be getting back," he said.

Ellen touched his arm, and stretching up on tiptoe she kissed him.

"We'll work this out," she promised him.

He managed a wan smile, wanting her words to be the truth. But the voice inside his head would not relent, and their future seemed eclipsed by his own dark demons.

Chapter 15

Jeffrey Vermont's twentieth-story apartment overlooked the famed glass cylinders of the Bonaventure Hotel and the surrounding downtown LA skyscrapers. He kicked back in his executive leather chair and chewed a pencil while staring out the glass wall. He used the den as his office, and had equipped it with the most expensive computer hardware and peripherals, along with the latest in telecommunication systems, embracing the work-at-home philosophy. His multi-processor powered PC was connected to the outside world by a heavily firewalled, ultra-high speed connection. He was ready to leap into action the moment any of his clients called to request his specialized talents.

Jeff considered himself the Red-Adaire of cyberspace. The term Hacker was not one he particularly cared for, although he admitted it was perhaps accurate.

In the past two years, since graduating college, a few lucrative, if slightly illegal, deals had brought him his independence and a prestigious address. He'd always liked L.A., despite what the press said about the smog and the crime. It was a frenetic, exciting place to live.

One of the phones on his desk beeped for attention, a small red LED flashing in the handset. His most secure line. The one he'd spent months designing and implementing. The incoming call could be coming from next door, but the signal would be bounced off a Hughes satellite, then redirected through the best fiber-optic connections across three continents before reaching him. The most challenging aspect of the system had been infiltrating various telephone companies' seemingly impregnable computers. Once he'd broken their security, he created his own encrypted line, with the added benefit that it cost next to nothing. His total billing came to $16.56 each and every month, regardless of how much time he actually spent on the phone. 1656 he had always considered his lucky number.

Tilting forward in his chair, he eagerly picked up the phone. Only five clients, his elite customers, knew the number. And whenever one of them called it meant big bucks.

"Hello?" he said.

"Ah, Jeffrey. Remember me?"

Jeff recognized the voice. He keyed up a record on his computer.

> PURDIT, Nicholas

> Special telephone line implemented at house.

He scanned a couple of pages on the display, recalling the work he had done to provide his reclusive client with a line as secure as Jeff's own. In fact, he had based his personal system on the one he'd developed specifically for Purdit.

"Sure, Mr. P. I trust there's no problem with your installation?"

"No. Your work was exemplary. In fact, I have another task for you."

Jeff grinned. Now that was what he liked to hear: a satisfied customer.

"Whatever you need," Jeff boasted. "How can I help?"

"I'd rather you came here to discuss things."

"Phone's perfectly secure, sir," Jeff said.

"Even so."

Jeff sighed.

"It will be worth your while, I assure you," Purdit said, his voice sibilant as a serpent. The voice kind of unnerved Jeff, but the man's money overrode any other considerations.

"You're the boss. No problem. When?"

"Today. This afternoon, say around three?"

"I'll be there."

"Good." The line went dead.

Jeff hung up, an eerie feeling crawling over his flesh. The guy was creepy. He remembered that now. Remembered how the man had watched him while he installed the phone, and during the days he spent on the computer at the man's house. House, Jeff snorted, the place was more like the Getty Museum. The guy had to be worth a freaking fortune. The thought provoked a small smile on Jeff's tanned face. This time he would be sure to relieve Mr. Purdit of a good deal of that fortune.

*

The man who occasionally called himself Nick Purdit clenched his fists. His knuckles beaded white. He didn't like the idea of involving anyone else in his plan for revenge. Using the young computer genius was tinged with danger. But there was no other choice. Purdit did not know what records Jeffrey Vermont might keep concerning the confidential work he had done. Records which might surface if the hacker met with an untimely accident, or simply vanished.

Fortunately, he knew Vermont's weaknesses. A voracious greed for life's finer things, and the sole necessity to acquire such possessions. Money.

Even so, what Purdit needed was illegal, and there was a possibility Vermont would refuse to help no matter how high the fiscal reward.

"Don't dwell," he told himself. After all, the boy would probably enjoy the upcoming challenge of breaking into the DMV computer.

The man's thoughts shifted focus.

Reaching down, he unlocked the desk drawer and pulled out a file. Laying it on the polished wood, he stared at Dr. Andrew Bernard's picture for a moment. Then he lifted the phone and made his next call.

*

The empty 73 freeway meandered across brushland as it skirted the Newport Coast community. Jeff kept his foot on the Porsche's gas pedal, feeling the surge of power as the needle swept past ninety and well into three figures. He backed off only slightly as he took the toll road's next off ramp.

Moments later, cresting Pelican Hill, he saw the ocean shimmering beyond a golf course rimmed with elegant houses. And soon he crossed the Pacific Coast Highway and approached a gated community, stopping outside the guardhouse.

"Jeff Vermont, my name should be on the list," he explained to the uniformed guard.

"Nice car," the guard commented dryly, regarding the car's garish neon orange paint. He took his time checking the name against the list on his clipboard.

Finally the guard ambled back to the gatehouse and triggered the wrought iron gates. They trundled aside.

"Blow me," Jeff muttered, flooring the gas. The squat, low-profile tires squealed, laying wide rubber burns on the concrete. In his rearview mirror, Jeff glimpsed the guard leap out of the gatehouse, glaring at the vanishing sports car.

He was still chuckling when he pulled up outside Purdit's palatial villa, beyond which lay the vast ocean. Now this, Jeff thought, is the kind of place where I should hang my hat.

Jeff stepped up to the hand-carved front door which reminded him of nothing so much as a medieval church or, he decided, a monastery. He pressed the bell. Through the heavy oak door, he heard its loud chime. Seconds ticked by, before his wealthy client appeared. Jeff couldn't help staring at the sickle-shaped scar on the man's cheek.

"You're late," the man commented sourly.

"The guard had a problem. No brain."

Purdit's lips pursed without humor. "Well, do come in, Jeffrey."

"Right. Thanks."

He stepped across the threshold.

Somehow the house managed to smell damp and humid. Hadn't the guy heard of air-conditioning? Jeff wondered. He followed Purdit, staring at the cast on the man's leg as he limped through the marble hall and into the dark study.

"Accident?" Jeff asked.

The man said nothing.

Jeff tried to think of something else to say, anything to break the oppressive silence.

"Any chance of a drink?" he ventured, his throat dry.

"Evian."

Jeff laughed. "Water? Don't suppose you've got any beer?"

"No."

Purdit sat down and waved Jeff into the seat facing the desk.

"Coke?"

"I didn't invite you over for drinks. I am in need of your rather particular services."

"Always glad to help."

Purdit's pinched face gave him a dour look. "Quite."

Jeff's mouth felt parched. "Maybe a glass of water would be good."

"Hmm." Purdit stood and hobbled over to a rosewood drinks cabinet. He pulled down the leaf, revealing a built-in cooler and a shelf lined with leaded crystal glasses. He filled two tumblers and handed one to Jeff.

"Cheers." Jeff sipped the refreshing mineral water. He'd forgotten that Purdit only drank water.

"My pleasure, I'm sure. If we could get down to business?"

Jeff nodded.

"I need to acquire certain pieces of information."

"From a computer someplace, right?"

"Please, don't interrupt. This information is held by the Department of Motor Vehicles."

Jeff whistled. "Not easy."

"Come now, Jeffrey. For a man of your talents?"

"Yeah, I'm not saying I can't do it. But it won't be easy, or cheap. You want to access someone's record?"

"Yes."

"You want me to get you in, then out their system. Only you don't want anyone, probably not even me, to know whose record you accessed?"

Purdit nodded.

"You see? That adds to the complication. I mean, if you're in there and you screw up..." Jeff let his words hang in the air.

For a moment, Purdit said nothing.

"I won't make a mistake."

"Fine," Jeff said. "What about my fee?"

"I thought you might have a figure in mind."

Jeff grinned. "Sure. Sixty thousand, cash or Bitcoin. Help pay for my toy outside." He could glimpse his car's pristine neon paintwork through the half-closed plantation shutters.

"Rather expensive, don't you think?"

"Hey, supply and demand, right? You could always get someone else," Jeff said and smiled.

The man opened a drawer and placed a stack of bills on the desk.

"Jeez, how much you got in there?" Jeff asked, his eyes wide.

"Enough. You can take this with you when you leave."

"What? Today?"

"Certainly. Once I have the information I require."

"Hey, Mr. Purdit, these things take time. I mean, I can use your computer and all, sure, but -"

He fell silent as Purdit's evil eyes narrowed.

"Perhaps I failed to make myself clear?"

"No," Jeff stammered, his stomach turning to ice. "I'll get started."

Purdit vacated his chair, and Jeff sat down. Pulling the keyboard and mouse closer he set to work. He checked the I.P. mask he'd installed previously, confirming it was still hiding Purdit's machine from the internet. Then he connected to his P.C. back in Los Angeles. Within minutes, he'd surfed through the Darkweb and downloaded a file containing information on government systems and access codes. He hadn't broken into the DMV system in a couple of years - the last time had been to remove the need to attend traffic school and clean his license.

"I need to know what information you want."

"I told you, that's not your concern."

"Well, do you have a name? Or do you want to use a plate to get someone's name?"

Purdit nodded, his expression enigmatic.

"And their address?" Jeff asked, receiving another curt nod for an answer. "Okay. So I could go in via the Police Department system. That thing's got so many holes," he laughed. But Purdit did not share the joke. Instead the man sat in silence, waiting.

Jeff forged ahead, choosing instead to probe the DMV's network. Seeking a backdoor into the recently updated system.

It took an hour to worm his way inside network. Two minutes later, he was ready and summoned his client to the keyboard.

"Okay. You don't want to spend too long poking around. Just enter the license number and the record should appear in a few seconds. Once you've seen what you want, hit control-C. That'll break the connection."

With the utmost confidence, he clicked the mouse and entered the DMV records.

Jeff walked around the desk and flopped into the leather couch and waited.

Purdit typed something on the keyboard. He jotted a note on a sheet of paper, which he promptly locked away in his desk drawer.

Should have asked for more money, thought Jeff. Even so, sixty thousand for a couple of hours' work. Who could complain? Only the IRS, who wouldn't see a dime.

"Done?" Jeff asked.

"Most satisfactory," Purdit said, sliding the cash across the polished desk.

"Always a pleasure," Jeff said as he loaded the money into his pockets.

"You'll see yourself out."

"No problem." Jeff reached over to shake hands.

Purdit waited a moment, then gripped Jeff's hand. The man's skeletal hand squeezed with a crushing force Jeff hadn't expected.

"Goodbye, Jeffrey."

"Right," Jeff left, flexing his hand to make sure it wasn't damaged. "Asshole," he muttered as he walked outside. Getting into the Porsche, he grinned. Purdit wasn't so clever.

"Man, if I want your secrets, I'll have them," Jeff said as he started the engine.

An hour and a half later, alone and back in his L.A. apartment, Jeff turned on his computer. He repeated the exercise he'd run through at Purdit's mansion. Only this time, when he entered the DMV computer, he accessed the transaction log. He quickly identified the call he had placed, and pulled up the license plate Purdit had paid so much money to identify.

Jeff had taken a small risk that the log wouldn't be checked during his drive home. But even if someone had checked, and for some reason been interested in this particular inquiry, they would only have traced the source to the police department. After which the trail would turn cold. The real risk was that the log would be cleared before Jeff had a chance to discover what Purdit was up to.

Fortunately the log had not been deleted.

Jeff noted the license number Purdit had secretly entered, then called up the vehicle's registered owner. A business.

>GRADE-A FX, INC.

>Sam Grady - President and owner.

He noted the name and the address of the business, then checked out Sam Grady. No criminal record. Not so much as a speeding fine. A family man with a Facebook account he rarely used, and a similarly Spartan LinkedIn account. Just a regular guy, who had sunk his savings into his company. A company which wasn't exactly doing great. Sam Grady was boring AF, Jeff thought. Then again, Purdit been willing to pay a small fortune to learn about such a seemingly innocuous man. Why?

Jeff's last act before leaving the DMV's network was to erase his entries from the transaction log. He was gone, more invisible than a ghost.

He picked up a Ticonderoga pencil heavily scored with bite marks and gnawed the end.

*

Armed with the make and model of Vermont's car, Purdit had made a call as he watched the young programmer race away. On the phone he discussed his needs with a highly specialized mechanic, an expert who had helped him some years before. The device Purdit sought, he was told, could typically be made utilizing a black market chip designed to defeat the automaker's speed-limiter. However, unlike other German car companies, Porsche did not restrict their vehicles artificially. Therefore, it would take about a week to manufacture and deliver the device, at a cost of several thousand dollars.

A bargain, Purdit thought as he placed his order using a fake name and account.

Chapter 16

Fittingly he was dressed in black. Black slacks. A black Ralph Lauren Polo shirt. He limped down the curving staircase, which led to the marble entry hall and open plan lounge.

His scarred face wore a heavy frown. Twenty minutes ago he'd tried calling Dr. Andrew Bernard's office again. An answering machine had picked up, and he had no intention of leaving another message. He decided to wait another ten minutes, then try the doctor's office once more before calling his home number. Too many damn doctors in Orange County, he thought, and in his exclusive gated community for that matter. Of course, like lawyers, they flock where the money is.

He glanced at the oil painting dominating the wall above the fireplace. Bright, almost gaudy in its colors. He'd paid a lot for the work, but it pleased him that he would be the only one to enjoy the artist's broad brush strokes and surreal images. He did not anticipate many visitors in the near, or distant, future.

The sparse furniture included a chaise and a glass coffee table, its edge intricately carved, as were the glass legs, curling below like waves. Both expensive pieces, and both subservient to the grand piano that dominated the space. The man had chosen a Schimmel concert grand having compared the sound with the likes of

Steinway. The Schimmel favored his delicate touch and carried an enchanting tone.

He sat, inching the piano stool a fraction closer, and played. He chose a random Mozart piece, K137. Tricky enough in parts to keep his mind off the elusive doctor. His fingers kissed the keys. Perhaps he could have been a concert pianist as his mother had wished. She had been a music teacher in a small town school, her talent wasted. The dreams she'd left unfulfilled, she had tried to pass on to her only child. He had learnt to play when he was four years old. And continued to learn at her side for the next eight years, despite the teasing he endured at school. But he hadn't inherited his mother's passion. He felt the pressure building inside his head again. The room seemed to shimmer and flash, and he squeezed his eyes tight.

A face. A man asleep in a hammock strung in the porch shade of a log cabin. The memory came fully fleshed. A sweet, bloody mist hung in the air, lingering. The gun blast echoed through the woods surrounding the cabin, where his father brought his son on summer weekends. Bringing the boy along not out of love, but because of a need to show off his hunter's prowess, as if proving his manhood. Only this time it was the boy who pulled the trigger - and another animal died.

It was a memory to be savored. He had waited until dusk settled over the Blue Ridge foothills. The weekend hunters stowed their rifles and camping gear and headed home late Sunday evening. There was little chance anyone would pay any attention to a solitary gun shot. The sound of gunfire had echoed in the forest all through the weekend.

The boy had been careful with the gun and the lethal cartridge. Only his father's prints were on them, just in case they were later discovered.

After firing the fatal shot, he swathed his father's shattered skull in plastic, wrapping tape tight around the neck to prevent the blood from leaving a trail, and dragged the corpse down to the lake.

Moving a two-hundred-pound dead weight proved far harder than he'd imagined, almost impossible for a thirteen-year-old boy. Exhausted by the end, he sank to his knees near the water's edge and weighed down his father's clothes with fistfuls of stones and pebbles, then hauled the body onto the jetty and finally rolled him into the lake. Peering down through the murky water, the boy watched a muddy cloud swirl in slow motion enveloping the body until it slipped from sight. Let the scavengers feed on him.

He hurried back to the cabin, and a few minutes later returned, hurling the gun and spent casing into the middle of the lake. The ripples faded slowly. The water still. Serene.

Idly, he wondered if his mother would be upset or relieved when she heard his father had disappeared. He would say his father had simply driven away without a word, leaving the boy alone in the cabin. Would his mother believe him? He knew she would. And she would be grateful. He had lost count of the nights he lay awake listening to his father beating her. Listening to her pathetic cries, begging him to stop. In the morning he had seen the dark bruises on her face beneath her heavy make-up. He'd seen the way she limped around the house, pretending everything was all right.

Well, everything would be perfect now. He'd seen to that.

That night he scrubbed the blood from the veranda, and took down the hammock. He lit a fire in the hearth, burning the blood-soaked cloth. Flames leapt high, devouring the cotton, embers rising with the smoke.

It was nearly midnight when the four-wheel drive Jeep pulled away from the cabin. It bounced along the dirt track, until at last the boy reached a switchback road that twisted through the foothills.

Fortunately, no other cars passed him that night, although he doubted anyone would have noticed the driver was too young to sit behind the wheel legally. He'd learned to drive two summers ago when they visited a man his father called Uncle Silas on a farm. One of the farm hands had shown the boy how to drive a tractor. It drove like garbage, but it had been fun. And useful to a degree.

Driving the Jeep, he misjudged one tight corner, the car scraping the low barrier. He caught a glimpse over the edge. Pine trees and loose scree disappeared steeply, swallowed by the darkness.

He eased his foot off the gas pedal, slowing to twenty as he approached the final part of his plan.

Another bend loomed. He shoved the gearshift into neutral and gripped the wheel until the last second. The barrier gleamed in the headlights. He threw open the door. And jumped.

Cold night air assaulted his face. Strands of hair whipping across his eyes, blinding him.

The Jeep demolished the barrier with an ear-splitting crash and soared into the air.

The boy hit the tarmac hard, his hands smacking the surface, flesh torn. His body kept rolling with momentum, carrying him to the cliff edge. He lunged frantically for what remained of the crumpled barrier and held on, desperate to avoid the same fate as the car.

Far below, the Jeep crashed to the ground, splintering sapling pine trees as it tumbled end over end.

The boy stared down, disappointed that it had not exploded as he'd expected.

The man's gliding fingers transposed the music, slowing the melody, changing key, morphing the piece into something primal, discordant.

Mozart had always been his favorite. A bright light that burned out too soon.

He struck a final ominous chord, leaving it hanging in the vaulted ceiling. When he glanced at his Rolex, he wasn't surprised to find he had been playing for thirty minutes instead of the ten he'd intended. Time often stopped when he played, as if the music itself absorbed you into a different dimension. But now he was finished, for there were important things to attend.

Despite, or perhaps because of, the green glow cast by the glass shaded desk lamp, the study felt somber, the walls papered with an angry swirling of reds and mauves. The window was hidden behind closed plantation shutters. It was a place for quiet contemplation, undisturbed by the world outside.

Seated behind the mahogany desk, he lifted the telephone handset. The landline appeared ordinary, but in reality accessed an electronic maze to bounce his calls around the world through a labyrinth of reconnections and satellite links for one purpose only. To ensure his calls were impossible to trace. He recalled Jeffrey Vermont's assurances that no call under seven minutes could be traced, not even by the most sophisticated algorithms the equal to those employed by the N.S.A. Indeed, the egotistical hacker had, without knowing it, staked his life on that fact.

The man dialed the doctor's office, letting it ring until the answering machine picked up. His lips compressed into a thin bloodless line. He tapped in Andrew Bernard's home number. After two rings he was rewarded by a faint click.

"Hello?" a woman's voice answered. "Hello? Is anybody there?"

He slowly replaced the receiver, pondering his next step.

Like many professionals, the doctor had two phone lines at his home, one domestic the other for business. The number the man had just dialed was the business line, and he'd not expected the man's wife, or maid, to answer.

He waited fifteen minutes and decided to call one last time. If the woman answered the call, he would risk speaking.

But the phone kept ringing, until a ubiquitous machine answered.

He slammed down the receiver. His fist clenched, nails digging into his palm.

"Playing hide-go-seek, doctor?" he breathed. Well, he could wait, for a while, and then he would pay the doctor a house call.

*

Officer Claire Sawyer sped along the freeway shoulder, the siren wailing as she passed the stationary ranks of cars and trucks which jammed all five lanes. She slowed as she approached the flares and cones blocking three lanes of traffic and the shoulder. A thin yet decisive barrier marking the line between the drivers going nowhere fast and the emergency crews racing to save lives. Claire silenced the siren. A young uniformed CHP officer shifted his motorcycle aside as she edged onto the gravel verge, parking as close to the accident as she could.

The scene was chaotic, with fire trucks and police cars, CHP bikes and the paramedics parked haphazardly. Beyond these vehicles was the reason for the chaos.

The first look often told the story in Claire's experience. A Kenilworth eighteen-wheeler, sprawled jack-knifed across three lanes, had ridden over a car. There had been no fire or explosion, luckily. Not so fortunate was the car's driver, who was instantly crushed to death. There must have been a large difference in velocity. Possibly the truck driver, after driving twenty hours nonstop, popping pills to stay alert, had succumbed to sleep. Illegal as hell, but she'd seen it before. A second sooner, a second later, and the Kenilworth would have plowed off the highway and into the bushes, except this time there had been a vehicle stopped on the shoulder. Perhaps the truck driver saw it, too late, and hit the brakes, unable to do more than watch as his truck demolished the car, crushing it beneath the cab. Or maybe the car had pulled off the shoulder onto the freeway, unaware of the massive truck thundering down upon it. Until a second later when it struck. Or, perhaps, the truck driver had done everything right, and the driver of the car had somehow caused the accident. There was too much activity right now to measure the skid marks from either vehicle.

Claire edged forward, feeling her stomach churn. Feeling that somehow the accident could have been prevented. A feeling that never went away.

Overhead two helicopters circled. Working no doubt for local TV stations, capturing the event. It would be on air in time for prime time. Just the thing to watch while eating dinner. Claire glared up at the disgusting vultures.

A compressor whirred beside one of the fire trucks. Claire stepped over a pneumatic hose snaking from the pump around the wreckage, and watched the crew working with the jaws-of-life. High-pressure cutters that could bite through the twisted, compacted metal debris surrounding the truck driver.

"Been at it twenty minutes," a voice at her shoulder commented.

She turned, surprised to see Mike Stadler on scene.

"Thought you were off today?"

"I was. Till I got stuck in that mess," he nodded at the trickle of civilian cars funneling past the accident. Rubberneckers, hoping for a glimpse of suffering they could report home before the news came on TV.

Claire nodded.

"Nasty," Mike commented when she didn't reply. "Dumb mother-truckers," he said.

Well, let's not jump to conclusions, Claire thought, letting him walk on ahead. She pulled out her old-school micro-cassette recorder, dictating as she observed the scene. Perhaps to other police officers, those not involved in traffic, it was just another accident. To Claire it was a crime scene, until proven otherwise, requiring acute evaluation. Using a vehicle to commit murder or assault was a surprisingly common occurrence, albeit more often found in neighborhoods than on the freeway. A neighbors' squabble turned violent. Or, in L.A., drug pushers had been known to resolve their differences with the hood of their car rammed against a rival who happened to be strolling along the sidewalk. Brakes failed, was the usual excuse.

Pincer-like jaws bit down on the metal tubing that pinned the truck driver's shattered legs. Mercifully, the man had been unconscious throughout his ordeal. An IV dripped fluids and drugs into his body, and a doctor was overseeing the man's painstaking extraction from the shattered cab. Claire glimpsed the driver. Blood soaked through a hastily applied bandage wrapped around his forehead, and a slick red gloss covered most of his face. Lacerations from the metal and glass debris which, she knew, would have exploded like shrapnel upon impact. Even toughened safety glass could do plenty of damage to soft flesh.

But it was the sight of the car that sickened and angered Claire. Not that there was much of the vehicle left intact. Keeping her emotions in check, she surveyed the destruction. She'd worked accident for over five years, and had seen most things. But sometimes it was hard to keep your distance, and the little voice inside her mind would whisper, that could have been anyone. Could have been you.

The car looked as if it had been crushed by a scrap yard compactor, bearing no resemblance to the shiny machinery seen in the showroom. Claire saw it had once been a Lexus, one of the curvy new coupes. A safe enough car under most circumstances, although personally she favored the German imports. But no amount of airbags and fancy crumple zones would have saved the occupants from twenty tons of unstoppable truck. The truck's front wheels had ridden up and over the car, which lay crushed between these and the rear axle of the driving cab. Parts of the car had been twisted vertically, its near-side front wheel bent grotesquely to meet the flattened roof. The roof squashed almost to the ground.

Moving closer, she pulled a compact DSLR from her pocket and took a couple of quick shots, the flash flaring on torn sheet metal. As she took her photographs, she spotted some debris lying under the trailer, just behind the front wheels. Bending down, Claire picked up a piece of metal that had been crushed and folded in half during the collision. The car's license plate, the number obscured. Digging her nails in the gap between the fold she tried to pry the plate open, to reveal the number.

"Need a hand?"

She glanced around at Mike. For a moment Claire thought about refusing, she could manage.

"Thanks." She handed him the sandwiched plate.

Pulling the plate open, he gave her a curt nod and went about his business.

Claire half expected to see the usual vanity number, the sort that proliferated in Orange County. I1PUTT, on some golfing fanatic's Porsche, or MOMSSUV on a gleaming sixty thousand-dollar Tesla, the soccer mom's car-du-jour. Instead it was just a regular DMV number.

"Hey," she called, strolling over to one of the CHP patrol cars.

The officer standing beside the car glanced around.

"Yes, ma'am?"

"Can you run this for me?"

Her voice carried with it the authority of the officer in charge. It might be *only* another traffic accident, but those officers on scene would do as she asked.

Claire moved aside as an ambulance reversed into position. The fire crew had cut away enough twisted metal to attempt freeing the truck driver. The paramedics waited nearby, ready to take charge of the dramatic race to the hospital. A race against time.

The driver would be in surgery for hours, Claire estimated. She wondered when the hospital would let her interview him. Not for some considerable time. And that was assuming he lived.

She made a note to check which hospital he ended up at. If the guy lived, he would provide the strongest evidence in the case.

As she walked around the back of the truck, a voice snapped her attention back to the scene.

"Best hose it down," an O.C. Sheriff's officer said to the fireman.

Claire's heart leapt into overdrive.

"Wait," she called, running toward them. "What's going on?"

"Gas leak," the officer stated.

Claire glanced at the tarmac. She didn't smell any gasoline. "Show me."

"Yeah," agreed the fireman.

"Right here." The officer pointed out a damp patch on the ground, a puddle so small she needed a magnifying glass to see it.

Great, thought Claire, you order the scene hosed for two drops of unleaded. If there had been any danger, then she wouldn't have hesitated. But in this case the guy was being too damn eager. Oh, just wash away any evidence. That was real smart.

The fireman glanced at the ground, then looked at her as if to say, You really want that washed down?

"Doesn't look like anything's leaking now," she started to say. Then she studied the puddle, the liquid was tinged with green. "Wait a minute." She looked at the firefighter and saw he was grinning back. "That's anti-freeze," she said. Diplomacy, she knew, wasn't her strongest suit, but she didn't mean to embarrass the guy.

"Huh?" The officer said. He stared at the puddle, then glared at Claire before finally turning and marching away, muttering under his breath. "Coulda been dangerous."

Mike reappeared from around the side of the crushed cab.

"Dangerous? Yo, Collins!" he called to the officer. "My kid pees more than that in his diaper. Now that's a dangerous liquid."

Officer Collins didn't bother to look back.

"I think you upset him," Mike told Claire.

"You think? Imagine a mere woman knowing such things?" she bit her tongue before she said something she might later regret.

"Whoa," Mike said, evidently not wanting to get into any sort of debate. He quickly deflected the subject. "So, what do you think happened?"

"Too early," Claire said as they walked away from the accident and edged along the shoulder, back to the initial point of impact. The Lexus had been dragged about thirty feet under the truck's wheels.

"No marks on the highway, prior to the impact," she noted.

"Trucker probably higher than Christ."

"Maybe. The hospital will run a tox screen."

Then Claire frowned.

She knelt down on the shoulder, pulling out her camera once more. Mike bent down too and inspected the abrupt black stripe laid on the rough surface.

"Not braking," he said.

"Accelerating," Claire agreed. Into her tape recorder she said. "Check traction control on Lexus. Limited slip, and anything else."

Mike nodded. "Could be. But why?"

Claire didn't know. It didn't make sense to her. But the tire mark suggested the Lexus had accelerated from rest, straight into the path of the truck.

"Maybe the driver misjudged the gap, the truck's speed," she offered. Or maybe he wanted to kill himself, she thought. It wasn't a common way to go. Sure, people might jump off an overpass, or leap in front of a speeding truck, flesh and bone impacting against solid metal moving at sixty-five. No contest. Quick and clean. But such cases were usually clearly suicide. Staying inside a car was different. Too many things could go wrong, or right depending upon your point of view. The suicide attempt could fail, perhaps at the expense of someone else's life. Or you might survive but suffer some nightmarish, crippling injury. Although, Claire admitted, if this had been a suicide attempt, then it had been one hundred percent successful.

Why? Why choose such a gruesome way to die? she wondered. What if the person had lived, suffering a broken neck, paralyzed for life. Or endured torturous agony, burning to death in a fire, the most terrible death Claire could imagine. Why not a bullet in the brain?

Don't jump to conclusions. That was one thing they had stressed at Northwestern, at the university's Traffic Institute, where she'd studied an intensive three-month course before transferring from routine duties to major accident.

Behind Claire, ambulance doors slammed. Siren screaming, it sped away.

Claire measured the black line on the shoulder. A blip of the rear tire, gaining traction, accelerating the Lexus into the traffic.

The truck driver would have seen it only a fraction of a second before the Lexus plowed under the cab - if her suicide theory proved correct. The truck driver had no time to react. No way to avoid the collision.

The noise and activity behind the two investigators increased. Claire stood, turning.

A tall crane maneuvered into position, preparations under way to lift the rig high enough so the wreckage beneath its wheels could be disentangled and hauled free.

As she watched the crane hook descend over the truck, the police officer who'd checked out the license plate marched over. Referring to his notebook he told her. "Car belonged to a doctor. Andrew Bernard. Fifty-one. Lemon Heights address. Car's a Lexus 400 SC – well, it was."

"What's the address?" she asked.

A doctor? What reason might the man have had for wanting to kill himself? *If* it had been suicide, she thought. Of course, there was a chance the doctor had not been the one behind the wheel. Perhaps a relative or friend had been driving. Nothing was certain until they pulled the trapped wreckage free and were able to identify the body.

High-tensile cables and guides ensnared the Kenilworth cab, the metal ropes twanging as the crane started to lift. Inch by painful inch the rig rose, its tires maintaining contact with the road until the suspension stretched twenty inches. As the truck lifted, so the Lexus clung to its mate, rising into the air. The car's shattered shell shrieked.

A fireman signaled the crane operator, and the winch declutched and whirred to a halt, the rig suspended three feet above the ground.

The huge truck seemed to be swaying, as if weightless, wafted by gentle currents of air. Very deceptive, she knew. If it should slip free, or a cable broke, then those firemen working with practiced proficiency, cutters snipping, slicing and sawing through the tangled wreckage risked being injured or crushed.

With a dying, creaking groan what remained of the Lexus juddered as the crew darted aside and fell free from the truck. The crushed car slammed onto the freeway. Everyone was lucky to avoid injury.

The crane ponderously swung to the right, carrying the big rig clear, although a paramedic was already ducking underneath the truck to check if by some unimaginable miracle there might be someone alive in the mangled wreckage.

It was no surprise at all when he glanced over at Claire and shook his head.

It had taken over an hour, but finally the twisted steel skin and shattered metal bones of the Lexus were loaded onto a flat-bed and driven away for later examination. The driver's wallet had been recovered and the ID confirmed the deceased was indeed Dr. Andrew Bernard - a reconstructive surgeon. Claire heard an officer making an off-color joke about the reconstruction necessary for the dead man, but she ignored such comments, understanding them for what they were. Ways for the men and women who saw such grisly deaths to cope, for there was never a way to forget. When she first started the job, those comments had seemed unnecessarily cruel and sick. Now they were background noise. She had her own way of handling it, every investigator did. You tried to push it away when the time came to go home. You never really could.

*

The killer had spent the night awake. He'd even driven between his house and the doctor's. And, from across the street, parked in his Mercedes, he'd watched the ranch-style home. He waited outside for nearly an hour, noting a Westec Security patrol that passed by. The driver barely glanced at the German motorcar. Like the battered VW the man used in the slum areas, here the Mercedes provided perfect camouflage. Burglars and prospective muggers were unlikely to be driving around in such an expensive vehicle.

The man studied the house, not really expecting to see any signs of life at five in the morning.

After the patrol passed by, he climbed out and crossed the street, skirting a pool of light cast by a street lamp and peered through the wrought iron gate at the driveway beyond. There were no cars in the driveway, and the garage door was closed, so he could not tell if the doctor had returned home the previous evening. It was possible the doctor had worked late, perhaps summoned to one of the local hospitals for some emergency.

Not knowing gnawed at the man. Questions swirled through his mind. Could the doctor have panicked and fled, trying to avoid his fate? Or did Bernard think he could simply not answer the phone and that his problems would go away?

I don't think so, Doctor, the man thought as he returned to his car, pulling the door shut.

It was risky to wait until the doctor decided to leave his house. The security man might cruise by again, and at some point even an unobservant driver might wonder about the Mercedes. So he decided to leave. Besides, he knew a safer place to confront his prey.

He twisted the ignition key.

Twenty minutes later he pulled into the underground parking lot beneath the high rent office building. Bernard's office was on the third floor, and he normally arrived on Saturday morning to catch up on his paperwork. At least that was the story the doctor told his wife.

The man smiled to himself.

Why did so many so-called professionals think they were above the rules? That they alone could dodge their taxes, creating write-offs for anything, charge their clients for time spent taking a leak, or cheat on their wives without ever being discovered. Keeping their illicit affairs behind closed office doors. These days, how could anyone be so naïve?

And this time, Doctor, someone did find out. And sadly for you, that someone was me.

He waited, his good humor dissipating rapidly, his frustration growing when the doctor's car failed to arrive after an hour. Then, shortly after ten o'clock, he was rewarded when he spotted Bernard's nurse driving her Toyota down the ramp and into her parking space.

The doctor would be close behind, he knew.

Another twenty minutes ticked by.

He wondered if Bernard had parked in one of the spaces outside, leaving his car on a meter. But that seemed improbable, when tenants could park in the underground lot for free. The man climbed out, locking the Mercedes, and strolled up the ramp. He put on his shades before stepping into the sunshine. Glancing up and down the quiet street he saw no sign of the doctor's car. Still.

Doubt crept insidiously into his mind once more. Had the doctor decided to pack his bags and leave? The man studied the building and made a decision. Although he'd hoped to catch Bernard alone, before the nurse arrived, he needed to make certain the doctor was not in his office. And if he wasn't, perhaps the nurse knew where the elusive doctor had vanished.

After all, if one person could tell him, it would be Bernard's lover.

Dr. Andrew Bernard, the brass name plaque pronounced.

The man rapped his gloved knuckles on the door. A moment later the door opened an inch and the woman's squirrelly face peered through the gap.

"I'm sorry, but we don't see patients on Saturdays," the nurse informed him.

"I'm a friend of Andy's," the man said.

The nurse studied him, unsure. "He's not here yet."

"Could I wait?"

"I don't think so, but if you'd give me your name, maybe a number? I can pass on a message."

"I tried calling him last night, and this morning," the man said, sounding concerned. "Still didn't get an answer."

The nurse eased her grip on the door, allowing it to drift open.

"I'm not sure where he is," she admitted. "He's usually here by now. I was going to give him a little longer before I phoned."

"I don't think we should wait," he said smoothly, inching inside the reception area.

The nurse nodded, allowing him inside, and stepping to the phone.

The man's clenched fist relaxed, fingers flexing.

"Oh, Stephanie, it's Celia. I was just calling -" Color leeched from her cheeks, her complexion turning as white as linen. The phone cradled between her shoulder and ear slipped free and clattered to the floor.

The nurse stared through the man. Her eyes wide, her pupils dilated. "Oh, God," she said. "He's dead."

The man's expression must have echoed her shock, for the nurse reached out and touched his arm, as if to steady him.

Dead? There must be a mistake. How? he wondered. Anger began to pall in his mind. His jaw clamped tight. Bernard had eluded him. Had eluded justice.

For a long moment he glared at the nurse. She had lost a lover. He had lost so much more.

Abruptly, he turned and stalked away.

A light stabbed his eyes, and his footsteps faltered. Bernard, you got away easy, he thought as he tried to fight the wave of nausea which threatened to drown him.

He breathed deeply, trying to think of something other than his defeat.

Bernard's mocking face gradually faded from his mind. In its place, he saw another.

The driver from that night on the road.

Sam Grady.

Chapter 17

For the first time in over a week Sam slept through most of the night, his dreams less troubled. The stranger who had confronted them on that lonely night did not loom forth to haunt him. The incident was perhaps beginning to fade, as Ellen had said it would. Although he could, when he closed his eyes, picture the barren stretch of road, the figure framed in the headlights, the body lying on the asphalt.

Sam rose from bed without waking Ellen and disappeared into the bathroom. Despite the welcome sleep, his muscles ached and he felt exhausted. A hot shower helped.

He looked in on Jason, who appeared mummified in his cotton sheet. The little boy murmured, on the verge of waking, before he rolled onto his side. Sam watched the faint rise and fall of his son's chest, his breath so quiet and peaceful it was less than a whisper.

With no real desire for breakfast, he texted a *Love you, Sam* note to Ellen as he headed out the door.

Traffic was light, and he made the trip to the office in record time.

"He should be here any..." Kathy glanced up as Sam entered the office.

He arched an inquiring eyebrow.

"Just one moment," she said to the caller before covering the receiver with her hand.

"A Mr. Purdit? He said it was personal."

Sam frowned. "He's probably selling. Just put him into voicemail, I'll call him back later."

"It sounded important. Something to do with your meeting in the desert last weekend?"

Meeting?

"He said you bumped into him in Palm Springs?"

His stomach suddenly lurched. Was that some kind of sick joke?

"Are you okay? Sam?"

"Yes, I'm…" Sam said. "I forgot, yes. Put him through. I'll take it in my office."

Heart pounding, hustled into his room, closing the door.

"Hello," Sam said warily as he picked up his extension.

"Hello, Sam," the sibilant voice replied.

"Who is this?"

"Sam, I'm disappointed. Don't you remember?" The voice cackled, maybe it was a laugh. "Our little incident on the road."

The image of the scar-faced man, with his black enigmatic eyes surfaced against Sam's will.

"You're – you're alive."

"How very astute of you, Sam. "

"But, how... How did you find me?"

"That's not really important, is it? Surely there's another question you want to ask?"

Sam frowned. "Listen, I don't know what you want. I'm sorry about what happened, but that was your fault as much as mine. If you hadn't attacked us-"

"Attacked you? A pedestrian against a two-ton vehicle. I don't think the police would look at it quite that way. Do you?"

Sam shivered, a tremor which shuddered through his body. He tried to calm his breathing. It wouldn't do to let the creep on the other end of the line know how scared he was.

"What do you want?"

"Ah, I knew you were smart. Yes, that is an excellent question."

"Well, you seem to have all the answers."

"Don't. Don't do that, Sam. Don't try to be too smart."

Sam bit back a reply. Breathed deep. "What do you want?"

"I think we should meet, Sam. To discuss compensation for my injuries. Don't you think that would be fair?"

"Look, I didn't mean to hit you. It was an accident, I swear."

"But you did hit me, more accurately, you tried to run me down like a dog."

"It wasn't like that. You know it wasn't."

"Maybe it was an accident, just as you say. So, let's meet like civilized men, I'm sure we can work things out. And you won't even have to travel. Why don't I stop by your home?"

"No," Sam blurted out. He didn't want the man anywhere near his family.

"Sam, I'm willing to put this behind us, but you don't seem to want to meet me half way."

"Yes, I do. I will, whatever you want, but not at my house."

"Very well. I'll come to your office."

Sam's voice caught in his throat. He didn't want that man showing up here either. But anywhere was preferable to his home.

"Okay. When?"

"No time like the present. Say four o'clock."

"Today?! I mean, things are kind of hectic here," Sam said playing for time.

"Four o'clock, Sam."

The line went dead. It took Sam a couple of seconds to realize the stranger hadn't asked for the office address – that he must already know where Sam worked. A chill coursed down his spine.

He hit the speed dial and called home.

"Sam?" Ellen answered.

"Hey, honey," Sam said trying to sound calm, but positive he sounded anything but.

"I missed you this morning. Is everything all right? Sam?"

"Yes, yes, I'm fine. Just wanted... I thought I'd give you a call, see how you're doing?"

Ellen laughed. "That's sweet of you, Sam. Odd, but sweet. Are you sure you're okay?"

"Me? I'm doing fine, considering..." His heart sank. He couldn't pretend. For all he knew that maniac might be wandering around his neighborhood. "No. I'm not okay."

"What's happened?" he could sense the tension creeping into her voice. "Sam, have you heard something? The police?"

"No. Not the police."

"Then what? Sam, tell me."

"That man. He just called. He called me here."

Silence.

Sam was about to speak when Ellen breathed. "He's alive? What did he say? What does he want? God, how did he even find us?"

"I don't know. But he wants to meet-"

"Are you crazy? We have to call the police."

"And say what to them? Excuse me, officer, but this guy I mowed down and left for dead on the side of the road just phoned me. I think he wants to blackmail me. Sure, I'd be glad to go to prison while you sort this mess out."

"That's not fair."

"None of this is fair. Ellen, I... I don't know."

"What if he's dangerous? What if he's got a gun this time, Sam?"

"If he wanted to shoot me, I don't think he'd have phoned first." He hesitated. "Listen, I think he knows where we live."

"He knows?" Her voice cracked. "God, Sam."

"But, I think if I give him some money, he'll go away. I mean, you saw him, a few hundred dollars will probably sound like a fortune. It's going to be okay," he struggled to keep his doubt out of his voice.

"Okay? No. What if he comes here?"

"He's not stupid. I'll pay him and he'll leave us alone."

"But what if he wants is more than we can afford?"

"I don't know. We'll figure it out, we don't have a choice. Let me find out first. Maybe he'll listen to reason."

There was a moment's pause before Ellen answered. "Be careful, Sam."

"I will."

Sam hung up leaned back in his chair, his fingers steepled beneath his chin, wondering what the hell he was going to do?

*

Someone coughed, clearing his throat, and Claire glanced around to face the doctor who had appeared from nowhere.

"Are you all right?" he asked, concerned.

"I'm fine," she smiled at the intern. "I was waiting for Dr. Stacey."

"Ms. Sawyer, right?"

"Officer Sawyer," she corrected, standing and offering her hand.

The intern shook hands, bemused by the formality. "I'm afraid Dr. Stacey's in surgery at the moment, but I was told to give you every assistance."

"I need to find out about a truck driver who was brought in. Frank DeSilva."

"DeSilva? His right leg was shattered in five places and he sustained three broken ribs. Some internal bleeding too, but he's stable."

Claire interrupted, not needing a list of the man's injuries. "I just need to speak to him for a minute."

The intern hesitated, rubbing his fingers over his bestubbled jowls.

"One minute. That's all. It's important," Claire said, offering the young man a warm smile. "You can stand right next to me."

Doubt tightened the muscles around the intern's jaw. "I guess it'd be okay, as long as I'm there."

"Of course."

Claire let him lead the way to the post-op recovery wing.

They entered the ward, and the intern drew the curtain around the truck driver's bed.

The driver inclined his head, and stared at Claire through the heavy bandages. His chest injuries were hidden beneath the sheet, his leg cast in plaster. But, despite the pain-relieving drugs he must have been prescribed, his eyes appeared alert.

"Mr. DeSilva?" she asked, keeping her voice soft.

"Yes."

"Officer Claire Sawyer," she said, producing her badge.

The patient merely grunted.

"I need to know if you remember what happened." She glanced at the intern, seeing concern for the patient reflected in his eyes.

For a moment she thought the driver would not answer, or deny any guilt. That was the typical pattern when people knew they'd made a mistake.

"I remember."

"That's good."

"That guy musta been drunk. I didn't even see him till…" he closed his eyes.

The intern edged forward. "Are you sure you're up to this?"

The driver nodded, staring at Claire. "Look, I'm doin' fifty-five, okay maybe sixty, slower than most of the traffic, you know?"

"Yes," said Claire.

"Next thing - this jerk pulls off the shoulder. No signal, no nuthin'. Right in front of me, wham! I didn't have time to hit the brakes. I mean, he was already un'erneath my wheels. Christ."

"You actually saw him pull off the shoulder onto the freeway?"

"Like I said, one second nothing, the next I've got a car diving under me. You think I'm lying? Think I was popping pills to keep on the road? Not me, lady. No goddamn way."

Claire hesitated, trying to read his eyes. "Okay."

"Good, 'cause not all truckers are speed freaks, you know?"

"I know. And thank you, you've helped."

She turned to leave.

"Officer?" The trucker called.

"Yes?"

"No one told me. The guy in the car, he has to be dead, right? There anyone else in there, I mean, kids or anyone?"

"No one else in the car, but yes, he's dead. He must have died instantly," she left the man to his own thoughts and tugged the curtain aside. She was glad to step into the corridor. The air suddenly seemed easier to breathe.

*

"Testing," Sam's voice came from his iPhone, using the recorder app. He'd hidden the cell phone under a couple of sheets of paper and had spoken in his normal voice. The sound quality was slightly muffled, but would suffice.

The clock crept toward four, and the hour slipped by with no sign of the man's arrival.

Sam felt a pang of hunger and realized he hadn't eaten all day. But his stomach was too jittery to keep down any food.

"Kathy," he said, punching the intercom. "Can I get a coffee in here?" Belatedly adding, "Please."

"Yes, sir," came the reply laced with sarcasm.

Sam sighed.

He crossed to the door.

"Sorry," he said, poking his head around the jamb. "I'll get-"

He froze.

The scar-faced man limped through the entrance. He leant most of his weight on an ornately carved walking stick. He wore an expensive black suit, which Sam guessed was Italian, dark silk shirt, and Ferragamo tie. His eyes remained hidden behind Ray-Ban Wayfarers. And when he raised a hand in greeting, Sam caught a discreet flash of the man's gold Rolex. Whatever the man might be, Sam realized he could cross poor off the list.

While Sam recognized the stranger they'd met that fateful night, the man certainly didn't act, or dress, like him.

"Hello again, Sam," the man said as if they were old friends.

"You'd best come through," Sam said warily.

"Two coffees?" Kathy asked.

"Very kind of you," the stranger said. His lips pursed in a thin smile.

Kathy smiled back. She even seemed a little flattered to Sam's amazement.

Inside Sam's office, the man accepted the seat and slipped off his sunglasses. His gaze touched Sam. His eyes black coals.

"See, we can be civilized."

"Sure. What do you want, Mr. Purdit?"

"Nick. Straight down to business. I appreciate that, I know you're a busy man, Sam."

Kathy knocked and elbowed the door open, carrying a tray.

When Sam glanced back at the stranger, he saw the man had surreptitiously slipped on his dark glasses.

"Thank you kindly."

"Thanks, Kathy," Sam said.

She smiled at the visitor as she left the room.

"So, are you going to tell me what you want?" Sam demanded.

"I'm not some sort of monster, Sam. I don't want to be unreasonable. I came here to ask for some small recompense for my suffering." He lightly patted his leg.

"You expect me to pay you?"

"That would seem a fair arrangement, considering what you did."

"What I did? What about you?"

"I don't recall leaving you for dead in the middle of nowhere, Sam."

Sam's pulse quickened. *Cut to the chase*, he thought. "Did you have a figure in mind?"

"Actually," the tightlipped smile reappeared for a moment. "I thought a settlement of fifty thousand wouldn't be out of order."

"I don't have that sort of money."

"Sam, please. Your life insurance policy is worth ten times that amount. I imagine you can borrow directly, or against the policy."

"How the hell would you know that?"

"Sam. I know everything about you. Everything."

Sam felt anger flare, his fists tight. Who the devil did this guy think he was? Barging in to his office, demanding money. And just what was the guy going to do if Sam refused? Call the police? Sam didn't think that was likely. Though he couldn't know for certain if Purdit was bluffing. And he couldn't risk that.

The man's eyes narrowed, studying Sam. His heavy eyebrows furrowed together, becoming a single dark smear.

"I can't pay that much," Sam said.

"Sam, such foolishness."

"You listen to me," Sam swiped away the sheets of paper, revealing his phone. "You want to go to the police? Well, you do that, and you can explain to them why you just tried to blackmail me for fifty thousand dollars. Did I get the figure right?"

To Sam's surprise the stranger relaxed, easing back in his chair.

"You think I'm joking?" Sam demanded. "You think this is fucking funny?"

"Oh, I'm sure you're serious. I come here to try and reach an amicable settlement, without involving lawyers and such unnecessary hassle for both parties. And you thought I was trying to blackmail you?"

"Wouldn't you call it that?"

"I thought you might be a man of honor. I suffered at your hands. I thought you might wish to make that right."

Sam studied the stranger. Despite his words, Sam didn't trust him. Not for a second. Purdit, if that was even his name, had a way of twisting, warping the truth. Yet, Sam now felt less confident about calling the authorities. Maybe, he thought, the man's request wasn't totally unreasonable.

"I can't afford fifty thousand."

"Then tell me what you feel is fair. That's all I ask."

"I don't know. I could raise ten, maybe fifteen thousand. If I do, I don't ever want to see or hear from you again."

"Fifteen," the man mused with irritating calmness. "Sam, that doesn't even cover my expenses."

"I've got some idea how much medical costs are. I'd say it was generous."

"Who said medical costs? It wasn't cheap to find you."

"You should have thought of that before you tried that stunt on the road."

"Sam. You're a businessman, let's split our differences. Twenty thousand five," he raised a palm to ward off further argument. "I'll expect the money within forty-eight hours."

Sam muttered. "Who do you think you are?"

"Think of me as your conscience." With that parting comment he rose and walked out the door.

*

Claire Sawyer strolled along a sterile corridor which looked like something out of a sixties hospital drama. Her footsteps echoed on the polished linoleum floor. Fluorescent lighting reflected off insipid walls interspersed with daylight falling through floor-to-ceiling glass blocks. She didn't particularly enjoy her visits to the County Coroner. Even the strong disinfectant couldn't hide the fetor of death which pervaded the building. She pushed open the door to the Coroner's office.

"Hello?" she called as she entered.

No one replied. The assistant's desk that doubled as reception was empty.

Claire glanced inside Marcus Fenster's office, but that too was empty. He would be next door, no doubt.

The autopsy room was lined with melamine cupboards and an ocher counter top ran the length of one wall. Large, grilled extractors hummed overhead. A steel table in the center of the room was haloed by a moveable surgeon's lamp.

As Claire entered, she heard a loud snap. Marcus glanced up at her and adjusted the tool he was using on a Latino youth who lay eviscerated on the table. The Coroner snapped another rib to allow further investigation into the thoracic cavity.

"Ah, Claire. Vanessa said you'd be dropping by."

"Marcus," she said.

"Autopsy's on my desk. I'll be wrapping this one in a few minutes if you want to wait."

Claire hesitated, morbid interest conflicting with her desire to escape from the formaldehyde-cloaked room as quickly as possible.

Marcus Fenster returned his attention to the body, and resumed reciting his report into the microphone suspended from the ceiling.

"The sharp upward angle of the entry wound, measuring approximately four-tenths, severed the pulmonary artery. Lacerations on the aorta. Rapid blood loss from the heart, death occurring within two minutes," he glanced at Claire. "Stabbing victim they brought over from Santa Ana. Gangs."

Claire nodded, and not for the first time wondered what made anyone want to cut open the dead. Creepy. "I think I'll go take a look at that report."

"Sure, sure," he returned to his dictation as she walked out.

Inside Marcus's office, Claire shifted in the hard armchair and read through the report. Cause of death had been obvious enough, severe trauma. With so many major injuries to Dr. Bernard's body it had been difficult to determine which had been fatal. Although Marcus believed the blow to the cranium had killed him. Nothing out of the ordinary.

But that wasn't what caught Claire's attention.

Marcus strolled in, removed his white coat, and was dressed like a regular guy, slacks, sneakers and a very worn Raiders T-shirt. She'd been taken aback by his unprofessional attire the first time they'd met. Now she was used to it.

"You saw the blood work?" he asked, nodding at the report.

"Yes. Sleeping pills?"

"Loaded to the gills. If the our doctor had stayed parked on the shoulder, we'd have found him permanently asleep at the wheel."

"Suicide."

"I'd say so, wouldn't you?"

Claire would, but questions still nagged at her. What would make a seemingly successful doctor want to swallow a bottle of pills, or drive in front of a truck?

*

"Why not pay him? I thought that was what you said?" said Ellen.

Sam stared at her. He had thought it through, after Purdit had walked out of his office.

"Because it wasn't our fault," Sam protested. "The guy was drunk or high. Besides, if you get down to it, he's got no proof."

"This isn't a law court, we know what happened. And if we pay him, he'll leave us alone. I don't like the thought that he's out there, and you said he knows where we live, Sam. How do you know he wouldn't try something? You don't know what he'd do, what if he tried to hurt Jason?"

Sam hesitated, then admitted. "I don't know if we can raise that much cash. He suggested I use my insurance."

"How much is it worth?"

"I don't know. But Purdit evidently reckons it's enough."

"How does he know?"

"This guy knows where we live and breathe. He knows everything."

"That's impossible," Ellen said. The fear and trepidation he'd seen in her eyes earlier returned.

He perched on the sofa beside her.

"The information's out there. I don't know, the Darknet, or something. Look, if we can get the money, pay him, maybe he leaves us alone. Maybe."

"But maybe he doesn't."

"I don't know. This guy's smart, but he's got to realize you can only push people so far. If he forces us into a corner, we'll go to the police. Take our chances-"

A creak at the foot of the stairs made them both spin around, Ellen yelping in fright.

Jason screamed as she startled him!

Sam's pulse hammered. He stood, his legs shaking, and took a deep breath before crossing the room, and scooping Jason under his arm.

"Hey there. You made us jump, scamp," he said, trying not to scold the child. After all, it wasn't the boy's fault his parents were so fraught.

"I had a scary dream, Daddy." Jason informed him once he was ensconced on the sofa.

"Tell me about it," said Sam with an unintended edge to his voice which he hurriedly softened. "You want to tell me? Makes it a lot less scary when you share."

It was midnight before they settled Jason back down to sleep. Sam knew his son had picked up on his parents' anxieties, and it had taken an hour to soothe away his fears.

In the bathroom, Sam found himself wishing he could do the same, and his nightmare would vanish.

He pulled on the T-shirt he wore to bed, then brushed his teeth.

Ellen hurled the door open and rushed in. Her face ashen.

"What?" Sam said, spitting out the toothpaste. "What's wrong?"

"The phone…"

"What?" He wiped his mouth, then held her arms. "Ellen?"

"It was him," she breathed, sagging against his chest. "He knows this number. Our home number."

He made to push past her, but she clung to his arm.

"He hung up," she said, looking up into his face, her eyes wide, pleading. Her whole body trembled, gripped by a desperate fever.

"What did he say?" Sam asked, running his hands gently over her hair, holding her close.

"He... He said, he needs the money tomorrow," a sob wracked her chest. "By noon."

"Noon? There's no way."

"He knew my name. Sam? He kept saying my name."

"Jesus." His mind unable to think straight. He couldn't process what was happening, or how fast his world was imploding upon him. This felt worse than the terrifying confrontation on that lonely road. Out there, they had been strangers. Now he was in their lives.

"Sam, what are we going to do?"

He whispered softly. "I'll get his money somehow. And after tomorrow he won't call us again."

*

Purdit sat before the grand piano and ran his fingers over the cool ivory keys.

Such a sweet voice.

"Ellen," he breathed as he stroked the keys.

A Brahms concerto lilted, filling the entrance hall.

The man closed his eyes while he played. He pictured the face he'd glimpsed a brief week ago. A face etched with such delicacy, it reminded him of a porcelain figurine he'd once bid for at an auction.

"Ellen," he hummed the name alongside the melody.

I can give you so much, he thought. I can make you happy. Give you what you deserve. You'll need a maid, perhaps a nanny. Well, he could live with such intrusions, if that was what she desired.

A sudden discordant note ruined the pure sound. A black wave of doubt obscured his reverie.

What if she didn't want him?

That would be foolish. Irresponsible, he decided. Surely she would see sense. Surely no respectable mother would wish her child to be harmed. He hoped such threats would prove unnecessary. He had no desire to hurt an innocent child.

Especially a child who had recently lost his father.

Chapter 18

Ms. Colleen Williams looked more like a mousey librarian than a VP of the bank, or rather, a Preferred Client Financial Advisor.

She continued her stoic appraisal of Sam's life insurance policy. Finally, she deigned to acknowledge his presence with a vague, unimpressed glance.

"I'm afraid the bank can't possibly advance a loan against this policy. Have you considered refinancing the equity line against your property?"

Sam shook his head. "I thought... is that a possibility? I thought it would take weeks."

Ms. Williams smiled, a disconcerting transformation of her face. Like the witch inviting Hansel to dinner, thought Sam.

"Two or three at most. I can arrange for the loan documents to be drawn up, and there's an excellent introductory rate for the first six months." Seeing the expression on his face, she paused.

"As I mentioned on the phone, I need the money today. In cash."

The woman's sour face curdled.

"I'd really appreciate anything you can do," Sam added.

Not bothering to hide a hefty grunt of annoyance, Ms. Williams started typing on her computer. After a while her expression softened once more.

"You do have excellent credit, Mr. Grady."

"Sam. Thank you."

"If you'll excuse me for just a few minutes." She got to her feet and headed over to the manager's office.

Sam helped himself to a cup of coffee and waited.

Twenty minutes later he was still waiting, the polystyrene cup empty, the rim scalloped where he'd idly picked away with his fingers.

After forty-five minutes, Ms. Williams reappeared. He gave her the warmest smile he could muster.

"Well, here we are," she said. "We've increased your credit limit, and you can take a cash advance-"

"Thank you. I can't tell you how grateful I am. You're a life saver."

She grunted at the hyperbole and slid a sheaf of papers filled with legal, microscopic print in front of him. "Once you've signed where I've highlighted, and initial each page."

He blinked. Aware that Mrs. Williams was staring at him, and still holding the pen in her hand for him to take.

"Is there a problem?" she asked.

"No. No problem." He took the pen.

Once he'd finished signing, she carefully perused his signature like some FBI profiler.

"I really appreciate your help."

Ms. Williams nodded curtly. "I'll arrange for your money."

Saturday morning and most people it seemed had better things to do than show up at work. There were only half a dozen cars, belonging to the owners of the various small businesses, parked in the lot when Sam arrived.

Entering the office, he flicked the lights on. Picking the mail off the carpet he dumped it in Kathy's tray. It could wait until Monday.

The digital clock on the wall behind her L-shaped desk glowed red, 11:52. He strolled past Kathy's desk and into his office, where he emptied his bulging pockets, piling the money on the desk.

Moments later he heard the outer door open.

"Purdit?" he said, returning to the reception room.

The man hobbled in. He leant so heavily on the wooden cane it flexed, and Sam could picture it snapping in half.

"I've got your money," said Sam.

"I didn't imagine otherwise."

Sam ignored the philosophy lesson. "How do I know you won't show up again?'

"Sam," the man's lips curled. "The money."

For a moment he considered refusing to hand it over. But he didn't really have a choice. The only alternative was to go to the police. And that prospect terrified him more each time he considered it.

Sam stepped back into his room and collected the money off the desk. When he turned around Purdit was standing in the doorway.

"Here. Take it," Sam thrust the money at him. "But I don't want to see, or hear from you again, ever."

The man coolly placed the money in the deep pocket of his black jacket. Then he looked at Sam, his piercing eyes narrowing.

"You should drive more carefully, Sam. Such recklessness. You weren't only risking your life. Think about your wife. You do love Ellen?"

Sam edged backward, his leg bumping the desk, halting his retreat. "Of course I do. You just leave us alone. I swear, you come anywhere near her..."

"I would never hurt a woman, Sam. You should believe that."

"Then leave us alone."

Purdit turned and limped outside. Sam watched him leave, his gut gradually relaxing, his fear ebbing. Yet he couldn't entirely shake the eerie feeling the stranger brought with him. A malevolence which seemed to cling to him, like the stench of a skunk to an animal which had been sprayed.

Through the tinted glass Sam watched the man approach a black Mercedes. As Purdit crossed the parking lot his body straightened and, before he reached the car, he was walking with little sign of discomfort.

Sam frowned. Confused. What was that about? Obviously the guy wasn't as badly hurt as he'd made out. Faking it, for twenty five thousand dollars? For money, it appeared, he didn't need. Sam's doubt and concern returned in full measure.

Sam sat down. He was shaking. He was unsure how long he sat there.

Becoming aware of his surroundings, he forced his rigid hands to relax. The white indentations where his fingernails had dug into his palms gradually faded to pink. For the hundredth time he wondered if he'd done the right thing. Ellen had agreed, but was it a smart move? They'd decided to pay the blackmailing bastard what he wanted, and just prayed he would leave them alone after this. Sam wasn't convinced that would happen, but if it didn't then his only recourse would be the police. He couldn't see another option, and he dreaded to think of the consequences of his own actions on that fateful night.

And to think, I was worried I might have killed that bastard-

Shit, he thought, realizing that he'd neglected to call Ellen the moment the man left. He hurriedly made the call. She picked up on the first ring.

"Sam?"

"He was here. He took the money," Sam said, trying to keep every ounce of tension from his voice.

"He's gone?"

"Yes, I don't know, twenty minutes ago. I've been sitting here. I felt sick. Thought I was going to throw up. Sorry, I should have called you."

"God, Sam," he heard her breath catch in her throat. "I hope he never comes back."

"I don't think he will," he said, praying rather than believing that might be true.

"Thank you."

"I didn't do anything, except give in to the son of a bitch."

"You know what I meant."

Sam nodded.

"Sam?"

"Yes, I know."

"Come home soon."

"I'm on my way." He hung up.

Maybe things would return to normal, he thought. God knew the chilling episode had caused enough disruption to his life, both at home and at work. And with Martin out sick for a couple of days they had fallen way behind schedule.

"Dammit," he said, suddenly remembering the penalty clause Aeon had insisted upon in their contract. How on earth had he forgotten? He could picture the purchasing manager rubbing his hands with glee if they failed to deliver on time.

He wouldn't be going home anytime soon.

*

Ellen was still in her bathrobe. She hated it when the day went like this. She'd been trying to take a shower all morning long, but Jason had kept demanding attention, and the housework seemed endless. Although for once, she admitted, she didn't despise the mindless chores. In fact, she was glad of anything which would keep her mind occupied and not thinking about that frightening stranger. Sam was right, she thought, he must have been drunk or out of his mind that night on the road.

Stop. Just stop thinking about it. She was going to take that damn shower and take a deep breath too.

"You okay, honey?" she called out to Jason. "Mommy's just going to dive in the shower."

No answer.

She'd left him in his bedroom, engrossed in a puzzle book and crayons.

Even so, she wanted to double check he was all right.

Tying her wrap around herself, she stepped out of their bedroom, and heard Jason laughing-

The sound distant.

He wasn't in his bedroom. What was he doing downstairs?

"Jason?"

She hurried down taking the steps two at a time.

The back door was open!

"JASON!"

Ellen charged outside into their tiny backyard.

Jason was swinging on the rope swing tire Sam had fixed beneath the sprawling Pepper tree.

He waved innocently. Happy as a clam as her mother would have said.

But Ellen's heart was in her mouth. She stormed toward him, and saw his smile crumble. "You can't be out here! You can't, not by yourself."

She grabbed his arm, harder than she intended and lifted him off the swing.

His lower lip trembled, on the verge of tears.

"It's okay, I was… I was worried when I couldn't find you. I'm sorry. I'm sorry. You're not in trouble. But you can't be out here alone. Only if mommy or daddy are here. You understand?" She rubbed his arm better.

He nodded and brushed his eyes. "Cos them's the rules?"

"That's right. And we don't break the rules, do we?"

Jason shook his head vehemently.

She hugged him tight. "Sorry I snapped at you, that wasn't nice. How about some milk and those yummy cookies grandma baked for us?"

That put a smile back on his face. That and an extra big hug.

*

The Mercedes' G.P.S. had guided him through the cookie-cutter residential streets. Everywhere the man looked all he saw were stucco town-homes daubed pink or off-white depending on the tract.

He'd pulled into one such community and parked in a visitor's space. A minute later he strolled down the quiet back alleyway between two rows of homes, passing backyards fenced in a vain attempt to provide some semblance of privacy even though the homes sat one on top of the other. Garbage cans and black trash bags were neatly aligned the length of the alley, tucked tight against the wood fences.

A child shrieked and laughed.

Purdit stopped to peer through a gap in the fence.

The Grady's son was playing, seemingly alone in the yard, holding onto a rope, imitating Tarzan.

Purdit's eyes swept the rear of the house, scanning the windows. Then, beyond the reflections, he saw her. She hurried through the kitchen like a ghost; a mesmeric mirage.

But the next instant, she dashed outside, shouting at her son!

Purdit's breath caught. As she ran, her robe flapped open. She hastily covered herself.

But Purdit felt a stirring denied for so long. Her body was like a dream. No, it was better than anything he could imagine. A dream made real.

It had been a fleeting glimpse. Her body revealed to him. For him and him alone. Did she know or sense that he was near?

The next moment, she was sweeping her son off the swing.

A mother protecting her young, thought Purdit as he watched the scene unfold. The boy looked about to cry, but she held him close, whispering words which Purdit couldn't hear. Then, hand-in-hand, mother and soon disappeared back inside the house.

Purdit sighed with longing and for a moment, he was tempted to enter the property. Then he heard an engine. A truck engine reverberating.

He glanced around as a blue and white garbage truck maneuvered into the alley.

Turning away, Purdit resumed his stroll, heading back to his parked car. Apart from an occasional twinge, his leg had not bothered him the past couple of days, but the walking stick had been a nice touch, he thought, a little melodrama to help convince Grady that he should pay. That he should do the right thing.

It had served its purpose, as indeed had Sam Grady.

Purdit opened the Mercedes door and climbed inside, the leather seat burning through his shirt.

The money wasn't much. A token, really. But, he knew, Sam Grady would pay more. And he would continue to suffer until Purdit permitted him the tranquil solace of the grave.

The tires kicked up wisps of dust as he pulled away swiftly and headed home. Already his mind was ticking through the details, plotting Sam's execution. It was always interesting to watch his prey twisting and writhing until they reached breaking point. He remembered Maitland, and the businessman's vain heroics. Luckily Maitland's aim had been poor, and Purdit's reflexes good. Otherwise... He shook his head, he had misjudged that time, and it had nearly cost him his life. That was a mistake he was not about to repeat. Within a week, he decided, Sam Grady would be dead and buried.

Leaving the cluttered low-rise offices behind, Purdit sped along MacArthur Boulevard heading toward the Pacific Coast Highway. The ocean glinted with silver light as he crested a rise that took him past the city's modern library, its roofline reminiscent of curling waves frozen in time, poised to break. He reached the PCH, then avoided the traffic by cutting through the quaint tree-lined back streets of Corona Del Mar. The flower streets as they were known colloquially. Within a few minutes he drove into the gated enclave overlooking the sand and sea.

He keyed the remote, opening his garage door as he approached, and vanished inside. Once the door closed, he took his original license plates out of the trunk and removed the false numbers. It would be stupid to underestimate Sam Grady's resources. If Grady somehow managed to trace the plates, or if he indeed decided to go to the police, then the DMV would show the plates belonged to a 1989 Ford truck. A dead end.

Purdit walked through the house and into the cool confines of his darkened study. There he sipped spring water from a crystal tumbler, rolling the frosted glass between the palms of his hands. Placing it on the desk, he pondered his next move, then dialed Jeffrey Vermont's number.

"Hello?" the hacker answered on only the second ring. "Mr. Purdit. Something I can do for you?" Vermont chuckled. "Need a line into the Pentagon or something?"

Purdit didn't laugh. "No. But I'm afraid my friend Sam Grady has been experiencing a little car trouble."

"I don't understand."

"Then let me explain..."

Chapter 19

"So what're you telling me?" Lieutenant Robert Smith asked, staring across his desk through gold rimmed spectacles, waiting for Claire to reply.

"Bernard's depressed. Leaves his office with enough sleeping pills to kill an elephant. Parks on the shoulder and starts popping them. As they start to kick in, I think one of two things happened."

"Go on."

"He's getting drowsy, realizes he's going to die, but then he changes his mind. Life isn't so bad, he's not ready to go, whatever. He panics, slams the car into gear to race for a hospital. Only he doesn't see the truck." She claps her hands together. "Only problem there is; why didn't he just dial 911? Call for an ambulance or something?"

"Maybe," Smith agreed. "What's theory number two?"

"He's on the way out, but then he starts thinking about his wife. How's she going to manage once he's gone? Their insurance policy, it's not going to pay one dime for a suicide. So, while he's got a some strength left, he starts the car. He waits until he sees this eighteen-wheeler and hits the gas. Pulls straight out. The truck driver's got no chance."

Smith kept nodding. "So suicide, whichever way you dice it. His insurance company's going to love you."

"I know," she said, dejected.

When she returned to her desk, she opened the case file. Inside were the series of photographs of Bernard's wrecked Lexus she had taken, an inventory of the late-doctor's personal effects found in the car; some crushed ancient CD's, a small notepad, some gum and twenty bucks in cash. The notepad had been photocopied. Most of the pages seemed innocuous, just notes to a patient, the hospital or his office. But one hastily scrawled entry struck Claire as unusual. She highlighted the entry.

11p. Meet at # PBA-312.

Beneath, were a series of directions heading from Orange County out towards Palm Springs.

Meet who? She wondered. And what was with the strange number?

PBA, what could that stand for? The first thing that entered her mind was a Post Office Box. Maybe Post Box A312? It didn't seem likely. Besides which, the directions seemed to lead to the edge of the desert, and Claire doubted there was a U.S. Post Office within five miles of the location. And what about the time, 11PM?

Strange bordering on downright weird, she thought. A meeting planned close to midnight on the edge of the desert. What was that about?

She decided she would take a drive out there, as soon as her time permitted, and once she'd discussed the note with Mike Stadler.

Chapter 20

"Are you getting up today?"

Ellen's voice whiplashed him.

Sam stirred for the third time, peering out from beneath the sheet. He hadn't returned home until two o'clock Sunday morning. The dead of night, after finishing a marathon without stopping for food or rest. And even after his intense efforts, they were still behind schedule.

"I'm beat."

"Really, well I don't want to be late." Rancor burned in Ellen's eyes.

"I already apologized, last night-"

"Don't, Sam. You said you were heading home, and ten hours later you show up. I needed you here."

"I'm sorry," he said. All he seemed to do these days was perpetually apologize for some mistake, real or imagined.

"I suppose you've forgotten we promised Mom we'd visit today?"

He had. "Midday, right?"

Ellen grunted, unimpressed that he'd recalled one small detail.

"Ellie," he said, "with everything that's been happening..."

His voice trailed away as Ellen shook her head. "No, Sam. You can find hours to spend at the office."

"I don't think that's fair," he sat upright, but didn't climb out of bed. Standing naked pleading his case didn't seem a strong move. "That's work."

"I know. But you've got to make time for us too. We need you as much as those damn computers. Especially now."

"Those damn computers are paying our bills these days."

"We never used to be short of money and you never used to spend all your time at the office, not when you worked for Pete."

"What do you want me to do? You want me to fold the company? Is that it?"

Ellen turned away. "No," she said softly, perching on the edge of the bed.

Unsure what to do, he reached over and touched her shoulder, expecting her to pull away. Thankfully she didn't.

"I can be ready in five minutes, and we can head over to your mother's, okay?"

Ellen nodded and, without looking at him, she slipped out the room.

Skipping a shower, Sam splashed cold water on his face, pulled on a loose fitting shirt and a pair of Levis, and hurried downstairs.

"Daddy." Jason rushed to meet him. The one constant in his life, thought Sam. Thank, God.

Sam tossed the toddler into the air, Jason squealing with undisguised delight.

"Careful," Ellen said, entering the hallway. "You'll hit his head on the ceiling one of these days."

He put Jason down. Ellen turned her back, and Sam pulled a we're-in-trouble-now face. Jason giggled.

"I saw that," Ellen said.

"Saw what?" Sam asked innocently.

She turned and regarded them both.

"Never mind. Are you ready?"

"Yes."

"Sam, you haven't even shaved."

Sam raised his eyebrows, knowing better than to argue. "I was trying to hurry."

Ellen shook her head in resignation and led the way outside to the car.

As Sam turned to lock the front door, his cell phone vibrated. He pulled it from his pocket, about to answer-

"Sam, we're already late."

"It might be important," he said, hoping that Martin was back in the office. Hoping that, maybe he'd be able to find the glitch that had slowed down the problematic rendering engine.

But when he glanced at the screen, he saw the message, UNKNOWN CALLER. He hesitated, then answered.

"Hello?"

"Hello, Sam."

The sibilant voice froze him.

"What do you want?" Sam breathed. He was well aware of his wife standing, staring at him. And he knew it wouldn't take a mind reader to know who he was speaking with.

"I thought to myself, it's Sunday morning, maybe the Grady family's gone to church."

"Maybe we're not believers."

"Then at least we have one thing in common," said Purdit. "Religion, nothing more than a salve to the masses."

"We don't have anything in common. If you don't hang up and stop harassing my family, I will call the police."

"Sam. We both know better than that."

"What the hell do you want?" Sam hissed.

"Your next installment."

"What? Listen you sick fu-" glancing at Jason in his car seat, Sam curbed his language. "I've paid you all you're going to get. You understand?"

"Surely you realized that first payment was only a gesture, a token. I think another eighty thousand would close the books on this unfortunate matter. Think it over, Sam."

"I've got to go," Sam said, and hung up.

"He wants more?" Ellen asked, though it was hardly a question. Sam nodded.

"Then what are we supposed to do?"

"I don't know."

He squinted against the bright California sunshine. Another day in paradise, he thought with bitter irony.

"Should I call mom and cancel?"

"No. We're going."

With a determination which surprised himself, Sam climbed behind the wheel. He was damned if this man, Purdit, was going to ruin their lives.

*

Lucy carried a wooden bowl heaped with salad and placed it in the center of the patio table.

"You really shouldn't have gone to so much fuss. Should she, Sam?"

Deep in dark thoughts, Sam nodded. "Sure, hon," he agreed to whatever question she'd just asked.

Lucy frowned, and Sam realized his stock answer hadn't been wholly appropriate. It was hard to concentrate on anything right now. Purdit's expressionless voice kept passing through his mind. What was the man capable of? Sam wondered, as he looked at his family. Sam knew he hadn't reacted well to Purdit's last phone call.

He shouldn't have flown off the handle, and he shouldn't have hung up like that. He should have kept his cool.

"So tell me, what have you two been up to lately?" Lucy asked, sliding her chair closer to the table.

"You know Sam," said Ellen. "Work, work, work."

Sam grimaced.

Lucy shook her head, the gesture striking Sam as condescending. "Sam," Lucy rested her bony hand on his forearm. "There's nothing as important as family."

Sam managed a feeble smile.

"Sam knows that, Mom."

"Of course he does, dear. But we all need reminding of what's really important in life. Don't you agree, Sam?" she gave his arm a gentle squeeze.

"Yes."

"When I spoke to Ellen yesterday, she said you were in the office."

"Mother."

Releasing Sam's arm, Lucy turned to her daughter. "What's wrong, dear?"

"Nothing. Sam has to work, that's all."

Grateful for the use of his limb once more, Sam attacked the cold cuts and salad on his plate, and did his best to ignore Lucy. The woman had a way of digging under his skin with her mightier than thou tone of voice.

"Well, at least you've taken today off," Lucy said, leveling her gaze at him once more. "We can be grateful for that."

Sam nodded, forced a smile, and chewed on a tough piece of chicken.

He felt his phone vibrate annoyingly in his pocket. Another text message. He'd been receiving them throughout the meal. Since hanging up on Purdit in fact. He was doing his best to ignore the man, and didn't intend to let Ellen know, at least while they were at her mother's.

He sneaked a glance when the next message came in. No Caller ID now appeared on the display. Sam didn't need an ID to know it was Purdit taunting him.

Enjoy your afternoon with the family.

He took another bite of Lucy's drab chicken, his mind occluded as he tried to think of his next move. He couldn't even contemplate how he might raise so much more money. It was impossible. Besides which, even if he could, he knew the blackmail would not stop. Purdit had demonstrated that in less than twenty four hours after he'd been paid off.

Money wasn't the answer.

He felt Ellen's hand on his, and a gentle squeeze.

The look in her eyes told him they were in this together. For that he was immensely thankful.

"You okay?" she asked softly.

Sam nodded. "We'll figure it out," he said, trying to sound confident.

The phone is his pocket buzzed again.

Chapter 21

Monday morning crept past, and the paperwork littering Sam's desk remained untouched. Sam gazed at the phone on his desk, then at his cell, waiting, and wondering as he rocked imperceptibly in his chair.

He'd received a solitary text message from his Unknown Caller. Two, seemingly innocuous, words.

Drive safe.

Using a pen, he stirred the muddy coffee he'd fixed earlier. He sipped the tepid brew, grimacing at the bitter flavor.

When was Purdit going to call again? Or, would the son of a bitch simply show up at the office unannounced? Sam couldn't face sitting in his office all day, waiting like a condemned prisoner. He felt he had to do something. But what? What could he do?

The office phone shrieked. Sam's hand flicked to the receiver, knocking it, sending it tumbling off the desk. Leaning over the desk, he grabbed the curly cord and pulled it back, just in time to hear the line click as Kathy transferred the caller.

"Grady?" a voice demanded.

Sam sagged in his chair, relieved to hear the brash, grating voice. It didn't belong to Purdit.

"Mr. Rogers," Sam said.

"Thought I'd check with you, Grady. You are delivering today, yes?"

"We're pretty much ready," Sam lied.

"Good. Good. What time will we have the final files?"

"I'm not exactly sure."

"Wait. Everything's good?"

He could picture Aeon's purchasing manager ready to pounce on the penalty clause. "Absolutely. Although we may need a little time to tweak a couple of things. I know you want the best, and that's what we want to deliver."

"Ah, a little extra time. How little?"

"We're giving everything a final polish. It's ninety nine percent there, but we aim for a hundred and ten," Sam felt his cheeks warm. He hoped Rogers would fall for his line of bullshit.

"Grady. Don't try any smoke and mirrors with me. I've been in this business too long. When are you actually going to deliver?"

Sam sighed.

"We should be finished today. I'll drive over as soon as we're done."

"That's fine, you're the one who paying the penalty if you're late. A grand a day, wasn't that what we agreed?"

Sam's heart sank. "Yes we did. I'll have it to you as soon as humanly possible."

"There ya go," Rogers replied before ending the call.

Sam stood, his legs weak under the weight of his worrying, and walked out the room.

"Trouble?" Kathy frowned.

Understatement of the year, thought Sam. "You might say. Did Martin come in yet?"

"He called while you were on the phone. Should be here soon. He said, he was working on things through the night."

Sam nodded and ambled along the short hallway to the demo room. The lights flickered into life as he approached the render farm. Cooling fans inside the computers hummed like a beehive. At the desk, Sam moved a mouse, activating a dormant graphics monitor, and slumped into a chair. Pulling the seat closer to the screen and keyboard, he called up the bug-ridden algorithm and tried deciphering the problem which Martin apparently had been unable to solve over the night.

Sam had better luck.

By lunchtime, although Martin still hadn't put in an appearance, Sam had debugged the program and produced the footage Aeon needed. Their manager was insistent about not trusting uploads to clouds or drop boxes, despite the inherent security, so Sam had no choice but to dump everything onto a flash drive and deliver it in person, like stepping back a decade in time.

As he drove, Sam glanced in his side mirror. A distinct chill gave him gooseflesh when he saw a shiny white police cruiser close behind.

Sam slowed to a stop at a traffic light. The right turn lane edged forward, and Sam turned on the red light.

The police car continued to follow.

God, it was always spooky when that happened. Sam felt as if he was being tailed. But the cop was probably en route to the golden arches for a quick burger. Sam tried to relax, slowing deliberately in the hope that the police car would overtake him.

It stayed behind, bumper to bumper.

Then, as Sam watched, the blue and red lights atop the roof flashed into life. The cop gave a single blip on his siren.

"What?" Sam swore.

Sam tried to remember if he'd gone over the speed limit before noticing the cop in his wake. He didn't think so. So why was the guy pulling him over?

Did I fail to stop at the red light? Sam couldn't remember. Maybe. That was probably it. He must have slowed down, checked it was clear, then swung through the junction without actually stopping. But that was the California way, wasn't it?

He halted next to the curb, never taking his eyes off his mirror.

"Stay in your car!" The police officer's voice reverberated through a loudspeaker.

"I am," Sam muttered.

"Lower your window, and let me see your hands. Driver! Both hands!"

Concerned, Sam did exactly as he was told. What was going on?

In the mirror, Sam watched the officer climb out, ducking behind the open car door. In his left hand he held a small microphone. A moment later his right hand appeared.

Sunlight glinted on the barrel of a gun.

Sam gagged. What the hell? This was no routine traffic violation.

Drive safe. The words came unbidden to the front of his mind.

Purdit. Had he gone to the police? Had he told them everything that had happened? Everything except his blackmail scheme, no doubt.

This made no sense. This was a mistake. Sam started to open his door.

"I can expl-"

"Freeze!"

His left leg partway out the door, Sam froze. He didn't breathe. For a moment, he didn't dare. His eyes flicked left, seeing the cop drop his microphone and move into a crouch, two hands on his weapon.

"Both hands! Keep 'em where I can see them!" the man ordered, inching around his own door, the gun never wavering.

Sam kept them there. Whatever the cop told him, that was what he'd do.

"Now, step out. Move slowly away from the car. Easy! Hands!"

His legs trembled so violently he nearly collapsed on the street. He managed a couple of shuffling steps away from the Buick.

A siren wailed in the distance, drawing closer.

"Lie face down, place your hands behind your head. Do it!"

Sam fell onto the tarmac in his hurry to obey.

He heard footsteps. Heard another car squeal to a stop.

Suddenly a weight slammed down on his back, between his shoulder blades. For an instant he thought he'd been shot, but then he realized the officer's knee had smacked down on top of him, pinning him to the ground. Something thin snaked around his right wrist, pulling tight enough to hurt. Then his arms were jerked behind his back and his left hand secured. He felt naked as the officer frisked him.

"What?" was all Sam managed to gasp as he was dragged to his feet and spun around to face two police officers.

Another officer emerged from Sam's car. "Looks clean."

"What?" Sam mumbled again, utterly perplexed.

"Quiet. Get in the car."

"Why? What did I do?"

"Get in the car." They led him to the squad car, opening the rear door. Giving him no choice but to duck his head and climb inside.

Sam sat down heavily on the solid fiberglass seat. The acrid smell of disinfectant threatened to overwhelm him. He gagged.

"Listen to me," the second cop said. "You listening?"

Sam nodded.

"You are being arrested for being in possession of a stolen vehicle."

"Stolen? It's my car. This is a-"

"Listen, I said."

Sam clamped down his retort. A sense of indignation started to bristle inside, replacing the stark terror he had felt up until now.

"What did you do with the weapon?"

"Weapon?"

"Look," the officer said, his tone exuding reasonableness, "we know you stole the car earlier this morning. The owner reported that you threatened him with a shotgun."

"I didn't threaten anyone. I'm the owner."

"You want to play the innocent? Fine. You're going to jail."

The cop started to shut the door.

"Wait! What's the owner's name?"

"Sam Grady."

"That's me, for Christ's sake."

The cop turned to his colleague. "You get this guy's ID?"

"Yeah." He handed over Sam's wallet, acquired during his frisk.

The second cop opened it, taking out Sam's driving license. "Carlos, you looked at this?"

"Give me second, will ya?"

Carlos looked. He blanched. "Sir," he reached into the car. Sam flinched. But Carlos merely touched his shoulder, helping him climb back outside.

"Mind your head, sir."

Sam stood, his hands still bound. Anger and relief churned his stomach.

Abruptly he turned away and vomited onto the tarmac.

Both cops stepped hastily aside.

"Sir? You okay?"

Sam managed to nod. He felt weak, drained.

"I'll get these off," said Carlos.

Sam's hands suddenly became free, and he turned to see the officer holding the plastic tie that had held him captive.

Carlos still regarded him with a degree of suspicion. "You file a report like that... I mean, did you get the car back and forget, or was this some kind of stunt?"

Sam tried to think straight.

"Stunt? No. And I didn't file any report."

"Well, you must have."

Sam snorted. "Anyone could have phoned pretending to be me."

But the officer shook his head. "The computer said you came in to the station in person."

"That wasn't me. I've been at my office all day."

Skeptical, the officer turned to his partner. "Check on the report on this one, Dave?"

"Will do." The other officer crossed to his car. He reappeared moments later, his expression one of total bewilderment.

"What's up?" Carlos asked.

"There's nothing on the computer. There is no report."

"That's impossible. We ran the plate a minute ago."

"What's impossible?" Sam asked, pocketing his wallet.

"There's nothing. It's not there. Nada."

"But..." Carlos turned to Sam. Genuine confusion on his face. "I don't know what to say, sir. I recognized your car from the description that came over the radio earlier this morning. We ran the plate. But I don't know, there must have been some... glitch. We sincerely apologize for the scare."

Sam held up his hand. "Forget it. I just want to go. Can I go, please?"

"Sure, yes. I really don't know how this happened. You feel okay to drive?"

Sam nodded. His legs had finally stopped shaking. "Yes. It's okay, honest."

Carlos stood before him, bewildered and shame-faced. "Real sorry for this. If you want to make a report?"

"What? No, that's… it was a mistake, like you said."

"Yes, sir. But I'm going to look into what happened here."

The officer stuck out his hand. After a moment's hesitation, Sam shook hands.

Climbing back inside the furnace heat of his car, Sam slammed his door and started the engine.

He shook his head in bewilderment. Cops had pulled their guns and arrested him, then discovered they'd made a mistake. He felt tempted to drive over to the station and file a complaint, but it was probably best to forget the whole incident. He wouldn't achieve anything by antagonizing the police, especially when he might need their help - if he couldn't persuade Purdit to leave him alone.

As he drove the rest of the way to Aeon, Sam wondered again about Purdit's seemingly innocuous text message. Could Purdit have filed the complaint? Perhaps later changing something on the police computer? Was that possible? God, what if it was a cop or something? Sam shuddered at the thought. Though a police officer driving such an expensive car, and wearing a five thousand dollar suit didn't seem likely. But Purdit might have pulled the necessary strings, and that itself was a chilling prospect.

Later, when he finally returned to his office, Sam sat in his car for a moment and made a conscious effort to relax, rolling his head, easing the tension from his neck and shoulder muscles.

Kathy had gone for lunch leaving a slim stack of phone messages awaiting Sam's return. Picking them up as he passed her desk, he went into the demo room. Martin had finally shown up, and was hard at work. Though he looked chagrined when Sam entered.

"I saw what you did," Martin said. "That was smart, shuffling the subroutine. Hey, you okay?"

"What?" Sam hadn't really been listening. His mind kept wandering back to Purdit. He couldn't help it.

"You look kind of peaked."

"Thanks. I'm fine," said Sam, flipping through the flimsy While-U-Were-Out message slips. He stopped abruptly.

Purdit.

The creep had called while Sam was out, and according to the message he would be phoning again in a few minutes.

"I'll be in my office," he told Martin as he headed out the room.

For once, Purdit kept his word. Sam had barely stepped inside his office when the phone rang.

"I'll get that," he yelled to Martin, although the programmer rarely, if ever, picked up the phone.

Sam shut the door and grabbed the receiver. "Grade-A."

"Sam."

His heart stammered when he heard his tormentor's voice. "What do you want?"

"A simple discussion."

"Why is it I don't I believe you?"

"But it's true. I'm sure we can work this out, Sam."

"I've already paid you everything you're going to get. You understand?"

"Sam, you sound flustered. Has something else happened?"

Wary, Sam didn't reply. Another of the man's twisted mind games. Perhaps the answer was not to play, Sam thought.

"A little trouble, perhaps?" Purdit probed. "A problem with your car? An unscheduled stop?"

Sam hesitated before replying. "I don't know what you're talking about."

"Sam, let's not pretend, shall we? Didn't your little adventure with the police earlier teach you anything about my power? You know, I could have as easily logged a report stating that you had killed a cop. Do you think they would have been quite so restrained?"

"You did that? That's not possible. How?"

"Does it matter? Your only concern should be to pay me the money you owe."

"I don't owe you anything."

Purdit laughed derisively. Abruptly, the harsh noise stopped dead. "Two days, Sam. That's all the time I can give you. And I'm being generous, so don't imagine you can take advantage of my good nature."

"Why would I give you another penny? You'll just continue demanding more."

"No, Sam. I give you my word."

"Yeah right. I've heard that line before, remember?"

"Sam, think of the alternative. Think what might happen if the police raided a suspected crack house in their usually tranquil suburb. You imagine there won't be a few trigger-happy uniforms crashing through your door at midnight. Think about Ellen and Jason, asleep and vulnerable. Sam, I can't believe you'd let anything like that happen. Of course, in the aftermath it would be discovered the police had tragically raided the wrong house by mistake. It's happened before."

"You're sick."

"I'll call again, tomorrow, with your delivery instructions. You really don't want to disappoint me, Sam."

Sam hung up as static bled from the receiver. *This can't be happening,* he wanted to scream.

How had that maniac managed to trick the police? What level of skills did that demand – to hack into the police database?

Purdit hadn't needed to spell out the consequences if Sam didn't meet his outlandish demands. Sam could easily imagine what might happen if there was a raid on his home.

And if anything happened to Ellen or Jason, he'd never forgive himself. His life wouldn't be worth living.

Chapter 22

Jeffrey Vermont's hand had quivered with excitement when he put down the phone. He had never imagined Purdit would go for it. But he had.

Jeffrey laughed. He couldn't believe the guy was upping his fee and delivering the cash in person. Not that the money was unreasonable, considering the risks he'd taken violating what was essentially the government's computers.

One hundred thousand dollars.

Sweet.

Jeffrey joined in with the music thumping from the ceiling speakers. He didn't know the words, but what the shit. From his computer he ramped up the volume, so loud he didn't hear the door-phone at first.

Killing the music, Jeffrey hopped up from his desk, and strolled passed the panoramic, floor-to-ceiling window as he ambled to the door.

"Yo?" he said.

"Mr. Purdit's here in reception," the security guard informed him.

"Send him up," he unlatched the door and left it ajar.

While he waited, Jeffrey fixed himself a Long Island iced tea, then mixed another for his guest and gave the cocktail-shaker one brisk shake.

"Good day, Jeffrey," said a voice at his shoulder.

Jeffrey almost dropped the shaker. He'd unlocked the door, but hadn't heard the man enter. Silent as a snake, Jeffrey thought.

"Hey," he said, recovering, and pouring the drink. He offered it to Purdit.

"Water."

"Oh, right. Sure," he whipped open the refrigerator beneath the wet bar. "Here you go."

Placing the unopened bottle next to Purdit, Jeffrey's eyes wandered to the large envelope the man was carrying.

"Don't look like much," he commented.

Purdit let the envelope drop onto the tiled counter. "You want to count it?"

Jeffrey shook his head, but he still wanted to see it all. He slid a miniature ice pick under the flap and ripped it open. Bundles of crisp one hundred dollar bills tumbled out.

"A pleasure, Mr. P," he said.

Purdit merely nodded and crossed the room to stand and stare out at the city skyline.

"Looks even better at night," Jeffrey opened a wall safe and placed the money inside.

"Imagine so."

"Anything else you need?" Jeffrey asked as he closed the steel door and spun the tumbler.

"I doubt I can afford much more," Purdit said dryly.

"Hey, value for money. That's what I provide."

Purdit sipped from his bottle and for the first time Jeffrey noticed the man was wearing driving gloves.

"What d'you drive?"

"Sorry?"

"What kinda car? Let me guess. A Bentley, right?"

"Mercedes."

Jeffrey nodded. "Like an AMG?"

But Purdit didn't answer. Instead he turned and walked past Jeffrey, heading to the door.

The guy didn't even turn around to say so long. Just let himself out.

"Well, thanks," Jeffrey called down the corridor as he watched the strange man stride to the elevators.

With a shrug, Jeffrey closed his apartment door.

At the bar he picked up the untouched Ice Tea and raised the glass.

"Fast money," he toasted before downing half the glass.

He unhooked his cell phone from his belt and tapped on a name.

"I was just thinking of you," his girlfriend's voice sounded husky.

"We're celebrating, babe," he said. "You wanna paint the town?"

"Totally." she paused. "Should I drive over to you?"

"No, no. I'll pick you up in twenty."

"Like twenty minutes? I need time to get ready."

Jeffrey shook his head.

"I'll drive slow, 'kay? Just be ready, all right. I want to have some fun."

He hung up and looked on the bar for his car keys. Where were they? He could have sworn he left them on the bar last night. Although Jeffrey had to admit his recollection was not one hundred percent, having spent most of the previous evening at a party just off Sunset. He knelt down and searched the tiled floor around the bar, even probing under the cabinet, in case he'd knocked them off the counter. But they were nowhere.

"Shit," he muttered, rechecking his empty pockets.

He sloughed over to the desk and grabbed the spare set out of the drawer. Screw it. He'd find the others later.

*

An annoying commercial played on the elevator's small flat-screen TV, the sound emanating from a tinny speaker, as Purdit watched the floor indicator tick down, descending below the lobby, gliding to a halt at 'P'. He stepped into a well-lit underground parking garage, clutching Vermont's keys as they jangled from a leather, Porsche Owner's key tag. Sleek, exotic sports cars peppered the ranks dominated by a glut of upscale SUVs. Automotive porn.

Purdit circled the visitor's area and casually confirmed the absence of cameras. On his arrival, he had checked in with the gate guard and handed over his driver's license. The man had been studious enough and inspected the ID against the list of names on his computer before raising the gate. But having passed through that one barrier, it appeared the building's management company considered other security measures superfluous. Purdit strolled past his own car, eyes still roaming the whitewashed walls and crannies as he continued along the first row of vehicles. The vent of a poorly sealed air-handler rattled, sucking out the noxious fumes that would have otherwise stifled the garage. Walking beneath the square vent, Purdit pulled a sealed electronic box, no bigger than a cigarette lighter, from his pocket. He turned the box over in his gloved palm. A thin, black cable emerged like a rodent's tail from the glossy unit and was terminated with a nine-pin adapter. It was the device he'd ordered over the internet and paid handsomely for, and it had arrived ahead of schedule.

Reaching the end of the row, he spotted Vermont's squat sports car parked in the furthest corner.

One last glance around the unoccupied garage and Purdit pressed the car's remote to unlock the vehicle. He lifted the rear engine hatch and peered inside at the unfamiliar engine. Digging in his pocket once more, Purdit removed a folded printout and reviewed the A,B,C instructions detailing how the device was installed.

Two minutes later he dropped the lid closed and walked away, dropping the keys on the ground, close enough to the Porsche that Vermont would find them easily.

Purdit drove his Mercedes up a short ramp to the automated exit. With a strained groan, the entire gate juddered and rose overhead. Satisfied with the morning's work, he slipped off his gloves as he drove out of the luxurious apartment tower and joined the hectic flow of traffic on West Fourth Street.

*

Jeffrey's girlfriend lived on the far side of the Hollywood Hills. As always, he was more than happy to drive the narrow, switchback roads and pick her up. Any excuse to hurtle up Laurel Canyon, he thought, hitting sixty in second gear before stabbing the brakes as he came upon a struggling motor home.

He was caught behind it with no immediate opportunity to overtake. With a sigh he glanced out at the view. Strumming his fingers on the steering wheel, he gazed at the hillside homes perched on their precarious pillars. There was no way, he thought that he'd pay millions to live in such a precarious location, especially given the area's renown for earthquake. Sheer insanity, he thought. Preoccupied, he almost missed a short, straight stretch of road when it opened ahead. With no oncoming traffic he floored the gas. The tach rose swiftly as he darted to the left and shot around the Winnebago. The needle clipped the redline as he pulled back to the right and took his foot off the pedal.

"Shit!"

The needle remained fixed in place. The engine screamed. Jeffrey's heart stammered. He jabbed the gas pedal, it had to be stuck. No luck.

The car rocketed toward the next corner.

He stood on the brakes, praying in vain that he could bleed speed fast enough as he clenched the wheel. Tires scrabbled for grip, squealing in protest as he tried to take the corner at over twice the legal limit. The car flew wide onto the wrong side of the road, clipping the low safety barrier. Metal shrieked like a Banshee. A whimper escaped his lips as he mercifully wrested control of the car. His eyes darted down at the sheer drop mere inches away –

A horn blared.

His attention snapped back to the road. Ahead loomed an SUV. He yanked the wheel as hard as he could to the right.

But there was no way to avoid the high speed, head-on collision that killed both drivers instantly.

Chapter 23

Sam felt exhausted, worn down by Purdit's constant harassment. His mind spun in a hundred directions as he drove along the freeway, skirting the Irvine office parks.

It was impossible to meet Purdit's ludicrous demands. Ellen argued that they had to go to the police. Tell them it had been an accident. But Sam hadn't told Ellen about the police pulling him over, arresting him, then letting him go. All an honest mistake, they said, except Sam was sure the entire incident had been orchestrated by Purdit.

Still, perhaps it would come to that, going to the police and admitting what had happened. Confessing to them that he had left a man he believed was dying on the road in the middle of the night. Sam noticed his exit looming at seventy miles an hour, he swerved across two lanes, barely glancing in his mirror, and raced up the ramp. A sudden clamminess crawled over his body, and he stared in the mirror, making certain a passing Highway Patrol car hadn't witnessed his reckless maneuver. Luckily there were no cops in sight.

Taking the off ramp, Sam pulled at random into the nearest parking lot and stopped. He sat there as the engine ticked over. He needed to think.

He contemplated calling the police, or perhaps he should think about a lawyer. He could explain the craziness that had happened and someone might offer some sane advice. An answer.

Yet he kept thinking of Ellen. Maybe she was right. He scrolled through the list of recently dialed numbers on his cell. He'd gone so far as to dial the local police department earlier that day, but had hung up before they answered.

With trepidation, he redialed the non-emergency number.

Sam was so nervous, at first he didn't realize anyone had answered.

"Sorry. I need to talk... I don't know. Is there a detective I can talk to?"

"If you can tell me the problem, I'll put you through to the appropriate person."

"I had a question, that's all really," his hand felt sweaty as he clutched the phone. His heart pounded, so loud he could scarcely hear what the woman was saying.

"Sir, if you could give me some details-"

No. This was a bad move. Stupid. He hung up.

Christ, what had he done?

What if they traced the call? Could they really do that with a cell phone? He didn't know, but certainly his number would have been shown as soon as the call connected. He should have thought it through. Should have bought a prepaid phone, what was that called... a burner?

"Damn," he muttered, tossing the phone on the passenger seat.

He needed to think straight. And he was doing a lousy job of that.

It was his responsibility to make sure Purdit didn't harm or harass his family.

His shoulders sagged with fatigue.

He was deeper in debt than he had ever been. All because of a stupid mistake, an accident. No, he decided, not simply because of the accident. Rather, because of the lunatic he'd injured, combined with Sam's own guilty conscience and fear.

The night before, once Ellen had drifted into a troubled slumber, Sam had lain awake, his sleep-deprived mind struggling to reason his options. He thought outlandishly about raising more money, if that was even possible, and hiring a bodyguard. In the middle of the night, he'd gone online and researched detective agencies that claimed to offer protection for home and family. Peace of mind. But he knew no one could be safe forever, not against a determined madman. Sam considered packing everything and moving, even to another state if they had to. But that would take time and planning. Besides, even if Ellen agreed to such a drastic step, Purdit had found them once and could probably do so again, no matter where they fled. The man's resources seemed unlimited.

Sam was at a loss.

*

Claire merged with the freeway traffic headed east toward Palm Springs. She'd spoken to Mike Stadler and he'd pretty much shrugged his shoulders. What you do on your time's your business, he'd told her, and if she wanted to play detective so be it. Claire had hoped he would have been more intrigued by the note they'd found with the deceased doctor. Of course such work, outside the scope of the accident investigation itself, wasn't their job. Besides which, she knew, Mike had plenty on his mind right now. His impending trip half way across the country to visit his estranged daughter and ex-wife had to be consuming his thoughts. However, one reason Claire had ended up in her line of work was her insatiable appetite for solving real world puzzles.

A car sped by probably doing close to ninety. Claire was used to drivers abruptly slowing with a telltale flash of brake lights, whenever they spotted a CHP black and white looming in their mirrors. Of course, in her plain-Jane Toyota, she was just another anonymous vehicle among the herd.

She drove by the scattered desert communities and a smattering of outlet malls that abutted the freeway. Then glanced again at the photocopy of the directions scrawled by Dr. Bernard.

Changing lanes, she took the Indian Canyon exit a few minutes later and turned north. Tumbleweeds blew across the road and the harsh sun bleached the surreal landscape where dozens of giant windmills stretched toward the low, craggy mountain range.

Pulling off the road, she took a gravel track. Why on earth would anyone want to meet out here? Claire wondered.

On the periphery of the windmill farm was parked a large, silver Greyhound bus. And, to Claire's bewilderment, nearby stood a group of a dozen people gazing skyward, busy taking photographs of the towering turbines.

Pulling to a stop behind the bus, Claire opened her door. A jackrabbit bounded away as she stepped outside and entered the oppressive heat of the afternoon.

A chirpy, bespectacled guy in his thirties, waved to them and ambled over. "Hi, can I help ya?"

"I was just wondering," Claire replied. "What's going on? What are you all doing out here?"

"Oh, we're out here most days."

 "Touring windmills."

The guy laughed, no doubt at the expression on her face. "That's right, I'm not joking."

Claire glanced at the bus and saw it wasn't actually a Greyhound. A sign pasted in one widow proclaimed, "World's #1 Windmill Tour". Whether that meant they were the best, or perhaps the only such tour, in the world, Claire wasn't sure.

"The future is now," he continued with the fervor of a green, Jehovah's witness. "Renewable energy. We've added Ivanpah to the list, you know? World's largest solar plant, right here in California. Amazing."

Claire, aware that she had become the focus of the tour group, offered a wan smile.

The guide pointed up at the nearest of the massive three-bladed windmills. "One of these puppies produces enough power every hour to run a home for a month. Fourth generation technology."

Claire looked up at the huge windmill, soaring some twenty stories overhead. Its gigantic propeller blade whooshed the air and she could almost feel an invisible tug of energy from the machine.

"I don't suppose P.B.A means anything to you?" she asked.

The guy smiled enthusiastically. "Sure. P.B.A Electric, they're a small startup. They own a farm, 'bout two, three miles north of here. Modern machines, but way smaller scale than these beauties."

Claire handed him the photocopied note. "And this number?"

"Each unit has a number, for maintenance. This'll be the third row, twelfth mill in. You know, like a matrix?"

"Okay. Thank you."

"Glad to help. Anytime," he offered what he must have considered a winning smile.

Claire nodded thanks again as she returned to her car and drove away.

Three miles further north, she again pulled to a stop, this time near a locked gate which blocked entry to the fenced off property. Ignoring the NO TRESPASSING sign, Claire clambered over and walked toward the array of windmills.

Unlike the previous machines, Claire was surprised how small these machines were. Though most of the blades were barely moving now the wind had dropped to a vague breeze.

She followed the stenciled markings, drawing closer to 312. But as she approached the pylon there seemed nothing at all unusual about it. No different to the others surrounding it.

Claire's shoulders sagged. What an utter waste of time this had been, she thought as she circled around the support. Then she stopped.

Here was a dry spattering, turned ochre by the desert sun, which could only have been one thing.

Blood.

Again, she wondered what possible connection there could be between a plastic surgeon who had seemingly committed suicide and a windmill farm in the middle of nowhere? She assumed Dr. Bernard had at some point come here, so was this his blood, or someone else's? Or, she thought, could it be just an animal or perhaps a large bird?

She glanced at the time, it was later than she'd imagined and she needed to get to work. Taking a few quick snaps on her iPhone, Claire jogged back to her car.

*

Purdit tailed Ellen's dark green SUV all the way to a small beach nestled on the edge of Corona Del Mar. He stood on the sand a few feet away from the base of a long flight of steps. The curved sweep of shoreline was sheltered by headlands and laced with rock pools where a handful of children scurried and played with tiny hermit crabs.

He watched Jason as the boy braved picking up one of the sea creatures.

"Be gentle," Ellen's voice carried on the breeze. "Maybe we should just put her back, sweetheart."

Purdit casually panned his long lens camera past her as she stood and glanced around. He felt her gaze briefly toward him, but with the camera covering most of his face, and wearing a wide brimmed hat, he felt confident she wouldn't recognize him. There was still a risk, of course. Yet it was worth it.

Holding her son's hand, she walked along the beach, passing by. The shutter snapped as he took another photograph.

He was a little concerned about her choice of skimpy beach wear, and wondered about Sam. What sort of man would want his wife strutting around in such sexy attire? In his judgment, the thin bikini straps, and high cut briefs, seemed too flaunty for Ellen. Although, he had to admit, she did look rather stunning. And evidently, he was not alone in his opinion. He'd noticed a sole lifeguard checking her out more than once since their arrival. And Purdit had been taken aback to see her offer the stranger a provocative smile in return.

Seagulls squawked overhead, and wheeled down to the ocean. Jason tugged free of his mother's hand and raced toward the water's edge, yelling at the birds and flapping his arms as if trying to takeoff. Ellen sprinted after him and caught him. She offered a warning, bending down so her face was close to his, although her words were lost in the wash of the waves.

Purdit's pleasant disposition evaporated when the lifeguard, bronze muscles rippling, sauntered in Ellen's direction.

Purdit lowered his camera, knowing he'd pushed his luck by staying this long, but he wanted to see what would happen next.

Mr. Muscles started chatting to her, pointing out to sea. Ellen nodded, listening intently. She glanced down at her son and said something. The boy lowered his eyes with a guilty expression, kicking ineffectually at the sand, before holding on to her leg until she finally scooped him up and perched him on her left hip. The lifeguard continued to smile and talk. His raucous laugh mingled with Ellen's girlish giggle carried across the beach. And with a final, dazzling smile, the lifeguard resumed his sauntering patrol.

Purdit didn't realize his fist was clenched until he felt a dull ache in his fingers. The pressure inside his skull too began to increase. The pounding pulse gradually drowning out the susurrant surf. He tried to relax, to concentrate on his breathing, but it was impossible. He spun around and began the long, steep trek back up to the quiet street where he had parked his car.

Laughter continued to echo in his mind. Taunting him. Mocking him.

Chapter 24

Sam's phone remained ominously silent.

He chewed on a thumbnail, elbows resting on his desk, and wondered what would happen once he had to admit to Purdit that he had failed to raise the eighty thousand. He only hoped he could convince the blackmailing son of a bitch that there simply wasn't any more.

Purdit had to know that.

But what if he didn't?

"Not my problem," Sam whispered, although he knew it was very much his problem. He recalled his heart pounding panic when he'd been pulled over by the cops and forced to lie down, face scraping the tarmac, his wrists bound by armed police officers. If Purdit could make that happen, then Sam didn't want to imagine what else the man could do.

The phone rang.

Without glancing at the screen, he snatched it to his ear. "Yes?"

"Sam?"

It was Ellen.

He breathed once more and tried to keep the tension from his voice. "Hey. You okay?"

"Yes. I meant to remind you, I'm meeting with Mom for lunch at Desert Hills."

"Today?" he'd forgotten all about her outing to the discount stores. He'd strongly suggested she cancel the trip, when she mentioned it a day or two ago, considering everything else that was happening in their lives. And with that man out there. But Ellen had been equally adamant, she couldn't let her mother down, especially not today – the anniversary of her father's passing some years ago. End of debate. "Right, yes. Do you know what time you'll be back?"

"No later than five, six," she promised.

"Just be careful, okay? Anything seems weird, call 9-1-1," he said, failing to keep his anxiety out of his voice.

"I will."

"And give Jason a kiss for me. Love you both."

His hand shaking as if from palsy, he picked up his glass of water and swallowed a Tums in a vain attempt to settle his stomach.

*

Nearly two hours after Sam had spoken to his wife, Purdit spoke softly into his car phone.

"Good afternoon, Sam,"

He'd parked his Mercedes in the expanse of pavement outside the entrance to Mikasa, one of the upmarket stores that drew a clientele all the way from the coastal cities to the Desert Hills Outlet mall. From his vantage point he had an unobstructed view of a dark green Ford Explorer.

"I trust everything's in order?" Purdit continued.

He detected a slight hesitation. "Please, you have to listen."

Purdit barely concealed a smile. "Sam. I hope you're not going to renege on our agreement?"

He continued to gaze at the empty vehicle parked less than fifty feet away. A sleek sports car pulled into the spot in front of the Ford, partially blocking his view. Purdit muttered a curse.

"I've been to the bank," Sam was saying, "I've been everywhere..."

"How enterprising," Purdit commented, lowering his powered window for a moment, then closing it against the day's dry heat.

"There's no way I can get that sort of money. I can't. It's impossible."

"I thought we had an agreement, Sam? The figure was not negotiable. Perhaps I didn't make myself clear?"

"Oh, you did, believe me. I got your message. But if I haven't got the money, how do you expect me to pay?"

Purdit pursed his lips. The money itself was unimportant, but he had to get Grady to travel to where he wanted him.

Alone, in the desert.

"Hmm," he mused. "No blood out of a stone."

"No," Sam replied.

"I'm not an unreasonable man," he paused. "I'm sure you tried everything short of selling your house."

"I did, I swear."

"Very well. How much can you raise?"

Again that hesitation. Then Sam spoke. "Maybe ten thousand-"

"Ten? Sam, really. Are you playing me for a fool?"

"That's all there is. I swear on my… I'm telling the truth. If you want it, it's here now. My office."

"Not your office this time."

Purdit scanned the frontages as shoppers laden with designer name bags ambled to and fro.

"I'll meet you, wherever you say. I just want this to be over."

Only half listening, Purdit peered at three shapes descending the concrete steps. Two women, one holding the hand of a child. Purdit smiled when he recognized Ellen.

"The road," he said into the phone.

"Road?"

"Surely you remember where we met, Sam?"

He heard Grady's rasping breath. "When?"

Ellen kissed the older woman on her cheek. The old lady said something, then knelt down and pecked the boy. Very touching. The old woman stood and strolled along the sidewalk, leaving the others at the curb.

Waving goodbye, Ellen checked for traffic as she and her boy crossed the road. Skirting the line of parked cars, she fished her car keys out of a black shoulder bag.

"I'll let you know," Purdit replied, cutting the call short.

He shoved open the door and walked briskly across the lot, cutting between two rows of cars to intercept Ellen.

She hadn't noticed him, her attention divided between the boy and looking out for traffic.

Purdit emerged beside the Ford Explorer, brushing her shoulder as he past.

"Sorry," he said, turning to her.

"My fault," she said, slowing and turning to face him.

She frowned. Suddenly her eyes widened in recognition.

"I'll scream. You touch me, come near us, I will scream."

"What?" Purdit reached toward her. He wanted to explain, he didn't mean her any harm. It had been Sam who was responsible for what happened that night. And it was Sam who would be punished.

Shielding her son with her body, Ellen fumbled with the remote, finally unlocking the doors. She lunged for the handle.

Purdit stepped closer.

"Get away from me!"

"Ellen, please."

"Mommy?"

She flung open the door, shoving Jason up and into the driver's seat. He scrambled back, clambering into his child-seat.

"Leave us alone!" Ellen screamed.

Out of the corner of his eye, Purdit saw an elderly couple crossing the parking lot. They glanced in his direction, uncertain as to whether they should become involved.

He held up his empty hands. "Please, Ellen. Listen," he sounded like a plaintive spouse.

The elderly couple continued on their way.

Ellen leapt into the car, shouting, "Put your belt on, Jason!" as she slammed the door and punched the lock. She stared out the window, her face a mask of sheer terror.

"I'm sorry. I'm sorry," he pleaded, but his words were lost as she revved the engine.

The car lurched backward, tires squealing.

Purdit watched her race away.

"Fool," he cursed himself. He should never have startled her as he had. He'd been stupid, and he despised stupidity. He would find a way to make it up to her. To make it right.

*

The Explorer shimmied and Ellen's heart raced as she felt the wheel slip in her grasp.

Behind her Jason was bawling.

"Your belt," she kept repeating.

Ellen twisted around, trying to see if he'd managed to buckle up. Thud. The front wheel clipped the curb. She fought to regain control, and was forced to lift off the gas.

Her eyes flicked to the rear mirror, afraid the madman might be following in his car, but she didn't see anyone close or in pursuit.

She was out of the mall, and jetting for the freeway entrance.

"Jason? Have you done it yet?" she asked, but he was crying too loud to hear. Then, the reassuring clink as Jason fastened his belt.

"It's okay, darling. Everything's okay. Mommy's sorry she shouted," she took the on ramp at sixty. Gradually her mind seemed to knit together.

Her phone - she needed to call the cops. Whoever that man was, whatever Sam thought they could negotiate, this was over.

*

The driver of the T-Bird pulled alongside a Vons delivery truck which was traveling in the rightmost lane of the freeway. Reducing his speed, he checked the GPS. He only took his eyes off the traffic for a moment. What the hell was the exit he needed?

The trucker leaned on his horn.

Startled, the T-bird driver's eyes snapped back to the freeway as a green Explorer rocketed across the truck's path, straight in front of the T-bird.

He hit the brakes.

He was a fraction late.

Tires screeched before an explosion of metal against metal ruptured the air.

*

"Sam!" Kathy yelled.

Sam lurched up from his desk, and dashed into reception. "Kathy?"

She held the phone in her outstretched hand.

"Are you all right?" He touched her arm.

"It's the hospital. Oh, God, Sam."

He snatched the phone. "Hello?"

"Mr. Grady?"

"Yes?"

"This is Desert Regional Emergency," a voice explained calmly. "I'm afraid your wife and son have been in an accident."

"Accident, what-"

"A car accident, on the freeway."

"No. No."

"Are you able to travel here, Mr. Grady?"

"What?" he couldn't think straight. Please, God, let them be all right. "Yes. Yes, I can. Are they..."

"Your son's going to be fine. A few bruises."

"What about Ellen?"

"She's in intensive care right now. Please have somebody else drive you if at all possible."

Sam closed his eyes, trying not to imagine the scene at the hospital.

"What? Yes, yes," he said. "Who's looking after Jason? Is Lucy there?"

"He's fine. Who is, Lucy?"

"Ellen's mother. I thought they were all together. Christ. I'm coming, I'll be there. Tell Jason, I'll be there."

"I can call her mother, if you have a number?"

"Yes, right. Thank you." He gave the woman Lucy's number and handed the phone to Kathy.

"Sam?"

Numb, and hardly aware that Kathy had spoken, Sam dashed outside, sprinting to his car.

Without slowing, Sam sped through an intersection as the light turned red, leaving a swarm of angry motorists in his wake. He cut across two lanes of traffic and onto the freeway.

"Ellen," he whispered her name, begging for the chance to make it right. And, all the while, an incessant voice kept telling him that it was his fault. That, whatever had happened, he was to blame. He raced north taking the toll road, oblivious to the speed limit. God, she was so far away.

Be okay. Please be okay, the mantra filled his every thought.

Ahead the afternoon traffic crawl became a quagmire when they reached the 91. He stabbed the horn and flashed his lights but was forced to slow down and weave his way through the crowd of cars.

"Come on, dammit!"

He felt like he was trapped in quicksand. Sinking deeper and deeper.

He punched the dashboard. "Let's move!"

Anger and frustration boiled over and he yanked the wheel hard to the right, and pulled onto the shoulder, and accelerated. He cut down the inside of the stationary cars, earning a flurry of horns, but ignoring them all. Up ahead, the relentless traffic started moving and he rejoined the freeway, his speed edging higher.

Chapter 25

Claire Sawyer was on routine patrol when the CHP dispatcher issued a report over the air, an incident less than five miles from her location.

Responding code three with lights and siren, she took the nearest ramp and made a high speed U-turn over the bridge, heading back toward Cabazon. During that time Claire received further details about the accident, including the fact that the 911 call had been placed from a cell phone. For once, thought Claire, technology was doing something useful. Some drivers were helping to save lives. Of course, there were far more drivers causing accidents in the first place through inattention, gabbing on their phones while driving, or worse still, texting. Still, she thanked whoever had called this one in.

Siren wailing, Claire reached the accident scene.

She was surprised to discover that both vehicles had already been moved, evidently to ease the flow of traffic leaving the mall.

She strode along the shoulder, and saw a PD patrol car was parked here, having arrived before the CHP. Likely as not the officers had been passing by.

"First on scene?" she demanded.

A young officer, barely of recruit age to Claire's mind, spoke up.

"Ma'am. Officer Heintzelman."

"Perhaps you could tell me, in detail, what the scene looked like before these cars were moved?"

The young cop winced, then opened his mouth, closed it again, and finally said. "Um."

"Any photographs would be handy."

"Sorry, ma'am. We just moved them out the way."

"Where's the driver of the T-Bird?" She already knew the other driver was in the ER. "Plus, I need to get some measurements and shots of the skid marks."

"He's over here."

"Thanks," Claire said, not hiding her annoyance.

The driver turned out to be a good-looking guy around thirty with olive-skinned complexion. He looked like he could be a yacht's captain out of Maui, but was probably a stockbroker out of Irvine.

"Hi," he said, dabbing his forehead with a blood-spotted handkerchief.

Claire glanced at the superficial wound. "You okay, sir?"

"No. Not really." He turned to stare at his car. "Just made the last payment two months ago."

He managed a weak smile.

Claire nodded. "I need to see your license."

"Sure." He fished it out of his denim jacket.

She noted his name, address, and noticed he was actually thirty-six.

"Can you tell me what happened?" Claire asked, making notes.

"It wasn't my fault. I mean, she shot out of nowhere, in front of that truck, cut me off," he said, pointing down the shoulder to a delivery truck. "I mean, I hope she's okay and all, but people like that shouldn't be on the road you ask me."

Claire nodded.

"I was driving along. Wasn't going fast or nothing. And, bam!"

His statement coincided with initial report. She would check his story with the truck driver next.

"What a mess," the guy muttered.

"Accidents always are. Thank you. I might need to ask you some more questions in a minute."

"I'm not going anywhere. Waiting on triple A."

Claire turned her attention to the freeway, as cars continued to drive past, slowing to watch the show.

The T-bird driver called out. "Excuse me, do you know if she's going to be all right? That woman and her kid?"

"I don't know."

*

Nearly two hours after speeding away from his office, Sam felt shattered as he pulled into the unfamiliar, downtown Palm Spring's hospital complex. His eyes flitted from one sign to another.

Emergency Care Unit.

He pulled in, but was waved away by an attendant who gesticulated to a notice, AMBULANCES ONLY.

Winding his window down, Sam yelled. "Where do I park?"

Following the attendant's brief directions, Sam sped around the low building, suspension smacking the speed-bumps, before he found a space close to the main entrance.

Running inside, he interrupted a receptionist who was talking on the phone.

"My wife and my little boy? Ellen Grady."

"Sir?"

"She's in Emergency. I don't know, I think Jason's okay. Where do I go? Please."

"I'm sorry, what was your wife's name again?"

Sam tried to calm down. "Ellen Grady. Look, she was in a car crash. I don't know if..." he couldn't bring himself to finish the sentence, let alone the thought. Please, let her be okay.

"Sir. If you'll go straight down the corridor, past the elevators, I'll have someone..."

But Sam was off and running before she finished.

"Hey, little buddy, how you doing?" Sam's heart was still racing as he stroked Jason's hair. The boy looked so small and vulnerable in the hospital bed. At least the children's ward was more welcoming than the sterile corridor near the operating theater, where Ellen remained in surgery.

For a long while he hadn't been able to decide if he should stay close to Ellen or come up to see Jason. But a nurse had kindly promised to find Sam the moment there was any news.

He perched on the edge of a wooden chair, drawing close to Jason's bed. He couldn't help glancing around every few seconds, wondering when the nurse would reappear. Anxiously dreading the moment when she did. He felt sick to his stomach with worry, but desperately tried not to show anything in front of his young son.

"Where's Mommy?" Tears filmed Jason's eyes.

"Hey, it's going to be okay. The doctors are looking after her. Making her better."

Jason gnawed his lower lip and nodded.

"How are you feeling, champ? You okay?" Sam asked again.

The boy shrugged. "When can I see Mommy?"

"Soon."

Sam stared out the window and rubbed his eyes, hoping Jason wouldn't see his own tears.

"I'll go try and find out soon as Grandma gets back."

As he spoke, the door opened, and Lucy stepped inside carrying a paper cup of steaming tea.

"Sorry I was so long," she spoke quietly as she shuffled into the room. Sam stood, so that she could have his chair, and bent down to kiss Jason. "It's going to be okay."

Then he gently squeezed Lucy's shoulder with what he hoped was reassurance.

"You all right?"

She nodded mutely. She seemed so frail that Sam wondered if he should get one of the nurses to check on her.

"I'll be back in a few minutes, okay?"

Again she merely nodded her head.

Sam glanced at Jason and smiled. His brave little boy smiled back.

"I'll look after Grandma," Jason offered, the comment pulling at Sam's heart.

"Thank you."

*

The corridor outside the OR was stark, lit by harsh fluorescents. As Claire approached a row of cloth-upholstered chairs, her eyes focused on a man seated alone on the endmost chair.

Claire stepped closer.

"Excuse me, sir? Mr. Grady?"

The man looked up. His face was pale, drawn, his eyes red-rimmed and bloodshot.

"Yes?" he said.

"Claire Sawyer." She offered her hand.

Reluctantly he accepted.

"I'm investigating your wife's accident."

No reaction.

"Is it all right if I wait here?"

Sam shrugged.

She passed a few awkward minutes in silence.

"Your boy-"

"Jason's okay."

Claire nodded. The child had been lucky, he'd been strapped in to his seat. The woman had not been so sensible. If she had been, Claire felt certain, she would have escaped serious injury. Often times she couldn't understand what people were thinking when they got behind the wheel.

"Did your wife usually wear her belt?"

"What? Yes, always. Why?"

Why not this time? Claire wondered. One of those quirks of fate perhaps. The one time you neglected to buckle up, was the time something happened. But in order to learn exactly what had happened, she really needed to speak with Ellen Grady. Her husband wasn't even a witness. Just another victim.

"Do you know how your wife-"

He glared at her. "Listen. No one's told me a thing."

He stood up and began prowling the corridor.

Claire wanted to say something, offer some sympathy. But words were of little use at times like these. Silently, she returned to the nurses station.

"Can you tell me how Mrs. Grady is doing?"

The harried nurse paused. "I don't know, I'm afraid."

One of her five desk phones buzzed. "No, no," the nurse said into it. "Dr. McFarland is coming over right now, he's doing the delivery."

The nurse hung up.

"Sorry."

"Any idea how long she might be in there?"

She gave a vague shrug. "It could be hours."

There was no way Claire could sit around. She pulled out one of her business cards. "Call me when you hear anything."

"Of course."

*

Sam watched the CHP officer leave, then glanced at his watch for the thousandth time. After the long, harrowing drive, he had been climbing stairs and walking corridors ever since he arrived, checking on Jason, then sitting quietly, praying for Ellen, in the corridor outside the OR.

One of the emergency care nurses brought him a cup of coffee.

"Thank you. God, I wish I knew what was going on."

"I expect Dr. Diaz will be out to see you soon," she told him.

Sam nodded, not knowing if he should believe her. He couldn't stand waiting a minute longer. He felt drained, exhausted physically and emotionally. All he wanted was to see Ellen again. To hold her tight and not let go.

He frowned, recalling the officer's question about Ellen wearing her seatbelt. Ellen was the sort of driver who put on her belt if she was simply reversing off the driveway onto the street. The idea that she might not have been wearing it at the time of the crash made no sense to Sam. No sense at all.

That was, unless something, or someone, had panicked her.

Drive safe, the words haunted his mind, and Sam wondered if perhaps he hadn't been Purdit's target. The thought chilled Sam to the quick.

*

The Mercedes was the only car parked in a quiet corner on the second level of the parking structure, hidden from the late afternoon sunshine.

Purdit's breath sounded hollow inside the luxuriant interior. He had passed out moments after his arrival, a wave of nausea washing over him, dragging him down. Down into the darkness, where the only flashes of light were the needle points of pain stabbing his eyes. He'd never experienced an attack of such ferocity.

The migraine attack began the instant he witnessed Ellen's car plowing into the Thunder Bird. He'd been following her and had just reached the freeway on ramp. He wanted to go to her. He'd been desperate to help her. But the sudden pain stabbed through his skull, crippling him.

The cops were on the scene seemingly moments after the crash, shortly followed an orange and white ambulance, its siren waning as paramedics rushed to rescue Ellen and Jason and spirit them from the scene.

Purdit had edged down the ramp. A cop waved him past the accident and glared when Purdit eased to a crawl. He toured the wreckage, then accelerated, determined to follow the ambulance to the hospital.

He fought against the overwhelming agony, struggling to keep pace with the speeding ambulance as it exited the freeway. Only when the ambulance swung into the hospital's emergency care unit did he relinquish pursuit. Slowing, barely able to see beyond the errant flashes strobing across his eyes, Purdit drove around the hospital to the parking structure and hid from view.

The pain intensified as he sat motionless behind the wheel, his head throbbing, pounding. Until, mercifully, he had passed out.

He awoke several hours later.

A spike of brilliance flared momentarily and faded from sight. Purdit white-knuckled the steering wheel, bracing himself for a renewed attack.

But the flickering agony did not return.

Eventually he forced his fingers to slacken their tenacious hold and leaned forward to rest his head on the wheel.

Gathering his strength, Purdit pushed open the car door, one thought driving him forward. He had to know if Ellen was alive.

His footsteps echoed across the concrete, the sound as hollow and empty as his emotions.

He cursed himself. He should not have waited to take care of Sam Grady. With Sam out of the way, Ellen could have been his by now. She would have been safe from harm. He could protect her. Save her. After all, he had managed to save his mother all those years ago.

If only he hadn't surprised Ellen at the mall... He should have thought things through. He should not have confronted her. But he'd felt compelled to reveal himself to her.

A chill evening breeze blew off the desert as he left the parking structure, a blood red sun sinking beyond the low-rise buildings.

A car stopped for him as he crossed the road and stepped into the hospital. He strode along a gray-carpeted corridor with its overhead signs at each intersection, and marched briskly past a bronze wall plaque engraved with hundreds of benefactors.

His pace slowed as he pushed through the double doors leading to the ECU. At the next intersection he stopped to steal a glance around the corner. As he'd expected, Sam Grady was there, dozing in a chair not twenty yards away.

Purdit pulled back from view. Somehow he needed to see Ellen. He only wanted to talk to her. Ellen would understand, he reasoned. She wouldn't be stupid. Not like his mother had been in the end. Despite the love he had lavished on her. Despite his protection and unwavering affection, his mother never once been grateful for the things he had done. Never.

Chapter 26

A muscle cramped in Sam's neck. He'd dozed off with his head propped uncomfortably against the wall.

"Sam Grady?"

Sam blinked.

Above him towered a doctor dressed in surgical greens. "I'm Dr. Diaz. I performed your wife's operation."

Sam stumbled to his feet feeling lightheaded. "Is she okay? Please."

Diaz scratched his bushy beard. "Your wife's suffered a concussion along with abdominal injuries. We've stabilized her condition. In fact she's doing remarkably well, though not all the way out of the woods yet."

Sam bit down on his lower lip. His mind was buzzing and he hadn't really heard the doctor's words properly. "But she's going to live?"

Diaz's warm smile helped reassure Sam. "Yes, and she should make a full recovery given some time."

"Is Ellen awake?"

"Yes. She regained consciousness after the procedure, but she's still very drowsy with the sedation."

"Can I see her?"

Diaz nodded, helping Sam as he swayed slightly. "This way."

They stepped into the recovery room. Subdued night-lights supplemented the twilight spilling through half-drawn shades.

Sam had never seen Ellen look more vulnerable. His chest filled with a desperate aching. Ellen and Jason, there was nothing more important in the world to him, yet how often had he treated them as second best putting the company and his own ambitions first? Like his wife and son would always be there in his life. It was impossible to imagine it otherwise. He knew he'd taken his family for granted, and the thought filled him with an overwhelming self-loathing. Not pity. Loathing.

An IV dripped a carefully regulated solution into his wife's wrist. Wires stuck to her temples and chest with metallic pads sent vital information to the machines that held her in their delicate web.

But she was alive, and the doctor said she would be okay.

"Thank you. God, thank you. Can I stay with her?" Sam asked.

Diaz nodded and, after checking one of the machines, left the room.

As the doctor's footsteps receded, Sam felt his shoulders sag. Ellen looked dead.

Yet when he sat down in the chair by the bed and took her hand, Ellen's fingers lightly squeezed back. Her touch was so faint at first he couldn't be sure he'd felt anything.

"Honey?" he leaned close to her, his voice barely above a whisper. "Hey, honey?"

Ellen's breath came as a sigh. Then she groaned, her face contorting.

Sam was about to fetch a nurse, when Ellen's eyes fluttered and opened, blinking in confusion.

Sam smiled. "Hey."

Brave-faced, Ellen managed a weak smile. Then a sudden panic flashed in her eyes. "Jason? Where's Jason?"

"He's fine. He's not hurt. Lucy's with him."

"Can I see him?" she whispered.

"Soon." He saw her grimace. "You need something?"

She shook her head. For a moment she looked away. Then she met his gaze, and there was something frightening in the way she stared at him.

"What?" Sam breathed.

"He was there," she said.

Sam frowned. "Who?"

Ellen closed her eyes. "That man."

Sam's heart fluttered, adrenaline coursing through his body. He straightened rigidly. "When? Today?"

"He must have followed me. I tried to get away. I tried, Sam."

Sam felt Purdit's invisible hands reaching out, tightening around Sam's neck, strangling him.

"If I hadn't gone there…" Ellen said drowsily.

"None of this is your fault. None of it," he whispered.

They stayed that way for several minutes until Ellen lapsed back under the fading waves of anesthesia.

He stroked his wife's cheek. "I love you so much. I'll be back in a minute," he promised as he walked to the door.

*

Purdit had waited long enough. Wandering the hospital hallways, spending time in the cafeteria, visiting the pathetic gift shop.

He was waiting for his chance.

His frustration mounted throughout evening, until, finally, he saw Sam leave her room. Purdit stirred from the couch in the ward's reception area where he was waiting, partially obscured from view by the fronds of a potted palm. He stood, leaving behind an unread copy of the *Wall Street Journal,* and walked past the nurses station.

"Excuse me," a florid-faced intern called out. "Can I help you, sir? Regular visiting hours are over."

Purdit turned and smiled. "I was told I could spend a few minutes with my sister?"

The young woman hesitated. "The patient's name?"

"Ellen Grady. I can't thank you enough for everything you've done. The accident… when I got the call. Well, it's horrifying when someone you love is involved."

The intern nodded. "You know her room number?"

"Yes. I was sitting with her earlier. Thank you again," he said as he walked away.

A minute later, he inched open the door to room 221 and stood at the foot of Ellen's bed. She was asleep. He felt a strong urge to touch her. To stroke her soft skin.

Moving around the bed he reached for the cool cotton sheet, one corner had slipped from her shoulder. Tenderly he lifted the sheet, covering her naked arm.

The door clicked.

Purdit spun, startled.

The policewoman he'd seen earlier stood in the doorway. A frown furrowed her brow.

Out of the corner of his eye he saw Ellen stir. He couldn't let her see his face. He walked toward the door and stuck out his hand. "Tom Chance," he said as if he had every right and expectation to be in the room.

"Ellen's my sister," he explained, glancing down at Ellen with concern.

"Oh. I'm Officer Sawyer, I'm investigating the accident. How's she doing? The doctor said I could ask some questions next time she's awake."

Purdit nodded. "Of course, of course. I just can't believe it."

"She's lucky, it could have been much worse."

"Quite."

The officer glanced around the room. "I can leave you two alone a while."

"No, that's all right. I was just going." He glanced furtively back at Ellen, looking blearily at them. "I promised Sam, my brother-in-law, I'd run a couple of errands for him."

The officer nodded, compassion and understanding lighting her eyes.

Ellen murmured something he couldn't make out, and the CHP officer moved toward the bedside.

"What did you say? Mrs. Grady?"

Purdit slipped out the room. He moved swiftly down the hall, and let his breath seep out. That had been too close.

*

Claire stepped to Ellen's side. "Hello, Ellen? I'm Officer Sawyer, I'm investigating the accident. Is there anything you want me to get for you?"

"No," her voice sounded fragile. "Where's Sam?"

Ellen's hand moved over the sheet, across her abdomen.

"I don't know." Claire pursed her lips. "I was sorry about what happened. Do you feel up to talking?"

Ellen swallowed, on the verge of tears. "It was all my fault."

She said it as a statement. No room for disagreement. And for all Claire knew, Ellen Grady was probably right. Certainly she shouldn't have been driving in such a reckless manner. But this woman didn't strike her as a maniac.

"What happened?" Claire asked. "Can you remember? Was there some reason you appeared to be driving so fast?"

Ellen nodded, her head moving imperceptibly. No doubt, Claire thought, the drugs were still clouding the woman's mind.

"He was there. The money wasn't enough. He came back."

Claire was about to ask what in the world she was talking about, when the door opened. Diaz's rugged face appeared, and the tall surgeon strode in.

"I see you've woken our patient," he said. Then his expression shifted to professional concern as he checked Ellen's condition. "I think perhaps, you should get some more rest. I'm sure these questions can wait. Can't they, officer?"

"Doctor," Claire spoke up. "If I could have a few more minutes?"

"Give her an hour," Diaz said, adjusting the IV controller, and increasing the LED readout slightly on the control box to .05. "Okay?"

Claire knew when to push, and when to admit defeat. And Diaz didn't seem the sort of person who took kindly to being pushed. "Get well," she wished Ellen before leaving the room.

Leaving the room, Claire pondered the woman's cryptic words. "He was there. The money wasn't enough. He came back."

Who? What man? Claire wondered, and what relevance did anyone's coming back have to the fact that Ellen Grady had been speeding out of a busy shopping mall, oblivious to other traffic. Had someone threatened her?

Claire strode down the corridor deep in thought.

Had someone else been in the car? she wondered. That didn't seem likely. Any other passenger would surely have been injured in the crash, or at the least would have been seen fleeing the crash.

Heading for the nearest coffee machine, Claire couldn't shake the feeling that something peculiar had happened to cause the accident.

Something she intended to ask Ellen Grady about before the night was over.

*

On his return to Jason's room, Sam found the doctor examining the little boy. It appeared he had suffered no lasting ill effects and could be discharged.

"When can we see Mommy?"

"In a minute," Sam promised.

After Sam signed the necessary paperwork, he carried Jason past the elevator as Lucy walked alongside, her head downcast.

"It's going to be okay," he told her for the umpteenth time.

When she didn't answer, Sam glanced back and saw that Lucy had stopped to press the elevator button.

"I was going to take the stairs?" he said as the elevator pinged.

She shrugged and Sam debated getting in the elevator with her, but he simply couldn't. He pushed open the stairwell door.

"I'll meet you," he said, again looking back, but the elevator had already closed.

Jason squirmed in his arms and he lowered him to the floor. They descended the steps together in silence.

"Visiting's almost over," a nurse told Lucy from behind a desk as Sam and Jason arrived.

"I know," said Sam. "We're here to see Mrs. Grady, my wife."

"I'm afraid she's probably asleep. Do you want me to check?"

"Can't we see her anyway?" Sam asked.

The nurse glanced at Jason and smiled. "Of course. Let me look in on her, one minute."

With that the nurse trotted down the corridor. She came back as promised, within a minute.

"She's stirring."

"That's wonderful," said Lucy.

"But please, you can't stay too long. I have to increase her sedative soon to make sure she gets plenty of rest tonight."

"Oh," said Lucy sounding defeated.

"No more than ten minutes."

"Thank you, my dear."

Scooping Jason up again, Sam strode down the corridor, forcing Lucy to walk double-time to keep pace.

The room's fluorescent lighting was on now, and he saw Ellen's faced was bruised and battered, but to Sam she had rarely looked more lovely.

She looked at her little boy. "Hey, sweetheart. Come here."

Ellen smiled despite her hurt as Jason rushed over to her.

"Mommy."

Ellen sobbed as she touched Jason's face and clutched his tiny hands. "You're okay? You're okay?"

Jason nodded.

"Oh, darling," Lucy gushed. "I was so worried. What ever happened?"

"Lucy," Sam said patiently. "I don't think Ellen's up to explanations right now."

Wearing her most put-out expression, Lucy demurred and remained at the foot of the bed while they all chatted quietly for the next few minutes. But neither Sam nor Ellen made any mention of the stranger who had entered and endangered their lives.

All too soon their time was up, and the nurse returned and dimmed the lights.

Jason gave his mommy a big hug. Sam saw her wince slightly, but he knew Ellen wasn't about to complain. He could see it in her eyes, she blamed herself for what had happened on the freeway. Logical or not, it was a feeling he understood all too well.

"You get plenty of rest," Sam gave her hand a loving squeeze. Then, leaning closer to her, he whispered. "None of this was your fault. You know that."

He met her eyes, and after a moment, she nodded. "I know, but... I know."

"What's this?" Jason wanted to know, pointing to the plastic IV tube that ran from Ellen's wrist.

"That's how Mommy eats while she's getting better," Sam said, stroking the boy's unruly hair.

Jason pulled a face. "Yuck. I'd want bananas. They're good for you."

Sam felt a deep sense of relief when his wife smiled.

"Yes," Ellen agreed. "The best."

Within moments of being given her sedative, she drifted asleep, and they tiptoed out the room.

It was already nine o'clock, and Sam suddenly felt famished. He couldn't remember the last time he'd had anything to eat.

"You want to grab something to eat?" he said to Lucy.

A broad grin spread across the boy's face. "Fries."

Lucy looked aghast. "Sam. It's bedtime. I can take him back home. He needs to sleep."

Sam wanted to argue - wanted to keep his son close in case Ellen woke up and wanted to see him again. And the idea of Jason getting into a car, driving on the freeway, it frightened him out of all proportion to the real risk. Yet he knew not only was Lucy right, it would be what Ellen wanted. She'd want Jason safe. Quite possibly she wouldn't want him at the hospital. It was a scary place for a young child. Sam knew that all too well from his own childhood. Recalling the hospital in Oakland, where his mother had lain in her final days. In his mind, these supposedly hallowed buildings were more closely tied to death than to recovery. He was just thankful that this time things would be okay. Ellen would be walking out of here in a few days at most. They'd been lucky. Of course, that didn't mean their nightmare was over. Sam couldn't see how it ever would be. A tunnel with no light at the end. He pulled himself from his dark reverie.

"Okay," he said, lifting Jason up. "Let's grab you some fries for the ride home with grandma, eh?"

Minutes later, Sam fetched the child-seat from his car and strapped it tight into the back of Lucy's vehicle. he triple checked the buckle and gave Jason a goodnight kiss as the boy dipped a greasy hand into the bag of fries.

"I'll be there when you wake up," Sam promised.

Jason nodded. He looked worn out. Poor little kid, thought Sam, and gave him an extra hug.

"Drive safe," he told Lucy without really thinking, until he'd spoken those ominous words aloud.

*

No one paid any particular attention to the orderly in his white lab coat, who pushed an empty wheelchair down the quiet second-floor corridor and into Room 221.

Inside the room, the orderly removed the IV from Ellen's wrist. Ellen stirred, moaning softly, but didn't wake. And soon her breathing resumed its slow, deep pattern.

The man rolled back her blanket and sheet, and maneuvered her relaxed body into the wheelchair.

Covering her with the blanket stripped from the bed, Purdit made sure *his* patient was comfortable, then wheeled her out of the room.

He nodded curtly at a nurse as they passed one another in the corridor, although the nurse was too preoccupied to notice.

He rode the elevator to the first-floor, then marched down the long corridor. Don't rush.

Most of the exterior doors had been locked for the night. The main entrance remained open, but he was no longer headed in that direction.

Instead, he pushed the chair down a little-used passage, and reached a fire door. For emergency use only.

His hands touched the push-bar. He hesitated one second, then shoved the door open.

An alarm wailed.

Moving quickly now, he trundled the chair through the door and into the adjoining parking structure.

Seconds later he unlocked his Mercedes and lifted Ellen into the back seat. He covered her with the blanket, pulling it beneath her chin.

Purdit discarded the lab coat, leaving it tossed over the wheelchair.

He climbed into the car, removed his surgical gloves, and pulled away.

They drove out the hospital grounds, headed into the night.

Headed for the desert.

Chapter 27

The sounds, the voices, surrounding him didn't make sense at first. As he stirred, blinking against the hard lights of the corridor, his brain snapped into gear, and he remembered where he was. He'd fallen asleep again on an uncomfortable plastic chair, and was paying the price. His spine protested as he sat up. A grunt escaped his lips as he tried to work some feeling back into his aching muscles.

Two people were staring at him. He only recognized the woman; the CHP officer who had spoken to him earlier in the night. Only he couldn't recall her name. The man standing next to her looked like another cop, but he was dressed in slacks and a polo shirt.

"What?" said Sam. "What's wrong? Ellen?"

Instantly, he was on his feet, his aching back immediately forgotten.

"Mr. Grady, please don't panic-"

"What's happened?" Sam exclaimed, his heart beating so fast he thought it'd burst. "Ellen?"

He looked around for the doctor, Diaz. Surely, if Ellen had problem the doctor or a nurse would be there to tell him. He looked at the stranger. "Who are you?"

"Detective. Ed Reed."

"What the hell's going on?"

Reed answered the question without equivocation. "Your wife. She's disappeared."

The words went in, but their meaning was as opaque as obsidian.

Sam shook his head, as if to clear it. "What are you talking about? She's in her room. Two-two-one."

Idiots. She was probably having some blood drawn or something.

He ran down the corridor. He needed to find out what was really going on.

*

Claire could see Grady didn't believe them. And why would he? At least until he saw with his own eyes.

"We need you to take a look in your wife's room," she started to explain.

"Where do you think I'm going?" He pushed past.

Claire and Detective Reed hurried after him.

Reaching the room, she watched as Grady stormed inside and confronted the doctor and nurse who had been instructed to wait with a PSPD uni.

"Where's Ellen?" Grady demanded.

The doctor, Diaz, seemed the calmest out of the everyone. "Security's looking everywhere. The police too."

Again, the shake of the head. Denial probably, Claire assumed as she watched Grady.

"I thought she was sedated. She can't have wandered off."

"We know. The medication could have worn off by now, it is unlikely."

"You're fucking right it is. This is insane."

Grady wheeled around to face Claire.

"We'll find her," Claire said, hoping she sounded more confident than she felt. This entire incident was one of the weirdest things she'd come across. The accident made little sense, likewise Mrs. Grady's words earlier. "The thing we need-"

"The main thing," Detective Reed interrupted, "is to remain clam. We need you to look around this room. Your wife's belongings appear to be untouched. But if something's missing. It could help us figure out where she's gone."

The anxious rise and fall of Grady's chest seemed to subside. For a moment earlier, Claire had thought the guy would hyperventilate and pass out.

An asthmatic cough, from someone entering the room, attracted Claire's attention.

A man built like an aging linebacker stood in the doorway, panting for breath. He wore a black uniform, looking to the world like a police officer. But his shiny lapel badge announced he was hospital security. Raul Sanchez.

"We'll find her, Mr. Grady," Reed said, then turned to the security man. "Anything unusual happen tonight?" he asked Sanchez.

"Yes," wheezed Sanchez. "Didn't think of it at the time. It was about ten o'clock, you see."

"What was?" Claire interrupted.

"One of the emergency exits was opened. Sets off an alarm when that happens."

"And does that happen often?" She ignored the detective's glare as she questioned the guard.

Sanchez shrugged and glanced sidelong at Diaz. "Sometimes the doctors, well, they work pretty hard hours. They're tired, in a hurry to get home, you know how it is."

"I know."

"When I checked the door, I didn't see no one around, and there's no camera in that part of the hospital. No reason-"

"Which exit?" Claire interrupted.

"Leads out to the parking structure. Didn't find nothing, 'cept a wheelchair which got left out by mistake," he remembered. "That's against regulations, but the orderlies are always doing that."

*

Sam sat on the edge of the bed where only a few hours earlier his wife had slept.

What in God's name had happened to Ellen? Where was she?

The question pounded his consciousness. It was his fault. Everything was his fault. Everything since that cursed night on the road.

Purdit.

He could think of no one else. Somehow Purdit was involved.

The man's gaunt visage rose like a specter before his eyes.

But why would he kidnap Ellen? Did he think taking her would force Sam to raise more money?

If so he was sadly mistaken. Sam had raised every penny he could, short of selling the townhouse - and that would take weeks probably if not months.

Besides which, if Purdit's motive was to extort more money, then why hadn't he called Sam to demand a ransom?

"Sir?"

Sam suddenly realized the detective was talking to him.

"Yes?"

"Do you know anyone who might want to harm your wife?"

Sam returned Reed's probing gaze. His mind tumbled. He was too afraid to tell the detective his fears. No longer afraid for himself, but for Ellen. What if Purdit had kidnapped her and the police tried to interfere? Sam knew in his gut that the crazed man was capable of anything.

"Harm? No," he said.

Detective Reed straightened his back.

One of the nurses sent to search the rooms reported in. "There's no sign of her."

Reed turned to the surgeon. "You're sure she couldn't have walked out of here?"

"I think that's highly unlikely, detective. She was in no condition to walk anywhere."

"Do you still need me?" Sam spoke up.

He saw the CHP officer frown when he asked the question.

"You have some urgent appointment all of a sudden?" the detective's voice was tinged with suspicion.

Sam shook his head, and kept quiet.

"I want to check out that exit," Claire said to the hospital guard. Reed nodded, the three of them heading out.

Where would Purdit have taken her? he wondered.

Suspended in a purgatory of his own creation, Sam sat motionless on the bed, trying to plan his next move. His entire world, his life, was crumbling around him. The only thing he knew was that he had to do something.

*

"You don't have to stay here any longer. Mr. Grady?" Claire Sawyer sounded more sympathetic after another hour spent discussing the myriad possibilities that might have taken Ellen from her room.

Sam felt sick from worry and lack of sleep, his mouth tasted stale and foul.

But at least he had a plan. And he knew where he had to go.

"I'll be at my mother-in-law's," he lied, jotting Lucy's cell number on a sheet of paper. He tried to keep his mind away from what he would tell her - or Jason.

Reed returned and took charge.

"Thanks officer." He turned his attention from Claire to Sam. "We'll let you know as soon as there's any news. Try not to worry. Most times there's an explanation and these things work out."

Sam noticed Claire Sawyer's silent surprise with that last comment. Not that Sam believed the detective for a minute. Sam was sure he knew the explanation, and it wasn't about to work itself out. The cops no doubt had experience dealing with "normal" kidnappers, Sam imagined. But there was nothing normal about the man who had abducted Ellen. Purdit would contact him, and Sam would pay whatever price was demanded.

Head down, he stepped between them and walked out the room.

*

Claire was about to leave when Reed reached out and touched her wrist.

"You finished?" said Reed, his eyes probing hers.

"Pardon? Something's definitely not adding up about any of this."

"That's why I'm here, isn't it? Best thing you can do is your job, and let me know the cause of that accident. Clear?"

As crystal, asshole, Claire wanted to say. Instead she settled for an enigmatic nod. He could take that whichever way he wanted.

Then she turned and marched out of the room.

She quickened her pace down the corridor.

"Mr. Grady," she hurried after him, determined to find out if there was something else going on. She'd been watching him ever since he learned his wife had vanished. His panic had been understandable. And Grady was frantically worried for his wife, that was doubtless true. Yet it seemed like he was holding something back. Though it was possible, Claire admitted to herself, that she'd simply misread the guy.

"Mr. Grady."

He took the stairs down, rather than wait for the elevator, not appearing to have heard her. Or deliberately ignoring her. "Sir!"

He was there. The money wasn't enough, she recalled Ellen's words.

Had Ellen been talking about her husband? Claire hadn't thought so at the time. But could she have been talking about her brother?

She could hear Mike's voice in her head as she followed Sam outside into the cool pre-dawn air. Not everything's some conspiracy. First Dr. Bernard, now Ellen Grady. Was she just seeing figments in the dark?

Maybe. Or maybe she was right, Claire told herself.

Had Ellen had some sort of argument with her brother at the shopping mall? Had that clouded her good sense? That was certainly possible. But that wouldn't explain her disappearance from the hospital?

She sprinted across the car lot.

"Wait a minute!" she yelled.

Still oblivious, Sam unlocked his car and climbed inside.

Claire ran and reached the car at the instant Grady started the engine. She banged her fist on his window.

Sam spun in his seat, and couldn't have looked more startled if he'd seen a ghost.

"Lower your window," Claire said.

Recognition dawning in Sam's face, he lowered the window.

"Do you mind turning off your engine?"

He sighed and did as she asked.

"Look, officer. I'm tired."

"I know, but I wanted to ask you a couple more questions."

"Okay, okay."

"Can you think of anyone who'd want to harm your wife?"

"I already told you and the detective, no."

Claire noticed Sam's eyes flick away for a fraction of a second as he spoke.

"Do you think her bother might know something?"

Sam frowned. "Ellen's brother? I don't see how, he lives in Iowa, last I heard. He and Ellen haven't spoken in years."

"You didn't know he's here? At the hospital, I spoke to him a few hours ago..."

Sam stared up at her, mute.

"Is something wrong?" Claire said.

"No. It's just... I didn't see him. I didn't even know he was in town. That's all."

"Mr. Grady, if you know something, if there's some history we need to be aware of?"

"No. Nothing like that," he yawned. "Look, can I go? I'll ask Ellen's mother to get hold of him and he can contact you."

"You don't have his number?"

A beat. "No, I told you, he and Ellen had a falling out. I really need to get back, check on Jason."

Claire nodded in acquiescence, moving away from the car. Every instinct told her that, despite Sam Grady's protestations, something was wrong. Very wrong indeed.

The car roared away.

Sam Grady was lying. Yet Claire had no idea why.

Instinctively, Claire turned and ran to her car. Thoughts wheeled through her mind as she flung open the door and leapt inside. She was one car behind the Buick, as Sam passed under the parking barrier and drove away.

"Come on," Claire muttered as the driver ahead ferreted out his credit card for the night attendant in her booth. Pulling onto the street moments later, Claire hit the gas. Some distance ahead she thought she saw Grady's car, slowing for a signal as it changed red.

Sure enough, it was him. Keeping to the left lane, and using what little traffic there was so early in the morning, she prayed he would be too tired to pay full attention to his mirrors. Her CHP black and white wasn't exactly inconspicuous.

Red turned to green, and she let the other cars pull ahead. She stayed far enough back that Grady would not be able to make out her vehicle in the darkness.

Claire reached for the dash mounted radio but hesitated before calling in. What was she going to tell dispatch? She certainly had no proof that Grady had done anything wrong, or that he knew something more than he was telling.

She wished she could have chatted things through with Mike Stadler, but he was thirty thousand feet in the air, well on his way to Michigan by now.

She eased further off the gas. Maybe she was chasing ghosts. But what if Sam knew more than he was telling? Something had seriously rattled him when she'd mentioned Ellen's brother.

She followed the Buick onto the main boulevard, still keeping her distance. Five minutes later she tailed him onto the 111, heading out of Palm Springs toward the Interstate.

Moonlight peeked through the clouds, adding an otherworldly silver sheen to the sands and rocks that littered the surroundings.

They joined the I-10. Claire felt sure Sam was heading to his mother-in-law's home.

But then, without signaling, he took a solitary off ramp.

Where the devil was Sam Grady going?

Switching lanes, she tried to keep his car in view without giving away the fact that she was tailing him.

She picked up the radio.

"Three-five-one."

"Go ahead, five-one," she recognized Keith, a dispatcher with a penchant for disregarding protocol on the air.

"I'm ten-seven."

"Okay," the dispatcher paused. "You all right?"

"Just need some personal time."

"Leave your radio on, and check in."

"Always do."

Claire debated turning off her headlights. Quite possibly Grady would notice her before long. On the other hand, she argued with herself, driving blind on this lonely stretch of road did not seem an intelligent idea at all.

What the devil were they doing out here? Claire wondered.

Maybe she should pull Grady over and ask him about his destination, and why he was going there. Was it possible he already knew where his wife had vanished?

She didn't think was likely, although he surely seemed to know more than he was telling the authorities. Even so, Claire couldn't believe that Sam Grady was directly involved in her disappearance. No, there was something else going on.

And then there was the *money*. What money, she wasn't sure.

She glanced out the driver's window as something caught the moonlight, reflecting in her direction.

Claire gazed at a long row windmills over a mile away. The tall pylons, similar to the ones she had visited near the tour bus.

Blood on the windmill.

Windmills, an unexplained suicide, a missing woman.

Claire felt an eerie shiver of a connection between the events, tantalizingly beyond her grasp. And, like the car she was following, everything seemed to lead deeper to the desert.

Where was Sam Grady going, and why?

Was he meeting someone all the way out here, perhaps as the dead doctor had done? Why would anyone do that? Except for some clandestine purpose, she thought. Presumably it had to do with his missing wife, but what if there was some other nefarious purpose?

Drugs? Might that be a possible link?

If Bernard had been selling prescription drugs, opioids maybe, then he'd want to make sure they met somewhere isolated. But his practice must have been making a fortune, and while that didn't rule anything out, it certainly made it less likely that he needed cash.

The money.

Blackmail? Could Bernard have been the victim of a blackmailer? A man with something to hide? Something he'd rather die than have come to light and ruin him? Had Sam Grady somehow been involved? Or Ellen's brother?

She recalled the blank look on Grady's face when she'd first mentioned the brother. As if he didn't have a clue what she was talking about. And meantime, poor Ellen Grady was missing.

Whoever had taken the injured woman from her hospital bed had to be sick, mentally unbalanced, she thought. She could hardly imagine what Ellen Grady was going through right now.

Briefly, Claire wondered if she was getting too far out of her depth. Mike and that detective, Reed, were both right, she was an accident investigator and nothing more.

But she was law enforcement, and if Ellen Grady was still alive, she needed help.

*

Sam notched open the front windows, a cool blast of air swirled into the car helping to clear his head.

His only thoughts were focused on finding Ellen.

Purdit could have taken her anywhere, Sam realized. But he had to start searching somewhere. And the only place he could think of was the scene of their confrontation, on that dark, terrible night a lifetime ago.

Sam's heart thumped when he glimpsed the headlights some distance behind. He had only been peripherally aware of them before. But now he felt sure - someone was following him.

The blacktop wound deeper into the desert, through denuded shrub trees, the road edge marked by crumbling asphalt and the occasional tumbleweed.

The road seemed as filled with terror as it had late that Sunday night.

He reached the fork where they had taken a wrong turn. A very wrong turn as it transpired.

*

Thinking about the desert, Claire recalled another strange incident. An abandoned car near the ramp Grady had taken minutes earlier. A car that had belonged to a cop, or rather an ex-cop, who was later deemed a missing person. She tried to recall the retired officer's name.

She radioed in and asked for the information.

In the distance, Grady slowed then took a tight right turn.

The dispatcher came back on the air. "Alex Casper. 1901 Yucca Way. Still listed missing."

"Thanks."

So, not a single missing person. Two people.

She took the right hand fork slightly too fast. The front tires squeaked.

Ahead, the Buick's brake lights flared a hundred yards down the road as Grady pulled to a stop.

Claire lifted off the gas, about to brake. But she realized that would probably draw more attention to her patrol car. Instead she accelerated, deliberately not looking at Grady as she raced by. She kept going until finally she curved around a long bend and the Buick's lights faded from her mirrors. Claire stopped and leapt out of the vehicle. She ran back along the edge of the road, darting among the sparse vegetation until she spotted Sam's car.

He stood, his eyes scanning up and down the road, as if he was expecting to see someone.

A meeting.

Ransom. The word flashed into her mind. Was Grady about to pay someone for the safe return of his wife? If so, how on earth could he have gotten the money? No, something else was going on, she felt sure. Not that any of this made sense.

Her hand dropped instinctively to her holster, and she flipped the release catch, the Smith & Wesson pistol readily accessible and fully loaded. She wasn't about to take any chances.

*

Sam's pulse still pounded. For one awful moment he thought the cop was about to stop.

He had held his breath until it disappeared from sight, then climbed out of his car.

He stared at the road, certain this was the place where he'd made a U-turn in front of Purdit's car. Sam looked farther along the blacktop, in the direction Purdit had come from. Using his phone, before he'd lost the signal, he had checked on Google Maps. This dusty road decayed to a dotted line, then vanished altogether a few miles from where he was standing.

What had Purdit been doing out here?

Sam had seen only a couple of distant ranch houses since leaving the freeway and he doubted there were many more before the road faded into the desert. Yet, it was possible one of them belonged to Purdit. And if that was so, then perhaps he would find Ellen.

*

Claire saw Sam climb into his vehicle, and sprinted back to her car. She fired up the engine, and was about to drive when Sam's Buick passed by.

Their eyes met.

Sam did a double take and braked to a stop.

She half-expected him to flee back to the freeway. But to her surprise he stepped out. Claire flung open her door, and leapt out poised to draw her gun.

"Hold it!"

Sam froze mid-stride. His face a study of complete bafflement.

"You followed me?" He sounded stunned by the simple fact.

"You said you were heading to you mother-in-law's. I can't imagine she lives all the way out here, does she? What's really going on, Mr. Grady?" Claire demanded, walking briskly toward him, her hand still resting on her gun.

"I... I'm looking for Ellen."

"In the middle of nowhere?" That's bullshit, she thought.

She was within ten feet when Grady moved.

Her hand grasped the revolver and she drew her weapon in a single fluid motion.

She brought the gun up swiftly, aiming along the sight, focusing on her target. But he didn't try to attack. Instead, his knees buckled and he folded, sinking to the ground.

His shoulders shuddered, and she realized he was crying.

Wary, she approached him and reached down, touching his shoulder with her left hand. He looked up, his eyes wide with dread, as if he was indeed staring into the barrel of a gun.

"This is a nightmare," he began.

Chapter 28

Thin slats of moonlight filtered through the bedroom's partially closed plantation shutters. The pale light fell across a woven Santa Fe blanket that trailed off the end of the wood-framed bed.

Purdit wrung the moisture from a cool damp towel and wiped Ellen's brow. She had stirred in and out of consciousness during the long trip from the hospital and since their arrival home.

"Ellen," he breathed as he touched the damp cloth to her feverish skin. "My Ellen."

He leant closer, close enough for his lips to brush her cheek.

She slept.

"I'm sorry," he told her. "I shouldn't have taken so long to rescue you."

A seeping breath escaped her lips, a silent moan.

He understood it was her expression of affection.

"Quiet now," he said, kissing her forehead. "There'll be time. Time for us to talk later. And don't worry about your boy. We'll all be together soon."

He crossed the paved floor, closing the door as he disappeared into the hallway.

Finally, she was with him. Finally, everything made sense to him.

*

At first, Claire Sawyer didn't know what to make of Sam's rambling story. His confession, of sorts. They sat in her patrol car, parked off the road a dozen yards behind Sam's Buick, and he spoke quietly, rarely lifting his eyes to look at her.

Even as she pieced his tale together, she wasn't sure she believed him.

"And you think this man, Purdit, he's here, someplace?"

"I don't know. But I have to start somewhere. I have to do something."

"You should have reported the incident."

Sam didn't meet her probing gaze. "I know. But I never thought anything like this would happen. We were both scared out of our minds. We panicked."

Claire started the engine.

"Wait," Sam said, startled. "I'm not under arrest, am I?"

"For what? No."

He reached for the door handle.

"Where are you going?" Claire asked.

"I have to find Ellen."

"Not by yourself."

She picked up the radio and called in.

*

Pre-dawn light rimmed the horizon and turned the ranch's stucco walls a soft pastel pink.

Inside, the open windows allowed a luscious breeze through the house.

Purdit sat in a chair by Ellen's side.

She remained asleep, as he had remained with her.

"My love, it's time to wake up," he urged, wiping perspiration from her face.

A guttural croak escaped Ellen's throat. "Sam? Where…?"

"No, darling, it's me, I'm here."

"It hurts, Sam."

"I'm not Sam!" his body tensed, his facial muscles rigid, jaw clamped tight. He heard a faint throbbing pulse inside his head.

"Wh- where am I?"

Purdit flinched as a spear of light pierced his eye. He took a deep, measured breath, forcing his body to relax. Willing the pain to subside.

Not now, he pleaded. Not another attack.

He gulped another deep breath and reached up to massage his aching head.

Ellen's eyes fluttered.

"Where am I?" she asked again, her head turning slowly, her eyelids fluttering.

She stared at Purdit.

And screamed.

His mother screamed at him.

Rage filled her eyes, suffused her face. Spittle on her lips. Like a creature possessed by the Devil.

The boy stood facing her in the kitchen, desperately trying to understand her anger.

"I did it for you," he tried to explain.

Why wouldn't she see that? Did she think he'd been blind to her suffering for all these years at his father's hands? Did she think he didn't care? Well, he had cared, and he had done something about it. He'd ended her torment. He'd done what she could not. Now, there could be peace. Peace and love.

"You're sick…" The words like a red ribbon of hate.

He watched her as she raised her hands to her face, stifling a sob.

The boy stared back at her. His momentary shock fading now, as his stomach knotted with anger.

"I did it for you. For us. Momma?"

"You stupid child. They are going to lock you away. I'll make sure they lock you away forever."

She advanced toward him. Righteousness filled her eyes, as if trying to penetrate his soul.

His voice came in a harsh whisper. "You should be grateful. You stupid bitch."

Her steps faltered. She stood no more than four feet from him.

He watched, as her anger wilted, slowly taken over by something more potent and primal. Fear.

But he didn't want her fear. He had only wanted one thing; her love. And for the first time he realized he would never have that.

He should never have told her the truth.

He should have kept his mouth shut.

But after seeing her suffer, this time because of him, he'd finally relented and answered the question she'd asked every day since his father had disappeared; "Do you think he'll ever come back?"

He had told her the truth, and this was how she repaid him. With her revulsion, with her bitter disgust.

A dull throb began to fill his mind, making it hard to concentrate. Light flickered behind his eyes.

He had done everything for his mother. Everything!

He'd saved her damned life. Killed the man who beat her.

And what thanks did he get? None. Instead, he'd had to endure her tears. Tears shed for a man who had abused her mentally as well as physically.

No one could take that, could they? Not even a saint.

She wouldn't stop moping about the house, no matter how hard he tried to convince her that they were better off. His father had gone, walked out on them. Good riddance, that's what she should have said. Instead, incredulously, she'd pined for him as if her heart had been broken. That wasn't right.

His head pounded like a tempest.

There was a knife. He saw it now for the first time. It was in his hand, blood dripping from the blade.

His mother's blood.

Then he looked down. Saw her lying at his feet. Blood, so dark it looked black, pooled beneath her, seeping into the worn wood floor. As if the floor itself was leaching the life from her body.

The boy who stared down at her wondered why she'd never appreciated the things he'd done for her.

Swaying, lightheaded, he rinsed the knife in the sink before returning it to the drawer.

He felt little remorse, only gratitude that the pain filling his skull had abated. Like a demon sated by sacrifice. By blood.

The boy was unsure what was happening to him, but he knew one thing; it was time to leave home.

Chapter 29

The tires crunched and cracked the loose dirt as the patrol car jostled along the track toward a ranch home. This was the third such place they'd found, this one set back over a mile from the road.

Inside the car Sam unbuttoned his collar, sweating despite the cranked conditioner.

Claire gave him another sideways glance and muttered something about obstructing justice.

"I did what I thought I had to do to protect my family. I was wrong." Sam said.

Claire regarded him for a long moment. Would she have done any different in his position? He wasn't law enforcement. He was scared, and rightly so from what she'd heard. "I can imagine the pressure you must be under. But you've got to understand, there's no proof that Ellen's been kidnapped. With the medication, there's a possibility she wandered out the hospital. That she's not out here at all."

"Then how come you're helping me?"

"Because… what if you're right?"

"Thanks," Sam said numbly.

Claire shrugged. "Here we are," she pulled up outside the house.

She opened her mouth to speak, but Sam said. "I know. Stay in the car."

"You're learning."

She got out and walked across the sandy path to the front door, each footstep kicking up dust.

Sam had to squint against the brilliant whitewashed walls, his eyes scanning along the frontage, shutters drawn against the heat that was already building up.

He pushed open the car door, but remained seated as he'd been instructed.

He watched Officer Sawyer press the bell, then rap her knuckles on the oak door.

No answer.

She knocked again and waited.

"Hello?" she called.

Sam heard a faint click, the noise carrying in the still air. A bolt being thrown back.

Claire rested her hand easily on her gun.

The door creaked, and slowly drew inward.

An old, wizened face appeared. The woman's leather skin was cracked and tanned a deep ocher by the desert. She stood hunch-shouldered.

"Whaddya want?" she demanded, not sounding a bit like a frail old lady.

"I'm Officer Sawyer, we're looking for a woman who may have been-"

"Ain't seen nuthin'," the old woman informed her, starting to shut the door.

"One minute, please." Claire stepped toward the door, blocking it with her foot.

"You got a warrant?"

"What? No, I only want to ask a couple of questions."

"Go away. No damn business interruptin', harrasin' an old woman."

"I'm sorry you feel-"

"And get your boot outta my door."

Claire withdrew her foot. The old woman slammed the door shut.

Turning to Sam, she mimed an action as if strangling the old woman, and walked back.

This search wasn't working, he thought. Where the hell was Purdit? What had he done to Ellen?

"Shit!"

He punched the dashboard. Then took a deep breath, trying to rein in his frustration. If he couldn't think, then he would be of no use, that much he knew for sure.

Twice the CHP officer had debated turning around and giving up. Both times Sam argued that they would find another home down one of the seemingly dead end tracks. And both times they had, even though one of the buildings was nearly four miles deep into the desert. But so far they'd found no sign of Ellen.

As the sun rose higher and the desert horizon rippled beneath the heat haze, Sam too wondered if his guess, his only hope, had been wrong.

Claire faced him. "She's almost certainly not out here," she said as if reading his thoughts.

"Then take me back to my car. I'm going to keep looking." Maybe he was wrong, but there was no way he'd give up. He turned to the officer. She looked as tired and drawn as he felt after the long night and no rest. "I have to find her."

She looked at him then with pity or sadness in her eyes, he couldn't tell which, but the look chilled him. It was as if she understood something he didn't. As if he didn't realize how hopeless it was - to search the desert was an impossible task.

He sat in silence as she drove back to his car. Maybe he couldn't convince Claire Sawyer, but in his mind, he knew Ellen was here. She had to be. And he wouldn't let her down, not this time.

*

"They'll be looking for me." Ellen craned her neck and looked over her shoulder at him.

"Not here," Purdit grunted, his pulse pounding inside his skull, nausea threatening to overwhelm him.

Purdit recoiled from an image that rose in his mind. His mother lying curled on cold tile. Her flesh cut and raw and bloody.

He pushed the memory away. He may not have felt remorse in that fevered moment many years ago, but he had so often in the time since. However, he'd learned, you can never heal the past. Your actions, your mistakes haunt you to your grave. But that pain perhaps could finally be salved. Through a love like he felt now. This was something pure, he told himself. Of course, Ellen would need time to adjust, he understood that, and he was prepared to give her whatever she needed.

In the meantime, he realized, he should have stolen some drugs from the hospital. Not to numb his own pain, he'd found nothing that helped his migraines, but a sedative to put Ellen to sleep before he passed out. There was no way he could trust her not to try something.

He had no choice but to tie her hands. "Sorry," he whispered.

"Ow!" she protested, her voice muffled as he turned her over, forcing her to lie face down.

With a pang of guilt, he slackened the electrical flex around her wrists a little, though not enough that she might slip free.

Beads of sweat stung his eyes.

"Why are you doing this?"

"I'll explain everything later," he promised, rocking backward as a dark wave rolled over him. He tugged on the wire and secured the knot. "You'll understand."

Ellen sobbed.

"Don't cry." He could barely focus. Needles of light blurred his vision, skewing the room around him, blinding him.

"Don't," he breathed, feeling the room tilt, and the darkness close in.

He saw nothing as he slipped from the bed, and felt nothing when his head struck the stone pavers.

Through her tears Ellen could see Purdit's crumpled body prone on the floor. For a moment she thought he was dead. Prayed he might be. But then she heard a shallow breath escape his bloodless lips.

She willed herself to stop crying, and to think.

A phone.

Somewhere in the house there had to be a phone. If she could call for help, the police would send someone to rescue her - only she didn't have any idea where she was.

She started to panic, but then realized the police could trace her call. She had to think straight.

Fighting to stay calm, she rolled onto her side. She tried to swing her legs off the bed, struggling with her hands bound behind her back, and gasped as a dagger of pain stabbed her stomach.

With a sharp intake of breath, Ellen levered herself up.

What if he woke and saw her trying to flee?

Don't think, she told herself. Move!

In agonizing slow motion, she knifed her legs off the bed and her bare feet touched the floor. Feeling frail and still woozy, she tried to stand, but toppled, losing her balance, and fell backward onto the mattress.

After another futile attempt, she rolled off the bed and landed hard beside Purdit. Her shoulder slammed the floor and another wave of agony coursed her body. All she wanted to do was cry out in pain. But she stifled the sound.

Purdit moaned. His face inches from hers.

Her heart froze.

If her hands had been free, maybe she could have found a makeshift weapon, a vase, or something, and struck him over the head. But her hands were bound and her legs too weak to stand. All she could do was snake her way across the floor toward the bedroom door.

The closed door.

She gazed at the daunting wooden wall, at the handle far out of reach. She wanted to shout, maybe someone would hear. Maybe they wouldn't. But if she tried, then Purdit would surely stir.

Somehow she had to get the door open and phone for help.

Ellen rolled onto her back, her hands digging into her spine. She squirmed along the ground until she was pressed up against the door. Straining, she shifted her arms, and shuffled her legs until she was sitting. Then she drew her feet under her. Pain spasmed. She wished she could clutch her stomach.

Taking a deep breath, her feet slipping on the chill pavers, she pushed, her back sliding up the door until she stood, leaning against it. She fumbled blindly behind her back for the doorknob, gripped it and pulled. The hinge creaked. She glanced at Purdit, but he didn't stir. The door swung open and she staggered into the dim hallway.

To the right she saw the front door some ten feet away. She was tempted to flee, but she knew she could not travel far or fast. Her best hope was to find a phone and dial 911 before leaving the house.

Hunched in agony, she turned in the opposite direction and lurched along the hallway. All the shutters were drawn, but shafts of sunlight speared the thin gaps between the shutters. She hadn't realized how much of the day must have slipped by while she lapsed in and out of consciousness.

She reached the kitchen, her eyes scouring the worktops, searching the walls. But she saw no sign of a phone.

Ellen held back her sobs and moved on to the next room.

A bedroom. His bedroom.

Strange, how desolate and bleak a room can feel. She shivered as she crossed the threshold. So achingly cold. As cold as death.

A silk black sheet stretched across the mattress showed no sign of use. Spartan furniture stood stark against the somber walls, the room void of any personal items. No photographs, no scraps of paper, not even a brush or comb. Desperately she glanced around the barren room for a phone but found nothing.

She lurched from the bedroom, hurrying toward the final door at the end of the corridor.

She was five feet away when she froze.

Ellen strained to hear a sound that she prayed was only her imagination. She looked over her shoulder, back at the bedroom where she'd been held captive, and listened. Nothing. She glanced farther down the passageway to the front door, wondering if she should flee or risk searching the last room. She heard something. Her eyes flicked again to the room where Purdit lay unconscious. Her rapid heart threatened to drown the faint noise. But then she heard it again. A groan.

Frantically Ellen glanced at the last unopened door. She took a single, silent step closer. Then stopped. She heard Purdit moving. If she fled now, perhaps she could make it to the front door. But what if a phone lay only a few feet away, beyond the last door? She stood, tormented by indecision.

Purdit called out. An inhuman cry of anguish.

Ellen turned from the final door and fled!

She stumbled back the way she'd come, toward the front door, each unsteady step threatening to send her flailing to the ground.

Praying the front door wasn't secured with a dead bolt Ellen ran past Purdit's bedroom, past the kitchen, and slowed.

She heard Purdit moving as she reached the open doorway into the room where she'd been held captive. She glanced inside.

Purdit's back was to the door, his hand groping the bed as he tried to pull himself to his feet. Ellen stumbled past.

Suddenly she tripped on the edge of a broken paver. Ellen felt the rush of air past her face. Unable to break her fall with her bound hands, she twisted instinctively.

The impact drove the air from her lungs. She writhed on the tile floor gasping for breath.

"Ellen?" Purdit's voice was indistinct, distant.

Frantic, she drew her legs up, trying to stand, but her feet slipped. There was no way she could stand while her hands were trapped behind her back. She curled on the floor, and drew her tied hands around her legs, under her feet and finally in front of her body.

With a surge of determination, Ellen staggered to her feet and lunged toward the front door.

"Ellen," he called after her, his strength no doubt returning. Ellen grasped the door handle.

The handle turned. She pulled, but the door remained shut.

"Oh, Ellen," he called. His shout sounded like those of a child taunting his chosen victim.

She threw a glance over her shoulder, expecting him to appear. Mercifully, there was no sign of him. Yet.

She spared a moment to look at the front door. A bolt secured the top of the door. Straining, she stretched up until her fingertips touched the metal. She barely had the strength to move it.

"Ellen."

The bolt slid free. Instinctively, she glanced back again.

Purdit stood framed in the bedroom doorway. A gash cut his forehead, blood darkening his cheek.

"Leaving so soon?" he asked.

Ellen twisted the doorknob.

Purdit stepped toward her, his black eyes aflame with menace.

Offering a silent prayer, Ellen tugged the door. It swung open, taking her by surprise, and she stumbled into the harsh light.

"Wait," he pleaded, his voice whining.

Ellen fled.

Her feet slapped the wooden porch, and she fell down two steps and hit the sand. She scrabbled to her feet.

"Ellen!"

Run. Run. Run.

The rhythm beat through her mind with every agonizing step. She did not look back, she did not dare. But she could hear him. And she knew he would catch her.

Run. Run. Run.

Chapter 30

Ellen's bare feet pummeled the hot sand and the small, sharp stones that littered the ground. Running blindly, she struggled to free her hands from the plastic flex. Straining until her wrists were rubbed raw. Until finally she pulled them free.

"Ellen!"

He sounded close.

She stumbled onto a dusty track. Lost.

"Ellen!"

She glanced down the slope and saw a car approaching. The vehicle looked indistinct, shimmering in the heat.

"Help!" Her voice sounded hoarse, and too weak to carry far.

She waved her hands desperately above her head.

"Over here," she gasped.

The car loomed nearer, suddenly recognizable. And her heart leapt. Blue and red lights flashed atop its roof.

Tears of relief streaked Ellen's face as she ran, stumbling toward the police car.

The car skidded to a stop a few yard ahead. A woman leapt out from behind the wheel.

"Mrs. Grady!"

Ellen collapsed against the car.

"A man… he's…" the words caught in her parched throat. Wildly, she looked around. He'd been right behind her moments ago, she was sure. She'd heard him shouting her name. Or had she? Could it have been a trick of the desert? The heat, the wind.

The woman officer drew her gun, her steady aim sweeping the barren terrain.

There was no sign of Purdit.

"I have to call this in, get some help out here."

Relief sapped Ellen's remaining strength. Her trembling legs buckled and she slumped to her knees.

The woman officer grabbed her elbow, then knelt down beside her, examining Ellen's injuries.

Claire Sawyer winced when she saw Ellen's hands. "Jesus."

Her wrists were bloody welts.

"Let's get you in the car. I've got a first aid kit-"

Ellen grasped the woman's arm.

"He's here. He was right behind me." A dry cough hacked Ellen's throat.

Claire again surveyed the desert. There were a few places someone might hide. Some boulders, a few large, low cacti. If the kidnapper was armed then he could easily have taken a shot by now. But she couldn't risk leaving Ellen to search the area. The most important thing was to get the injured woman inside the patrol car and radio for backup.

Gun at the ready, Claire edged around to the rear of the car.

Ellen maneuvered into the shade offered by the vehicle and sank to the ground. She heard the trunk lid click open.

Ellen curled her legs beneath her chin. Wary, her eyes kept darting, caught by tiny movements in the desert. Eddies blown by the wind kicked up miniature dust devils and blew dried scrub across the gritty sand. But there was no sign of Purdit. He'd vanished.

"Here we are," Claire called and a moment later the trunk slammed closed.

As Ellen shifted her feet under her and tried to stand.

A shadow fell over her.

"Let me help you, Ellen."

Ellen froze. The man's voice sounded so calm, so reasonable. She tried to swallow, but couldn't.

"Please," she croaked as she looked up.

Purdit smiled down at her.

Her eyes flicked to the knife in his hand, and fixed on the long, jagged blade stained with blood.

"Don't hurt me. Please don't," her simpering plea sounded pitiful even to her own ears. She'd always considered herself strong and capable, but now when she needed it most, she felt weak and afraid. A victim.

Purdit didn't answer. He simply smiled at her.

Ellen stared past him, as if expecting to see the officer who had miraculously found her.

"Wh-where is she?"

"In the trunk," Purdit answered nonchalantly as he opened the rear door. "Let's get in."

Ellen didn't move.

"Is she..." Ellen couldn't bring herself to utter the word. Dead.

Purdit grabbed her arm, lifting her to her feet. Firmly but gently he forced her into the rear seat of the police car.

"Actually, she was still breathing. Remarkably resilient, the human body. Although I fear her wound is fatal. Never killed a woman before..." He hesitated, his smile vanishing. He knew that was a lie, and didn't Ellen deserve the truth? Hadn't that been one of his silent promises? He was no longer sure. No longer sure of anything.

He slammed the door and opened the driver's side.

Ellen fumbled for the handle, fingers scrabbling. She tugged the handle, throwing her weight against the door.

It remained stubbornly locked.

Purdit shook his head in mild amusement.

"We'll take your friend to her final resting place."

Ellen punched the door, desperately wrenching the handle back and forth.

Purdit idly turned the ignition key and started the engine.

As he drove, Ellen became aware of a faint tapping sound. Regular, yet it didn't sound mechanical. The noise was coming from behind her. A feeble tapping against the back of her fiberglass seat.

*

At Sam's desperate insistence, they had split up, able to cover more ground in two vehicles. He'd been surprised and beyond grateful that Claire Sawyer had changed her mind and agreed to continue the daunting search.

Although, he had to admit, the desolate land had taken on an eerie feel now he was alone, and unarmed.

Claire was searching the sparse ranch properties to the north, Sam to the south, and they had continued to work their way down the cracked blacktop, disappearing on forays deep into the desert at every dirt track. Sam had driven four miles only to find this particular track vanished, obscured by years of wind strewn sand, with no building in sight.

Returning to the road he stopped and checked the time. Nearly two o'clock. He headed west, to the meeting point they'd arranged, and pulled off the road to wait. Claire had his cell number, but when he tried to get a signal the phone failed. So, at Claire's insistence, they had agreed to meet here every hour on the hour. She had given him a walkie-talkie and instructions on how to use it, explaining its range was limited to only a few miles at best. She'd also radioed in, despite having come off duty hours earlier, and told dispatch she was following a lead. Sam was well aware that the only thing they had to go on was his hunch.

"Just don't change the frequency, okay?" she had instructed him, adding that he should only call her if he either found some trace of Ellen, or in an emergency.

The black transceiver had blurted static once, but otherwise remained silent.

Sam's fingers anxiously rubbed the steering wheel.

With the windows wide open, he kept the engine running. The air conditioning worked sporadically, straining with the hundred and ten degree heat. Sweat drenched his shirt.

He checked the time again and wondered if Claire had discovered something to delay her return. Reaching over, Sam picked the walkie-talkie off the passenger seat. He was about to press the button to transmit when he saw her car approaching and relaxed his grip. Claire's car jounced along a rutted track, nearing the blacktop. Sam squinted despite his sunglasses as the sun dazzled off her windshield, raising a hand to cover his eyes.

The car reached the road some distance away. But instead of turning right and driving to meet him as he anticipated, the CHP cruiser turned left, and sped away spewing dust.

His heart stammered.

As the car had turned onto the blacktop, he'd glimpsed a terror stricken face peering out the rear window.

His wife's face.

Without hesitating, Sam accelerated, pursuing the patrol car into the desert. As he drove he kept trying his cell phone, repeatedly stabbing 9-1-1 in vain. He had to reach the police.

"Come on," he pleaded.

There was no signal. No one coming to help.

Chapter 31

Purdit spun to face Ellen.

"What? What did you say?"

Ellen turned slowly and stared into his eyes. "Nothing."

Purdit's eyes narrowed, not trusting her. He'd heard her gasp a moment earlier as they reached the road, and he'd seen a car. For a second he wondered if the car also belonged to the CHP. But no, it had been a plain, nondescript vehicle. He hadn't seen the driver, but he had an idea who might be behind the wheel. And no doubt Ellen had visions of that person rushing to her rescue.

Purdit grinned as he touched the cool metal barrel of the service revolver he'd taken from the female cop after he'd stabbed her and watched her collapse forward, falling into the trunk.

Beautiful as a ballerina's final bow.

He glanced in the rearview mirror, the road behind obstinately obscured by a rooster tail of dust. His gaze turned to Ellen. She was huddled in the corner, her mouth chapped so badly her lips were bleeding. He knew how thirsty she must feel after the chase she'd led him on. There had been a large bottle of water in the patrol car, but he'd needed most of that to slake his own thirst.

"We'll get you some water soon," he promised.

She nodded vaguely and muttered something incoherent. She was becoming delirious, he knew. Heat exhaustion and dehydration were quick and merciless killers in the desert. Yet she had survived, and he had found her again.

It was destiny.

Like the fate of the cop.

"It's time," he said to Ellen, though he could not be certain she heard.

Time to show her his special place. The hidden Cathedral where those who sinned, believing themselves above the law, met their fate. Perhaps then, she would begin to understand him and his lifelong dedication.

Not that he could tell her everything. Especially not about her husband's fate. He was fairly confident the nondescript car they'd seen belonged to Sam. And now it was time to lure his prey. Soon Sam Grady would become another mysterious disappearance.

And Ellen would be his alone.

*

The Buick jolted and bucked as it hit every pothole in the aging asphalt. It was easy enough to follow the cloud of dust in the cruiser's wake as the sandy blacktop meandered east, until the road itself finally petered to an end. Here a fresh set of tire tracks lead farther into the wasteland.

Sam glanced at the walkie-talkie. Would someone hear if he radioed for help. Then he froze. The only person who would probably hear would be Purdit.

He couldn't take that chance.

Again he cursed his cell phone, trying it once more in a futile attempt to get a signal.

What had Purdit done to Claire Sawyer? He prayed she wasn't lying somewhere in need of help. For a split second he wondered if he should have gone to look for her.

"God," he breathed. What was he supposed to do?

Sam stomped on the brakes, his car skidding in the sand, sliding to a stop mere inches from where the sand and rocks tumbled away. His mind had wandered for a moment and almost ended in disaster. Most likely, Purdit had driven this close to the edge, before turning to parallel the arroyo, hoping for Sam to meet an abrupt demise. Shaken, Sam shifted into reverse and nudged the gas pedal. The rear wheels spun for a second before finding some grip.

He continued to follow the tire tracks, although the wind was picking up and already obscuring them in places. And then the trail led back to the edge - and disappeared. Trying to control his anxiety, Sam stopped the car and climbed out. Leaning against the wind, he stepped to the edge, and looked down. Here a dangerous trail arced steeply downward, to the arid riverbed, and there he saw the police car, parked facing a low cliff on the opposite side.

Sam watched as Purdit stepped out of the police car and strode around to the trunk. The lid swung up, and Purdit dragged something out.

Sam gagged.

A body. Officer Claire Sawyer. Motionless and bloody.

Disgust choked like bile in his throat, and he couldn't help glancing away.

By the time he looked up again, Purdit had disappeared.

Sam frowned. That was impossible. Keeping low to the ground, he hurried along the ledge, eyes scanning for any sign of movement near the police car.

Ellen was trapped inside.

He didn't know where Purdit had gone. But if he could reach the police car before the madman returned...

He needed to hurry!

Hunched over, Sam scrambled down the incline to the baked riverbed.

He was less than a hundred yards from the police car when he heard scree skitter. He dropped to the ground, using what little cover there was in an attempt to hide. Moments later, he spotted Purdit emerge from a patch of darkness part way up the cliff, his boots dislodging the loose gravel as he walked.

Sam lay motionless, feeling exposed.

Purdit left the cave and crossed to the police car.

He opened the door and helped Ellen out.

"Come with me," he said, leading her by the elbow. "There's something you need to see."

The desert wind carried his voice.

"Please, you don't have to do this," Ellen tried to tug her arm free but the gesture was futile.

Purdit led her across the brief stretch of flatland to the rubble beneath the cave entrance.

"Why did you have to kill her?" Ellen's voice cracked.

"Why did you have to run?"

Ellen sobbed and stumbled. Purdit caught her before she hit the ground and pulled her to her feet.

They scrambled over the loose rocks piled at the base of the cliff.

His pulse jacked and his chest tight, Sam watched them disappear inside cave.

Crouching low, he followed.

The entrance was like a gaping, black maw. He didn't want to go anywhere near the cave, let alone venture inside. But he kept moving closer. Drawn by a desperation which warred with his own claustrophobic fear.

Beyond the mouth, he could see nothing. The gloom palled thick and dark. Feeble fingers of sunlight groped a few feet into the cave entrance, showing only a rocky floor and a slight downward slope.

Sam shivered despite the heat as he peered into the murky confines beyond the opening.

No choice, he kept repeating to himself, willing his body to move. He had to step inside, but for a moment he felt paralyzed.

Straining, he listened for any sounds of Ellen or the madman who had taken her prisoner. How far did the cave stretch? Sam wondered.

He heard nothing except his heart pounding in his ears.

Forcing himself to move, Sam edged inside the cave.

Taking one step, then another, he felt a suffocating cloak settle around him, shrouding his body. The air fetid and stale.

Sam concentrated on his deep, measured breaths, trying to push away his trepidation. His hands balled into fists of determination. Then, with one final glance back at the reassuring daylight, he ventured into the dark.

*

Purdit yanked Ellen's arm again, and wondered if he should force her to move in front. They were nearing the narrow passage.

The beam of his flashlight played over craggy walls. He placed the flashlight on the ground and pulled the stolen revolver out of his pocket. He wondered if he could pull the trigger if she was so foolish as to gamble her life.

"I don't want to hurt you, Ellen," he warned.

"Then let me go."

"I could never do that."

He pulled her to him, so close her breath touched his cheek.

Then he forced her to squeeze past him, their bodies pressed together as she moved ahead.

"Please, don't do this," she whispered again.

Tightening his grip on her arm, he forced her to bend down, and to enter the fissure, the passageway leading to his Cathedral.

The waving beam of light from Purdit's flashlight did little to guide Ellen. She crawled and clambered through the narrow passage, shards of rocks digging into her hands and knees. Only one thought kept her going. Sam. She had seen Sam. And he had seen her, she felt sure of it. But what could he do? Did he even know where she'd been taken? And even if he managed to contact the police, how long would it take for them to arrive?

Abruptly she emerged in an underground chamber.

Water droplets echoed in the darkness.

She stood, lightheaded with exhaustion and gripped the wall to help keep her balance. Purdit crawled out.

Ellen looked around the vaulted chamber of rock, following the flashlight. The beam panned down the far wall some twenty yards away, then swept closer and touched the cavern floor nearby.

Ellen's stomach tightened.

On the ground lay the police officer who had tried to save her.

"God. No," Ellen sagged against the cold rock.

"Come here," Purdit ordered as he walked over to the body.

Somehow Ellen found the strength to move away from the wall, her feet shuffling across the floor to where Purdit was standing, close to the edge of a dark crevasse that split the floor.

"This is where they go," he said, turning to face her.

"They?" she stared at him. A single thought beating inside her head. Keep him talking, keep him occupied, no matter what that meant. Just keep him talking.

"They thought they were so clever, so superior. But they weren't. Don't you see?"

"Yes," Ellen lied.

"Do you?" he turned on her, eyes alight. "I wonder. Do you think we were meant for each other? You don't know how hard it's been. How long I've been alone..."

He reached out, his fingers stroking her face.

Ellen froze.

"Ellen," he breathed.

Abruptly, he pulled away, playing the beam of light over the cop.

"First things first."

He moved toward the injured officer, then looked at Ellen.

"You can help me if you wish. I think you should."

Ellen tried to shake her head, but she couldn't move.

"I... I can't."

Purdit's eyes narrowed.

God help me, Ellen prayed.

"Ellen? Shouldn't we help each other?"

Terrified, she nodded and stepped forward to help him drag the body to the crevasse.

As she touched the woman's hand, she felt Claire's finger twitch. Ellen stifled a scream. Had to fight every impulse in her body. Claire Sawyer still clung to the last threads of her life.

Relentless, they neared the edge.

Ellen stumbled deliberately. Anything to stall what was about to happen.

"Get up," Purdit ordered.

Her grip tightened around Claire's hand. She couldn't let him do this.

Purdit reached down and pried her hand free.

"Time to say goodbye to the dearly departed."

"No," but her voice was a whisper.

Ellen closed her eyes in silent prayer as Purdit pushed the poor woman over the edge. She heard a dull thud as the body bounced against the unseen cliff. A loud splash echoed a moment later.

Ellen sank to the ground, clutching her hands to her face, unable to hide her sobs.

Pain vanished like an ugly dream, all-encompassing one moment, washed away the next. The pain gone as the shock of the icy water shattered her consciousness.

As she fell, she had hit the rock wall once and then the chill water had broken her fall with a stunning jolt. But she was too weak. Too weak to swim.

For a moment her head broke the surface. She gasped the air like elixir.

There was no light.

Pitch black, like nothing she'd ever experienced. Darker than when the trunk lid had slammed shut and entombed her. Trapped, her eyes had finally adjusted, and she could make out thin cracks of daylight where the rubber seals had perished. Now, buoyed by the icy water it was almost impossible to tell up from down. She felt herself start to sink, and she knew this time would mark the end. She tried to kick her legs but they felt so numb it was impossible. Her arms flailed as she slipped below the surface.

Her fingers scraped rock.

She must have landed close to the edge. Her fingers probed blindly, seeking a handhold and finding a ledge as slender as her last hope.

Mustering her strength she pulled herself toward the ledge. Shivering. So cold, so desperately cold. Claire began to drag herself from the black water's possessive grasp.

A trickle of warmth kissed her cheek. She tasted the tannic sweetness of her own blood as is touched her lips.

Even as she escaped the cold grave, so her body relinquished its grip on the world. Her consciousness waned.

Blind. Sam felt his way along the cave wall, tripping over stones and rocks. His progress was both painful and slow. Ahead, once, he thought he heard Ellen's voice, desperate and afraid.

His hand stretched forward. And met solid rock.

He probed the wall, expecting to find a passage leading off at an angle. But all he found was the back of the cave. A dead end.

Panic surged through his mind. He must have missed a side passage, somewhere in the darkness behind him.

He started to turn when he heard a splash.

The disorienting sound seemed to come from below.

Sam crouched down and reached out again. His hand passed through open air, and like a blind man he fell forward into a low crawl space.

Entering the constricting fissure consumed him with abject fear, the rock closed tight around him like a coffin.

"How many?" he heard Ellen ask. The sound of her voice was enough to spur him on.

"Does that matter?"

"Yes."

"Not enough."

Sam edged forward, he felt hot, his breathing shallow. His hand accidentally flicked a loose stone.

"What?" Purdit's voice took on a different tone. Alert.

Sam gritted his teeth, his body rigid, motionless.

"I..." said Ellen, "I didn't hear anything."

Purdit did not reply.

Sam edged deeper into the nightmare gloom.

Ellen couldn't help glancing at the passage entrance when she heard the faint sound of rock on rock.

She let Purdit run his fingers through her hair. And tried to smile, her jaw quivering. She blinked rapidly to hide the tears which filmed her eyes.

Purdit's fingers brushed her neck. His voice as soulless as a vampire's kiss. "We'll be together. The way it should have been."

Sam reached the end of the eternal passage. There was light cast by a flashlight lying on the floor. The glow illuminated a large cavern. And standing near the middle of the chamber he saw Purdit holding Ellen, his back to Sam.

Hardly daring to breathe, Sam crawled from the passage, his hand closing around a hefty rock.

Purdit was twenty feet away.

Ellen opened her eyes and saw Sam-

Gripping the rock, Sam charged.

Purdit sensed another presence before he heard the man's footfalls.

He shoved Ellen away, not meaning to push her so hard, but he had to draw his gun.

Pulling the revolver from his belt, he spun to meet his attacker.

He glimpsed Sam's face, his features contorted with anger, then saw the rock in Sam's hand as it swept down.

Purdit pulled the trigger.

Sam's body jerked backward, his momentum faltering, the bullet hitting his shoulder, spinning him around.

Purdit took aim and smiled, about to fire again when he heard Ellen's frantic scream-

"Help me!"

Purdit twisted around, searching, unable to see her. Then he dashed to the edge of the crevasse and looked down. He'd pushed her here – over the edge!

She stared up at him, her fingers fastened around a tenuous sliver of rock.

"Ellen!" he shouted.

Dropping the gun, he lay down and stretched over the edge and reached for her.

"Reach up."

"I can't."

He could barely see her pale hands clutching the rock.

Straining to reach as far as he could, his fingertips brushed hers.

"Take my hand."

Sam rolled onto his back. A few feet away, he watched Purdit lean over the edge. And heard Ellen's pleas for help.

His eyes fell on the discarded gun beside Purdit's prone body.

Ignoring the fiery pain that threatened to engulf him, Sam clawed and crawled his way toward the gun.

Purdit's fingers closed around Ellen's hand. He gripped with all his might and pulled.

He lifted her until her body emerged from the shadows, and with a final heave, he hauled her to safety, to lie beside him.

"It's over," Purdit breathed.

"Ellen."

Purdit twisted in the direction of the other voice.

Sam's voice.

"Ellen, move away from him."

"Sam."

She scrambled away from Purdit.

Purdit looked up at him. Unafraid, despite the weapon Sam was holding.

Purdit started to get to his feet.

"Don't move," Sam's fingers tightened on the gun. Pain stabbed his shoulder.

Purdit stood. Tall, his back straight. His arrogant smile mocking Sam.

"I'm warning you, I'll shoot." Darkness passed before Sam's eyes. He swayed.

Purdit turned to face Ellen.

"Do you want him to do that, Ellen? Could you live with that? Could you live with a cold-blooded killer?"

Ellen stared at Purdit for a moment, then turned to Sam.

"Shoot! Sam!"

Sam's vision blurred. He wanted to pull the trigger, but felt himself falling.

Ellen stepped toward Sam as he collapsed to the ground, the gun spilling free and clattering across the floor.

"Sam!"

Purdit laughed.

Ellen dove for the gun.

Her fingers closed around the handle.

Purdit stared at her. Confusion in his eyes. "Ellen?"

She pulled the trigger.

A deafening explosion filled the cavern. Purdit reeled backward, eyes wide with shock.

His left hand clutched his stomach, his right arm still outstretched, reaching for her. He staggered back, his foot suddenly disappearing over the edge of the crevasse.

"I did everything." Blood dribbled from his mouth as his last breath escaped. "Everything for you."

His eyes rolled toward the roof and he tumbled into the abyss.

Ellen heard his body smack the water far below.

She moved toward Sam, then stopped.

A faint cry rose from the crevasse. For the briefest moment her pulse raced fearing it was him. Then she recognized the sound, a woman's agonized cry for help. Lord, thank you. Somehow the officer was still alive.

"We'll get help!" Ellen shouted into the depths.

Epilogue

"You're sure about this?"

Pete Ashby stood in the Gradys' driveway and bent down to speak through the open car window.

Sam tapped the steering wheel, eager to move on. He glanced at Ellen and she nodded. "We're sure."

"Certainly appreciate everything," Pete said for the tenth time. "I mean, it's a pretty good customer base you've given us."

"You paid more than it's worth, Pete." Sam had already thanked his friend for the generous offer to buy his company. An offer Sam had accepted without reservation. Although he would miss Kathy and Martin.

"You guys take care of yourselves, okay?"

"We will," Ellen said, leaning across Sam. "Tell Anne I'll call her soon as we get settled in Marin."

Marin County, mused Sam. It had been a long time since they'd left and moved south, drawn by the lure of... Of what? he wondered now. The chance to be his own boss? The high-tech smog of LA and the OC? He wasn't sure anymore, but one thing was certain. It was good to be heading north, escaping the memories of this place.

The removal truck, laden with their possessions, pulled away from the curb to begin the five-hundred-mile haul to the house they would rent while searching for somewhere to buy.

Perhaps it was a step back, a retreat, returning to the Bay area, to work for somebody else again. But Sam wanted time to spend with his family, time to see Jason grow up, to help Ellen recover. To help them all heal.

Sam started the car and glanced in the mirror at Jason, the boy dozing in his car seat, his head lolled to one side.

With a brisk salute to Pete, the new President of Grade-A FX, Sam turned to Ellen. She was already occupied with one of her word puzzle books. At least one thing was returning to normal, he thought with a faint smile.

While their furniture sped north on the Interstate, Sam drove leisurely along the meandering Coast Highway.

Two days ago, they had paid a visit to the hospital where Claire Sawyer had been in intensive care for so long. Now she was confined to a wheelchair, her spine broken when she'd hit the crevasse wall. The doctor's said there was hope that she might walk - but Sam doubted they had looked into that woman's eyes. If they had, they would have seen something far stronger than hope, a raw and primal determination. On the day of their visit, Officer Claire Sawyer had received the Governor's Medal of Valor, a fact that largely escaped media attention.

Ellen interrupted his thoughts. "Ever wonder who he really was?" she asked.

Sam shrugged - what did it matter? The news reports had speculated for weeks about the true identity of the serial killer, but no one knew. His name was false, he possessed no Social Security number, and his prints and dental records had revealed nothing.

"Or how many people…"

"Honey," he said softly. "We can't keep doing this."

Of course it had been impossible to avoid the sensational headlines which flooded the TV and internet in the wake of the gruesome discovery. Reports on the lives Purdit had claimed had been updated daily at first. Until, mercifully, the news cycle had moved on. But those horrifying reports had stated the remains of more than two dozen victims had been recovered from the pitch dark, underground lake.

And Sam had little doubt that the final figure would be higher.

"You're right," said Ellen. But a glance at her told Sam she could never forget, and of course neither would he.

However, they were headed toward their new life.

Literally, thought Sam with a smile remembering their last visit to the doctor and the good news, when Ellen's obstetrician had examined her. One day, Jason would have a brother or sister.

A new beginning.

AUTHOR'S NOTE

Although I wrote an initial draft of NOWHERE TO HIDE over a decade ago, the manuscript was never finished. Between raising a family, moving home, and changing vocation, the book remained on my shelf, with the promise to pick up the pages again and see the story published. My sincerest wish is that you enjoyed this novel, while I'm working on the next.

ABOUT THE TYPEFACE

Printed in Garamond font and named for sixteenth century Parisian engraver Claude Garamont, whose designs helped establish what is now called the old-style of serif lettering.